AVAILABLE LIGHT

STEVE HOSELITZ

Published by Saron Publishers in 2023

Several stories in this book were previously published in
Penthusiasm. They include *Before Christmas, Childhood
Memories, Your Car My Car* and *The Days of Chars*
They are reproduced here with minor amendments

ISBN-13: 978-1-913297-40-4
Also available as an ebook
978-1-913297-41-1

Saron Publishers
Pwllmeyrick House
Mamhilad
Mon
NP4 8RG

www.saronpublishers.co.uk
info@saronpublishers.co.uk
Follow us on Facebook and Twitter

CONTENTS

FOREWORD

None of my school teachers would have anticipated this collection of my stories: I scraped an English O-level at the third or fourth attempt. Notwithstanding which I have spent most of my life as a journalist.

After I finished working full-time on newspapers, I decided to try to master the craft of writing fiction.

I was helped enormously by a group of modest, kind, unassuming, talented writers who met every week as a local group, the Penthusiasts. My thanks for their friendship, fortitude and forbearance. Encouragement is gold dust.

It was the rigour and experience of writing with them that encouraged me to dredge-up most of the stories and poems in this book.

Some are purely the result of exercises in writing in a different voice, with a new idea or to a subject we were all working with. Others are pure flights of fancy.

Even the more auto-biographical stories, grouped at the end, are generously lubricated with the oil of fiction.

Readers need to be aware that this is only evidence of a journey and I make no claim to having arrived anywhere.

The title of the anthology comes from a *BBC* radio interview I heard many years ago: an artist was asked if her paintings were true to life.

'They are not, but one can only paint with available light,' she replied.

ALGARVE DREAMLAND

Felicity sighed and pushed opened the door, wincing at the grating noise as it scoured over the tiled floor. The musty smell would linger for several days despite opened windows and air fresheners. She disabled the burglar alarm, kicked off her red sling-back sandals and padded through into the lounge area, avoiding dead flies.

Some tiles were beginning to lift. Two of the chairs, which used to be dark rose, were now sun-bleached an ugly shade of yellowy pink. Something very unpleasant was wafting across from the kitchen area. The patio doors ground very reluctantly open and in the bottom of the kidney-shaped pool there was the usual collection of wind-blown rubbish and a brown rain-residue.

Silvino had said he had mended the pump but he certainly hadn't cleaned out the pool or filled it. Another chore on the 'welcome to my villa' list. *I'll get some of them done today and leave the pool to fill overnight,* she said to herself, almost out loud since there was no one to hear. It would take three days to fully warm up: hardly worth the effort since she'd be flying home on Monday.

She picked her way over the hot paving to the edge of the terrace. Weeds were now the only thing growing where she'd once struggled to nurture a border. Two rose bushes were dry and very dead. The apartment block, which robbed them of their former uninterrupted view of the sea, seemed even taller. Instead of the ocean, the view was of balconies with washing lines. Perhaps it was only to be expected, despite what the selling agent had said when she and PJ viewed what was then just a vacant plot all those years ago.

It had been his dream to live there permanently. It was never hers.

Back inside, she let the kitchen tap run until the dirty sediment had cleared from the water. Even clear, it tasted awful. She took down one of the glasses from the shelf – his old favourite beer mug. The first thing he would have done when they got to the villa would have been to open a beer, back when they went to the villa four or five times a year. The Babycham glasses came later, she remembered. It took her back to when she stayed there with her friend, June, during that very hot summer, nineteen eighty something, or perhaps the early nineties. PJ had had that big contract. The Darcy Flyover. That was the one summer he missed coming to the Villa back then and God, it was hot. The air conditioning couldn't cope. And the almost non-existent heating system couldn't cope with the winters, either. 'I'll upgrade it when we retire out here,' he used to say. No wonder she'd been only been back once to Lar Feliz since his funeral.

He would have turned in his grave if he had heard what that slimy valuer had offered. Luckily, she had found out by then she didn't really need the money. Typical PJ – he had kept both her and the Inland Revenue in the dark...

And now, there were those who still didn't want her to sell.

'Keep the last two weeks of June free for me and Sam,' Andrew said when she told him she was thinking of turning it into a holiday let. 'And a week at Easter.' *Not slow to ask, that one... I spoiled him as a child,* she now realised.

The door chime broke her reveries.

'I was seeing car,' Silvino said, his imperfect English a contrast to his perfect tan. 'I worry maybe not you.'

'Thank you, Silvino. I really appreciate you keeping an eye on the place for me.'

Rather quickly he handed her a bill for his management and repairs. More than she had expected, especially with the weak pound. *That didn't take him long, I've only been in five minutes,* she thought. Still, he was good for security. She was going to ask him to sort out the patio door tracks but at those prices... and the bathroom needed re-doing, too.

When he had gone, she went back out to the small hire car, lugged her suitcase into the bigger of the two bedrooms and started unpacking, putting her clothes in neat piles on the bare, plastic-covered mattress. She found what she was looking for. She took her iPad and charger through to the lounge, plugged it in and sat down with it on the sofa, gazing out across the patio and beyond. What was she going to do about everything, she wondered...

* * *

It must have been almost an hour later when she awoke, damp with sweat and with a slight headache. Her neck hurt because of the awkward position in which she'd flopped and her sunglasses had slipped off. She narrowed her eyes against the bright light and pushed her hand down between the bulky faux-leather cream cushions to try to find them. A coin, something else – yuk... She got a damp cloth from the kitchen and removed the cushions. That's when she saw it: a small, faded envelope with her late husband's name on it. The handwriting looked somehow familiar. Turning it over, she saw that a letter was still inside.

My Darling Paddy,
I have had the most marvellous week at the villa.
I can't face going home to Morden and Malcolm - you have been such good company and we have had the best time ever together, haven't we, sweetheart?
Sun, sea and you know what, it is not just a cliché is it...?

Trembling, Felicity turned the page to read the signature: June with kisses! Her friend June! Her close friend June, her best friend... The friend she'd spent the summer with, here in this very villa.

Stunned, she stared blankly out of the room. PJ and June? No, it couldn't be... Never, no, not them. She could not imagine it. Then the tears came, tears of confusion, of hurt, of anger... Her whole body was heaving and shaking. Her mind in overdrive, thoughts rushing in, doubts, conjecture, distress. A horrible, terrible jumble: and here she was in this villa, his bloody villa; all alone in it.

When had he been here with June? How often, how, why... why June of all people? She had no idea how long she sat there with that dreadful letter in her hand. But when she got up out of the chair, it was already getting dark outside. And after the confusion and anger that had raged inside her, there came an emptiness. An almost total emptiness.

She put some water in the kettle and found a jar of instant coffee in the cupboard. Got a mug out and a teaspoon from the drawer. No milk. *I'll get some in the morning...* Mechanical. Making herself do it all deliberately: any concentration completely gone.

Coffee in hand, she went back to the chair and read the letter again. She didn't think PJ had ever been to the villa without her. How come... and June... The same June who'd spent the summer with her here. What a cow, what a bleeding double-crossing cow!

She counted back the years in her mind. When had he had his stroke? Three years ago this May. So this must have been at least four years ago. When their son, Andrew, was about to start his last year at university. When she'd spent several days in Liverpool helping him find a flat. Was it then? Or when she'd visited her brother in Dorset and PJ had carried on working? Was he working? Or was it all subterfuge? When else could it have been? She had to know.

The letter was undated, the envelope blank except for his name, written and underlined in that lavender-coloured ink June always used. Handed to him perhaps; certainly never posted. Paddy, for God's sake. No one

13

called him Paddy. Made him sound like an Irish labourer. He'd been PJ. Always PJ. She'd never heard anyone call him 'Paddy'. His mother called him Patrick, not Paddy.

And if they had been together here, what was going on between them back in Surrey? She took her mobile out of her bag and without thinking, selected June from her contacts. The number rang. Then it hit her. What was she going to say to the cow? 'When were you here screwing my husband?'

She disconnected the call before it was answered, not really realising just then that she would leave a missed call trace. *I'm not ready to confront her now. I need to think some more about things. Who else knew? Why June? Who else had PJ been here with? Who else had he 'done it' with? There would be others, wouldn't there? And for how long? Wasn't I good enough for him? Mother of his children? Cooking his meals, ironing his shirts, cleaning his house? Listening to his grumbles - always grumbles, the negative, nit-picking sod. Fussy and mean... And then I nursed him, after his stroke. More than a year. Fifteen miserable months. Where was bloody June then, eh? Not by his bedside, changing the sheets, washing him, feeding him. Full time. If I'd known then, the bastard. Life support, I'd have given him bloody life support. Between the eyes!*

Her mobile phone buzzed on the table. June's number, one she knew so well, calling back. *Let it ring. Let it bloody well ring.*

* * *

When Silvino called round for his money three days later, Felicity was dozing in the sun-lounger. The Big-Ben door chime woke her; she had not been sleeping well. She'd had long nights fretting about June and PJ.

14

The image of them together in this house, in their bed, on the sofa, anywhere, everywhere. Doing it. She couldn't get the images from her mind.

'Come in, Silvino, I've got your money here,' she said. 'By the way, I've something to ask you,' trying to sound nonchalant. 'A few years ago, before my husband was ill, do you remember him coming here with my friend June, you know the blonde lady, a bit overweight, who was with me all one summer.'

Silvino thought for a moment then his face lit up. 'Oh! Yes! Was when Mr Oregon (his way of saying O'Reagan) had open car.'

'Open car – what do you mean?' Felicity queried.

'He had red Mini cabriolé, we call,' Silvino explained. 'Was here perhaps three, four days. Was not OK?'

Not slow to catch on, our Silvino. 'No, everything's fine,' she said rather too quickly. Trying hard to sound as if she meant it. *So the love cheat had hired a convertible, had he? Who was he trying to impress? Don't answer that.*

'Was that the visit in August or in November – I've lost track...' she quizzed.

'Was late in year, November perhaps, like you say. Little sun – why need open car, I think.'

'Thank you, Silvino, I thought it must have been then...' covering her tracks clumsily. 'By the way, I may be selling Lar Feliz sometime so if you hear of anyone looking for property, please let me know – you have my email address, don't you?'

'I have details,' Silvino said. 'Early summer good time to sell to get bigger price. Your villa very good. But I need look at alarm system now. Not change since I have made him in – is what you say?'

15

Felicity could feel a big bill coming again... but if she sold up, she'd be shot of the damned cuckold's love nest and Silvino's bills, too. So she agreed to let him service the alarm system, fix the bathroom tiles and the patio doors – in fact, all the jobs which would need to be done before she could be rid of PJ's wretched dream home, now a nightmare villa.

* * *

Back home in Morden, Felicity found it impossible to settle back into her normal routine. Thoughts about Lar Feliz, PJ and June were pretty much a constant intrusion. Never more so than after three or four weeks when the postman squeezed a package through the slot in Felicity's front door. She looked at the stamps – Portugal – and cut through the sticky tape to open the bulging envelope. Inside was another bill from Silvino, this time not quite as bad as she expected, telling her that he'd 'complemented change' to the alarm and enclosed a small video cassette tape 'from old system which is no need. Now use IP,' whatever that meant.

So far, she'd avoided any contact with June, shying away from an inevitable confrontation. By now, her former friend – love cheat and prize cow as she now thought of her – must have known something was up: that disconnected phone call and the normally so-reliable response to messages were so completely out of character. And normally Felicity would meet June for their Thursday shopping outing and again at St Mary's on Sunday. June was bound to suspect something was up. *I hope a guilty conscience is giving the bitch an anxious time,* Felicity reflected.

It had been a good, dry, late summer and June's loss was Felicity's garden's gain... It provided her with the necessary distraction and as a result, her borders had never looked tidier. When Andrew and Sam came for lunch one Saturday, Andrew noticed how good the garden was looking.

'You seem to have found a new lease of life, Mum,' he remarked. If he even noticed his mother's complete lack of sparkle, he certainly didn't comment on it. Lunch consumed, the couple were making their way out through the hall when Andrew noticed the tape on the hall stand.

'What's this, Mother?' he laughed. 'You can't watch old films on your TV any more. This format wasn't any good even back then.'

'It is not an old film, darling. Silvino sent it from the Villa,' Felicity explained. 'He's upgraded the alarm to help the sale. I should have put it in the bin.'

'Can I have it?' Andrew asked. 'My old system uses tapes like this. They're obsolete and hard to find,' and with a brief brush of cheeks, he and Sam were gone.

* * *

June and Malcolm Troughton were among the most regular members of the congregation at St Mary's. Malcolm was a sidesman and June did the flowers in the church three times a week. The vicar, Revd. Jack Hayes, wished he had more parishioners like the Troughtons. Always ready to lend a hand in a crisis, he had rarely met a more reliable, well-balanced couple in his twenty-eight years as a minister. Which is why he was always quite happy to allow Malcolm to use the church hall for the annual exhibition of local Shuttermasters Photography Club. Large, tasteful, black-and-white and colour photographs always filled the walls. Landscapes, studies, a few almost abstract images and some carefully selected portraits. Never anything that could not grace spaces in the church itself, never mind the adjoining hall.

This year, the club's 20th anniversary, the exhibition was being opened by Tom Davies. The name did not mean much to the vicar, but to those in the know, it was quite a coup: Tom trained under David Bailey and some of his work had made it into the National Portrait Gallery. There was going to be quite a gathering – the South London Press was sending a reporter.

And Revd. Hayes had been so pleased when Felicity got back in touch after all these weeks and asked if she could decorate the hall with flowers for the exhibition opening...

'You haven't been ill, have you?' the vicar asked before handing over the key on Friday. 'Your friend June said she hadn't seen or heard from you recently either... I was going to call round the day you rang.' Felicity brushed him aside with a few platitudes about being busy sorting things out.

* * *

It was sunny but cooler at 10.30 on Saturday morning. The vicar and Tom Davies were at the door of the church hall, ready to declare the exhibition open. So too were members of the public and many of the members of the Shuttermasters Club, plus quite a few parishioners, including June and Malcolm, of course. There was no sign of Felicity, who had been *so* busy the evening before with flowers. She had not returned the key to the vicar until almost 10pm.

Revd. Hayes give a little speech and a blessing and Tom Davies said a few words about the blossoming of photography in the digital age... and then the exhibition was open. On the left wall as you came in was the expected series of nicely framed studies, many of which had been awarded prizes in the regional finals run by the *Amateur Photographer* magazine. It was the facing wall which was not as one might have expected. It appeared that all the framed photographs had been taken down and stacked carefully to one side. Now filling the entire wall were three huge, poster-size prints. The first was a blow-up of a very fruity, handwritten letter to a man called Paddy signed by a woman called June. The second was an AlgarveCars rental agreement showing, if you cared to look, a Mr Patrick O'Reagan and Mrs June Troughton as named drivers. The third was a grainy, indistinct time-stamped still, taken from what appeared to be some type of surveillance system showing the inside of a villa with a man and a woman, apparently in an embrace and a state of undress.

The display must have puzzled most of the visitors, but not quite all...

DEAR RUSSIAN SEX GODDESS

From: justanordinarybloke@hotmail.com
To: youngvirgin@iwillalwaysloveyou.com
Subject: Re: Russian sex goddess for love and more

Thank you for your recent unsolicited email which somehow avoided my junk-mail filter.

I suspect that you have your wires crossed somewhere because you refer to me as 'your superman' which I think you would doubt were you meet me (which is not going to happen, by the way)!

You offer to send me sexy pictures from an obscure website in Canada but at my age, that is not an appropriate way to get acquainted. Actually, it never was at any age.

Then you ask if I know that 'the loveliest girls in the world live in my country'. I don't, but in any case, this is an entirely untested matter of opinion.

I guess it depends what you are looking for, but I have learned that loveliness is a far more profound concept than just physical appearance, which is what you are hinting at in your saucy message.

You wonder if I 'would mind to finding a young and nice girl like me is'. Good luck with your English lessons. You are getting there.

Actually, since you ask, I have 'found' several young and nice girls – who are my granddaughters. We are certainly not acquainted in the way you are suggesting, of course, but thank you for checking, anyway.

I suspect that the web-link you attach would take me somewhere on the internet where I really don't need to go or see and quite probably something entirely unwelcome might attach itself to my laptop. Your email address is totally implausible – youngvirgin@iwillalwaysloveyou.com is much less credible than what might be more appropriate if you are really whom you sign yourself as. If what you say is true about your vital statistics why not try 'TashaKempinskya 362236@gmail.com'!

I am a little puzzled as to how you got my email address in the first place, but I think I have read that lists get traded on the inter-web. If I were you, I would ask for a discount. You are most unlikely to find your 'stud' if most of those you contact are in the same age group as me!

Personally, I believe your whole approach is flawed. If you are really looking for 'a kind and love-giving husband' in the West, it might be better not to link yourself to what appears to be a very seedy porn website. Believe you me: it is not marriage which will be uppermost in the minds of those who are likely to look at your provocative poses.

Anyway, I hope things go well for you and that you are not being brainwashed about what is going on in Ukraine. I know a thing or two about the Nazis and your politicians' description of the people of Ukraine is very wide of the mark.

Best of luck,
More-Robin-Than-Batman

DREAM JOB?

It is my first day at St Michael's and Year 12 seem almost as nervous as I am. They all know each other, of course, so I'm the stranger.

I have introduced myself and told them briefly what they'll be studying. It boils down to The British Empire for paper one, an in-depth study of Italy and Fascism for paper two and I'm just about to explain paper three when Mr Calman, a deputy head, knocks and enters. I remember him from my interview: the overlord of the humanities. He is a short, portly man with a bushy moustache which is a darker colour than his grey hair. He speaks with the hint of a Scots accent: 'Miss Parkin,' (I'm Mrs and it's Parkins with an 's') 'could you please come with me to the school office.'

I think my mouth drops open for this is, well, it is extraordinary and quite out of order in front of the seventeen pupils who are having their very first lesson of A-level history. But I am new and relatively inexperienced – this is only my second job. I am just wondering what will happen to the class if I go with him when another teacher arrives. She is a much older woman wearing a tweedy, knee length skirt and a lemon-yellow blouse. She gives a knowing nod to Mr Calman.

I leave the classroom with the deputy, who is mumbling an apology of sorts for 'the most unfortunate but rather urgent interruption.' I am completely unnerved by this and it suddenly flashes through my mind that something terrible may have happened to my husband, Mike.

'Has there been an accident?' I blurt out. Mr Calman, clearly in no mood for further explanation, shakes his head. 'Nothing like that – don't worry,' he says without looking at me and strides ahead through the still unfamiliar corridors. We turn left, then right and I am lost. We end up at the office of the headteacher, Donald Plackett. He's a demure man in his fifties with a completely shaved head, a light grey suit and rather prominent crooked teeth.

Why have I been hoiked out of my very first class? I am about to find out but first I am offered a seat, at which signal my guide, Mr Calman, retreats with a mumbled grovel to no one in particular.

'Miss Parlin,' Mr Plackett starts, getting both my name and marital status wrong, 'we have made a very unfortunate mistake, for which I am truly sorry.'

I wait for more but I am at least relieved that Mike is not dying in the casualty department of the county hospital.

'You see, we offered you the job in our history department when, by some completely inexcusable administrative mistake, we had already taken on another teacher for the same vacancy. It only became clear to us today when both of you turned up.' He stops and looks down at a sheet of paper on his desk. 'Instead of history, how would you like to be part of the religious education team, we have an opening there.'

I am about to kick that idea into touch when he continues. 'I see from your details that you did an A-level in divinity and we could offer you a bit more money on a higher point on the scale to make amends...'

Much as the modest financial up-lift would be welcome, it is not religious education that I want to teach, that I am cut out to teach or really qualified to teach. I am a history teacher. I want to stay a history teacher. I have spent most of the long summer brushing up on the topics I have been engaged by St Michael's to teach.

'I don't understand, Mr Plackett...' I start to say. I have been to meetings with other members of the history department before today's start of term. There was no confusion then. No double-booking. But he is not going to let me finish.

'It really is our mistake and we need to make things right for you and of course, for our pupils. They must always come first. Always.'

He may be right but I'm not sure how that squares with what is going on.

'I tell you what, why not meet Miss Leech? She leads the RI team. You'll get along really well, I'm sure. She's a lovely person.'

'I couldn't possibly...' I try to start again but Mr Plackett is not listening or waiting. He's picked up his desk phone and is making a call, smiling at me all the while in what he obviously thinks is a friendly way. His teeth really are very crooked.

'Why can you never get anyone when you want them,' he says to phone itself, replacing the handset, and he turns away from me and towards the side door which has remained open all the while.

'Caroline,' he sort of sings out and a woman a little younger than me emerges almost immediately in the doorway.

'Can you check when Miss Leech has a free, please, Caroline... You've met Miss Palin of course, haven't you?' using a new, wrong version of my name, and no, Caroline and I have not met before.

'Of course, we'll sort this all out very soon,' he tries to reassure me. 'You are going to be a most valuable member of staff, I can tell.'

Valuable is the last thing I am feeling. Worthless is nearer the mark.

'Mr Plackett. With respect,' (which I am not feeling), 'I came here to teach history. At my interview, I was told the school wanted me to take the A-level class in particular. It is wha...'

But yet again he is not going to let me finish. 'Yes, yes, all so very true. I completely understand. We have messed up. I can only apologise. Really. But meet Miss Leech. Meanwhile we'll sort things out. You can be sure.'

Actually 'sure' is not what I am experiencing at all.

He hardly pauses before summoning Caroline again. 'Miss Palin will meet Miss Leech while we sort things out here. She'll go with you now,' and I have been dismissed.

Caroline looks almost as confused as I, but she's perhaps more used to this type of situation and we both file out of the head's study.

She beckons me out into the corridor, where it seems we are unlikely to be overheard. 'Are you in the union,' she asks conspiratorially.

'No. Do you suppose I need to join?'

'Try to see Martin Sherman, he's the union rep here. I'd better not say any more,' and she slips back into the outer office.

I am left in the corridor, like a World War One solider abandoned in No-Man's Land. It seems a long way back to the trenches in the staff room, somewhere down the same corridor. I wander along, feeling that my career as a teacher has crashed. What I had been offered seemed like a dream job. Now it is becoming a nightmare.

I find the staff room which is occupied by one other person, whom I have not met before – but that's hardly surprising. I've met almost no one. We look at each other and he smiles. 'You're new, aren't you?' he opens. 'I'm Greg - physical education.'

'Hello, I'm Emily, Emily Parkins. It's my first day and I'm in the history department. At least I think I am.'

'Oh! I know what you mean – first days are like that, aren't they?' he replies. He hasn't the first idea of my predicament but I don't care to explain, so I nod shyly.

'Must go,' he says, putting his large mug in the sink. 'Nice to have met you…' and he's gone.

* * *

It is now Tuesday lunchtime and I am back in school, but not yet teaching. I have another meeting with Mr Plackett in about ten minutes. I've just finished talking to Martin Sherman who has been really helpful. I've filled in the form to join the union but technically I'm not a member yet, so he can't formally represent me. I feel it's my own fault in a way because I should have joined when I had my first teaching post two years ago. It's just that there was no union rep at the last school. Martin has no idea what is going on in the history department, except that another new teacher, Mrs Callaghan, is now taking the Sixth in history, according to what he understands. She's not in the union and he says so far, no one on the school grapevine knows much about her. I wonder if she's the tweed-skirt-woman who came into the room as I was ushered out.

I managed to meet Miss Leech yesterday in the late morning. She had been told to 'make time to see me' and was clearly a bit resentful, but I think she knew it was not my fault and tried to be pleasant when I explained what had happened. She didn't understand what was really going on any more than I did but said that she'd welcome almost anyone – they had found it hard to fill the post. I was still far too confused to say anything much, but I certainly do not want to be *almost anyone*. After that, Mr Calman told me I should go home and the school would contact me 'very soon to straighten things out'.

I phoned Mike as soon as I was off the school premises and tears just poured out. He couldn't believe what I told him and came home early. I rechecked my one-year contract: 'History Teacher'. No quibble about that. Then we talked about what had happened but got no nearer to understanding what was really going on. He could tell that the whole St Michael's dream was turning sour for me. 'It's probably just a little glitch and will be sorted by tomorrow,' he tried to suggest.

'It's the way they handled it as much as anything,' I moaned. 'And I thought St Michael's was a top school. Perfect catchment area. I'm not so sure, now!'

So here I am.

Caroline comes down to the staff room to meet me. She can't meet my eyes. 'Something unexpected has come up,' she says. 'Mr Plackett is very sorry but he's had to postpone your meeting. He wants you to come back this afternoon at four-thirty.'

'So what about my classes today,' I ask, already suspecting the answer.

'They've been covered,' she says, still avoiding my eyes.

'Is it Mrs Callaghan?' I ask.

'Yes… I must go. I can't say any more. Come back at four-thirty. I'm sure they'll sort you out then.'

I wonder if I'm a re-incarnation of Katherine Howard, suddenly out of favour and about to lose my head…

I try to get hold of Mike but I know it will not be easy. He usually turns off his mobile while working. I leave a message – he will probably turn it on again in the lunch break.

I don't want to stay on the school site until this afternoon, so I walk into the town centre. It is at least a couple of miles but it is pleasantly warm today and it looks as if it might stay dry, unlike the forecast which predicted showers.

I've been mooching around the shops, getting more and more miserable, when Mike rings. I tell him that I've been fobbed off. He's very vocal and rightly angry, but it doesn't actually help. 'I'll pick you up from school after your meeting,' he promises. 'I'll wait in the car park.'

I don't feel like catching the bus home so I buy a sandwich and go to the public library. They've got Dairmaid MacCulloch's book on Thomas Cromwell on the front shelf and I sit down and start reading. It is fascinating and the time passes more quickly than I feared.

It is spitting with rain as I walk back to St Michael's, very light precipitation that on a warm day makes the atmosphere heavy but I don't really get wet. However, I am dripping with perspiration when I get to Mr Plackett's office. Is it the weather or anxiety? The pupils have left for the day but Caroline is still in the outer office.

'He's just finishing a phone call, I'll tell him you're here.'

Mr Plackett comes out shortly after. He's wearing the same light grey suit but today his shirt is black. I briefly wonder if it is an omen.

'Mrs Parkins, it is Mrs, isn't it? I'm sorry about this morning,' he opens, this time getting both my name and marital status right. Is it a good sign? 'We are in a bit of a cleft stick and it has rebounded on you, I'm afraid.

'I won't go into all the tiny details, but when our HR department computerised their system before the summer, they got things a bit mixed up. So you got the offer of a job when we had already appointed someone else.' He laughs, perhaps nervously, and I find myself staring again at those crooked teeth.

My dander is up, as they say, but I speak as politely as I can muster: 'Mr Plackett, I accepted the job after your school wrote to me offering me an initial one-year appointment as a history teacher. That's really all I want to teach. I'm prepared to be flexible to a degree, but I'm not happy about teaching RI full-time for a year. It is not what my contract states.'

He looks flustered. Perhaps he's not used to young female teachers being so bold.

'Well, of course, there are bound to be some times during the year when one of the other members of the history department is unavailable, off sick or something. You'll be first reserve, ready in the wings, so to speak.'

My heart sinks. This is going to be impossible and my eyes are beginning to fill.

'I joined the union yesterday, Mr Plackett, and Martin Sherman will be advising me. I…'

He doesn't let me finish.

'Of course, everything we do is entirely in accord with agreements and best practice guidelines, Mrs Parlin.' (My name has changed again.) 'It's entirely up to you, of course. I'd probably be in the union too, in your shoes. In the meantime, we will want to use your undoubted skills elsewhere in the school. It'll give you and us a chance to get to know each other better.'

This is not what I want to hear…

'Bob Calman, you know him, of course, will have a work schedule ready for you tomorrow morning. Let's call it a temporary glitch while we sort you out properly. How's that?'

I wonder if he was asking me or appealing to a cricket umpire.

I give it one last go. 'I really want to teach History – exam level. I turned down other job offers to come here to do just that. I made that…'

Again, he doesn't let me finish. He never has, I realise.

'Quite so, quite so,' he says and now I feel patronised and a bit silly. 'Well done!' Is he congratulating me or himself? And he shows me to the door.

I leave, feeling perhaps like Thomas Cromwell, ill-equipped to survive the terrifying unpredictability of Henry VIII and his toxic regime.

Mike is my beacon of strength and sanity, waiting for me in our Micra in the school car park. As he sees me approach, he gets out and gives me a much-needed hug. 'How was it?' he asks and now the tears really do flow.

When I have gathered a little composure, I tell him all about it.

'They're fobbing me off, I can tell. I'm not the gullible fool they're taking me for. And Plackett doesn't ever let me finish. He doesn't even get my name right half the time.'

It is pouring out of me.

Mike takes me home, gives me a big bunch of flowers, and talks sense. 'Your union rep, what's his name, Sherman, will see that they play fair, I'm sure,' he says.

I'm not so sure. Is this their Operation Mincemeat or my Agincourt moment?

We open a bottle of wine with supper and I start to relax.

'We'll get through this,' Mike says.

'Maybe, but I don't want a Pyrrhic victory,' I stress.

* * *

It is Wednesday morning and fortunately, the alarm goes off on time. I am woken from a strange dream in which I am on an Ottoman galley at Lepanto. All is lost. Mike takes me to school himself, no bus ride today, and gives me a reassuring hug.

'I'll keep my phone switched on… Remember you're worth more than any of them,' he says.

31

I'm a bit early and I wait in the staff room for Mr Calman. I wait and wait. It is after 9.30 when he arrives, obviously flustered by something.

'I'm sorry to do this to you, Miss Parkins, but please go home and wait for us to call you. I can't say any more. You are on full pay, you know. I'm so sorry.'

He is not going to say any more and there's no point in staying. I try to find Martin Sherman, but he's teaching and I leave a note in his pigeon-hole.

I wander out of the school grounds. It is cooler than yesterday, overcast but dry, and I decide to walk home. It takes me just over an hour. This is starting to be something of a recurrent nightmare, isn't it? Not so much a battle, more the Wars of the Roses.

I spend the day in the house. We moved in during the early summer and there are still boxes to unpack. I ring Mike and tell him about school developments.

'Are you OK,' he asks, obvious concern in his voice.

'Sort of,' is my answer. I should have said, 'Not really.'

Caroline rings just after three. 'I know this is a highly irregular, Emily,' (wrong-footing me with the use of my first name) 'but could you possibly come here after school at six today to meet the chair of governors, Dr Hawthorne?'

Anything is better than limbo and, very puzzled, I agree, immediately ringing Mike to update him. He'll be home in time to take me, he promises.

I spend the next hour or so looking up what I can about Dr Rosemary Hawthorne, OBE, on the internet. She is also chair of a higher-education body I have never heard of. There's not much else about her I can find out. In desperation, I ring Hilary Spencer, who was my supervisor while I was at Sheffield doing my diploma. I haven't spoken to her in over a year but we always got on really well. She listens carefully, makes reassuring noises and says she'll find out what she can and get back to me.

I kick myself for not contacting her sooner.

I shower and change and Mike is punctual as usual. Just before six, I'm back in school. I've been told to go to the head's office and I knock on the door.

I'm feeling strangely resolute. Ready for battle. Belligerent even. Wellington comes to mind.

Dr Hawthorne opens the door herself and invites me in with a grave smile. She's a tall, graceful Black woman, wearing a well-tailored dark blue suit. 'Do sit down, Mrs Parkins,' she says. 'This is Mr Bellingham. I hope you don't mind if he sits in on this. I'll explain everything.'

I nod agreement. As if I had an option.

'St Michael's owes you a huge apology,' she opens. 'This must have been awful for you, and on behalf of the governors, I am truly sorry for what you have gone through.'

I am warming to Dr Hawthorne.

'What you'll probably most want to hear is that from tomorrow, you'll be back teaching history here, as you had expected. Your timetable has been reinstated in full. I'm sure you are really well prepared and we are lucky to have you.'

I can't believe my ears and I am welling up. I blink away tears.

'I'm afraid I cannot go into all the details about what has happened here now. We are still going through a process. But Mr Bellingham has just taken over from Mr Plackett and is the acting head with immediate effect.'

Mr Bellingham, who looks as if he's in his sixties and has a tidy, white, close-cropped beard and a shiny pate, smiles across at me and says, 'I hope you understand that none of what has happened here is in any way your fault and St Michael's should not have put you through this. You have joined a great school with a proud history and I will make sure it stays that way.'

More is said, but I am now lost in emotion and not taking much in.

I am back on my original timetable from tomorrow morning. I am riding away from the battlefield victorious. There may have been casualties.

Mr Bellingham accompanies me to the car park where Mike is waiting. He makes a point of going up to Mike, introducing himself and apologising to him for 'what you and your wife have been through these three days'. Like me, Mike is lost for words.

Driving back in the car, we are relieved and confused. What has happened to Mr Plackett? Where did Mr Bellingham spring from? What is going on? I tell Mike the story of Stonewall Jackson's success at Chancellorsville in 1862. He usually likes my historical anecdotes.

* * *

St Michael's is a buzz of intrigue and rumour for the next few weeks. No one seems to know for sure what has gone on but Mr Plackett is on 'garden leave' and Mr Bellingham quietly gets on with his job at the helm. There appears to be no truth in the story that my 'problem' was caused by computer glitches in the HR department. Neither the part-time HR administrator nor Mrs Callaghan are around now and there is speculation about the teacher's 'romantic' connection with Plackett, much of it entirely fanciful, some of it possibly true. I have a sneaking suspicion that Bob Calman knows more than most, but he is being discreet. I may find out more this evening when Mike and I meet Caroline and her boyfriend for a drink in the pub.

OUT OF PRACTICE

It is Sunday afternoon and the snow outside is falling quite steadily but, thankfully, not settling.

The forecasters say it will stop before the evening when it will get colder. I am concerned about this because I have to go in to the office tomorrow, actually for the first time this year. I will need to use the car, and I don't relish having to clear the drive or motor on icy roads. I am due in at 10, so no slouching round in my 'comfies'. Back to the routine, hey. Early breakfast, a shave, for God's sake. Clean white shirt, tie!

I have had several days to speculate about why I am to attend the partners' meeting. Until last year, it was not that uncommon for all us middle-rankers to be asked to sit in on the quarterly meetings and be updated by one of the 'four suits', as we refer to them, on some aspect of practice development.

But since we started working from home, at first only a few days a week, back last March, none of us has had to attend a partners' meeting as far as I know. I don't even know if such meetings have taken place. Probably not. Or maybe on Zoom. I didn't much care until a few weeks ago.

Kendrick rang me one evening, not long into the New Year, to ask me what I had heard, which at that point was nothing. He said the word was that the firm was letting people go.

When I started working from the home-office, as I now call the spare bedroom, there was such a backlog of cases to finish that there was, as usual, too much work, not too little.

But during the course of 2020, that mountain has been slowly whittled down, with no thanks to the courts, which are being exceptionally slow and unhelpful. Now those cases which can be settled have been, in the main. Others, which have to go to proceedings, are stuck in a hopeless queue. And, according to Kendrick, who seems to have his ear to the ground, very little new work is coming in. Even conveyancing is down to a bare minimum, he says.

When he first alerted me to the prospect of some 'blood-letting', I assumed it would be on the basis of last-in-first-out and that several juniors and trainees would not be made up. Now I'm not so sure.

Evans & Kitson (actually there are three Evanses and one Kitson) is, I suppose, a successful legal practice. In this small town, we are well known and mostly well respected. Down in Cardiff, we might seem stuffy and old fashioned, which we are, but here in Builth Wells, we fit in perfectly. Anyone who is anyone knows Gwynne Evans; most know his two sons, Rhodri and Dafydd; and although Cameron Kitson has only been with the firm a few years, he is no longer really regarded as an outsider.

There are seven of us 'middles', eight if you include John Parsons, who is a consultant. I hear the family-law team is still pretty busy, but there's me and Kendrick on farming and commercial and we have both had to do all types of other stuff these last few months.

Molly says that I worry too much, but then she doesn't see the big picture. You see, I think they might try to save more money if they let one of us go, rather than a newbie. Glenys, our practice manager, didn't give me any idea about why they want me to come in, and, I suppose typically, I didn't ask. Molly says that I should have.

At the time... Oh! I don't know. Perhaps I thought they'd got one of those more sensitive or technical cases that they needed to brief me on in person. But now I have had time to think, I realise that old Mr Gwynne wouldn't do that at a partners' meeting, would he? So now I'm left worrying and wondering. Something gives me the feeling that Kendrick may know more than he's letting on, too.

Actually, at the back of my mind, I have the feeling that this might be the end of me and 'EEEK' as I think of our firm. I am fifty-nine, but sometimes I feel older, especially these days. When I started out, I expected to retire at 60, but nowadays... Parsons is somewhere in his seventies. Funny thing is, since I've been working from home, I have got used to being here all day. So has Molly.

Can't pretend that I'm looking forward to tomorrow, though...

THEY DIED IN THEIR MILLIONS

They died in their millions, those ancestors of ours
And now we buy poppies; and now we place flowers

They marched in their lines, then died in a trench
The Germans, the British, the Russians, the French
The political elite, those masters of war,
Heard of the deaths and said, 'Send in some more'.
And when it was over, the end of the game,
The lawyers wrote treaties apportioning blame.

They died in their millions, those ancestors of ours
And now we buy poppies; and now we place flowers

And the wise and great promised peace evermore,
And they called their mistake 'the war to end war'
But listen, my darling, to the radio news:
They're killing the gypsies, slaughtering the Jews,
So it's back into battle with shiny new guns
This time we'll teach them, those terrible Huns

They died in their millions, those ancestors of ours
And now we buy poppies; and now we place flowers

Johnson and Bush, Thatcher and Blair
They all said that bombs would make the world fair
And now it's civilians who die in their scores
Mothers and children, the victims of wars
But ask any parent who weeps for a son
Whether peace is delivered at the end of a gun

They died in their millions, those ancestors of ours
And now we buy poppies; and now we place flowers

They stand at The Cenotaph in their shiny new shoes
Then walk to the Abbey in their ones and their twos
Security tight, a sermon ensues...
Solemn expressions for televised news
Then it's back to business for the mongers of war
Not enough weapons? Well, let's make some more

They died in their millions, those ancestors of ours
And now we buy poppies; and now we place flowers

The gentle, the peaceful, the kind and the good
Know that these weapons can only spill blood
And yet we still make them, sell then abroad
And the same politicians all grin and applaud
Arms sales means jobs and votes that are dear
But the guns that <u>they</u> sell will kill <u>us</u> next year...

They died in their millions, those ancestors of ours
And now we buy poppies; and now we place flowers

DEATH AND TAXES

He was so obviously pleased with himself. Veronica sensed that as soon as he came in the drawing room. His chest puffed out inside his mustard-colour waistcoat, redness in his cheeks emphasising earlier excess at The Red Lion.

'Your lunch with Paul went well then?'

Graham grinned. 'I should say so. Between us, we've cracked it.'

She knew better than to press her husband further. He'd fill in the details when he felt like it.

'I could murder a black coffee,' he said, slumping in his usual chair. Veronica went through into the kitchen and idly picked a few grapes from the fruit bowl while she waited for the kettle.

Her thoughts were miles away from Ballington Hall and the estate when the phone rang. She picked up the extension: 'Two-one-nine.'

'Hi, Mum. What's new?'

Matthew's calls were rare. Unlike his sister, Susan, he had little time for the niceties of the landed gentry or farm talk. He was regarded as a black sheep by his unsympathetic father.

'Lovely to hear from you, darling. Is everything OK?'

'Yes, fine. We're just going to have breakfast and I thought I'd see how things are back in perfidious Albion.'

They chatted on about nothing much. The kind of call Veronica loved but rarely had with her transatlantic son.

'Your father appears to have made a breakthrough,' she told him. 'Are you sure you are happy about all this.'

'Quite sure. I don't approve, anyway. Glad I'm out of it all.'

Veronica let that hang there. The last thing she wanted was to stir things up. Graham would come down on her hard if he thought she was doing that.

They talked for just a little longer. Afterwards, she made the coffee and went back into the drawing room. Predictably, Graham was asleep in his chair, snoring.

She left a cup when he'd be less likely to knock it over and went into the new conservatory. The sun was getting low and she gazed out, enjoying the warm autumn light just catching the tops of the hills. Their own land as far as the eye could see. A lifetime's work, improving the estate until it was the envy of Cumbrian landowners. She was still elegantly good looking. The struggles of the past didn't show. Perhaps those expensive balms did work, after all.

* * *

Graham had changed into something more comfortable and they were sitting at the scrubbed-wood kitchen table. Dressed down for a light supper after such a heavy stint at lunchtime. Cook was off so it was scrambled eggs on toast, smoked salmon on the side. Veronica had taken off her Harrod's green apron.

'Paul's found another of his loopholes,' Graham mumbled through a mouthful of egg. 'This one's the biz. I just need to live till I'm seventy-five… You may need to have another few years, too.'

Veronica smiled weakly. 'I'll do my best.'

'We transfer the whole shebang to Susan and Jason. Everything. Now. It'll all be in their names. We'll have no assets. Nothing to pay the greedy taxman.'

'Isn't that a bit risky?'

'Only a tiny bit. Jason could turn over his tractor, I suppose. Life's a bloody risk. But not a certainty like grasping taxes, is it?'

'But where will we live?'

'Here at the Hall – nothing will change really. Just the deeds, the certificates, that sort of stuff. Paul thinks we might have to pay the two of them a peppercorn rent, just to keep HMRC sweet.'

Veronica was not happy. 'What about Matthew?'

'He said he doesn't want anything. I'm taking him at his word,' Graham said, trying not to sneer. Underneath he'd been bitterly disappointed that his only son had not wanted to take more interest in the farm, but the two had clashed from when the child was quite little.

She knew better than to raise more objections and she understood her husband's motivation. When he had inherited everything, the estate had been run down. Barely productive. The Hall in bad repair. The death duties were crippling.

Back then, they'd talked about selling up and starting again somewhere else. Possibly even abroad. But the Ballingtons went back to the 17th Century. Through good times and bad, the family had held onto a sizeable part of east Cumbria, from Sedbergh almost to the Dales. And so, with grit and determination, they soldiered on. Graham was both reasonably shrewd and very lucky. He admitted only to the former. Veronica, loyal, intelligent and with better judgement, quietly helped keep the project on course, a role which was barely acknowledged. She's been brought up to marry well, cook tolerably, ride elegantly and breed copiously. She'd done all of these, none to excess, but she was much shrewder than her husband and had kept him on course, allowing him all the time to feel he was in charge.

* * *

'Are you sure you won't finish them?' Susan asked her mother. They were in Betty's in Harrogate, pigging out on afternoon tea. Their usual table was surrounded by carrier bags from the day's purchases. Veronica thought her daughter might show more restraint, too. She was getting rather broad in the beam.

'Quite sure, darling. You know where it shows!' Hint, hint.

'You're still lovely, Mum. No one would guess your age.'

'Thank you, dear.' Long pause. 'Has your father said anything about what he discussed with Paul?'

'No.'

'Well, I better not say too much. You and Jason, you're OK, aren't you?'

'Yes, of course we are. Why do you ask? What's this about?'

'It would be better coming from him. I don't know all the details. We're handing over the estate to you...'

'What?'

'Death duties. You know what your father worries about. He and Paul have come up with this scheme.'

'What scheme?'

'We give everything to you two. Now.'

'Now!'

'Seems so.'

'Oh! My God!'

'Don't let on that I've said anything, will you?'

'Of course not. Mum, have you thought this through?'

'I think your father has.'

'Oh! God, Mum, I don't know if we're ready for this.'

'Nor do I, darling, but you know your father. There'll be no stopping him now.'

They asked for a refill of tea and talked some more. Both had a sense of unease and stuck to the topic of furnishing the conservatory during their two-hour drive back to Sedbergh.

* * *

It had been one of those days. No 97, a big awkward beast, wouldn't go in. Unsettled some of the others. Jason hoped it wasn't the start of something. Then he noticed some teat-end damage. Things come in threes, don't they, he thought to himself. He was right. The storage tank thermostat was playing up. That would cost. Lose this tankful. Then a repair. And it had rained all day, like it did in Cumbria. Steady, not hard, but the ground was a mess. To cap it all, Taylor had not turned up. Didn't ring, just didn't arrive. He'd no time to sort out that waste-of-space. Have to see to the broken fence himself. And everything else.

It was later than usual when he came down after his shower. Long and hot. The kitchen was scattered with her purchases. Nothing on the cooker.

'Susan,' he bellowed.

'In here, dear,' but she could hear the irritation in his voice. 'Just coming…'

The sushi she'd brought back for supper was not well received.

'I don't want this foreign muck when I've been working all day,' he spat. 'You could at least have brought a curry to microwave.'

She laughed. 'You mean you want different foreign muck?'

He smiled back. Anger gone. 'You've been on a spending spree, I see.'

'I have, and I've something really big to tell you.'

'You're not, are you?'

'Not what? Oh! That! No, I'm not… but we are going to be rich!'

'You've won the lottery!'

'No. Dad's going to give us the estate. You mustn't say anything. It's not official. But he's going to give it to us now. We don't have to wait. We won't have to share it with my brother.'

'What-d-you mean "Now"? He's not ill, dying, is he?'

'No, nothing like that. He's avoiding taxes.'

'So? What? He's giving everything to us. Now? The Hall, the estate, everything? Where are they going to live?'

'I don't know the details. We'll have to wait until it's all official. But he and Paul, you know Paul, have worked it all out.'

'Bloody Hell.'

'You mustn't say a word. Promise. Mum told me in confidence. Even she doesn't know the ins and outs.'

Jason was speechless. No more days like today, wet, muddy and unrewarding. Money issues over. The good life, just around the corner.

* * *

'You're sure you don't mind?' Susan insisted.

She was on the phone to her brother in Los Angeles.

'Listen to my words. I'll say them again. I. Don't. Want. Any. Of. It. Clear enough?'

Brother and sister rarely talked. Other side of the world. It wasn't that they didn't get on. They'd just gone their different ways.

'If you change your mind, then what? It'll be awful.'

'Listen, Susie' – no one else ever called her that – 'I have made a different life for myself out here. I love teaching at Pepperdine. Jon and I are settled. We're not coming back to be lords of the effing manor.'

'Yes, but the money… you know…'

'Get yourself on a plane. Come out here. Sunshine. Fun. Great people. We do fine. What do I want with any of that?'

'We might just do that – come out to see you, Matt. Me and Jason. Once this is all settled. I haven't seen you since our wedding.'

'Be great to see you, Sis. I just hope it's really what you both want…'

It was, wasn't it? The Hall, the land, the money, the status. While they were both young enough to enjoy it. To start a family. Three children. She'd always thought three would be good. Maybe four. Perhaps Mum and Dad would move into their farm. It wasn't bad. Could be a nice home for a retired couple. There would probably be enough money around to do it up. Mend the roof where it was starting to go. Add some nice touches. Dad might even want to help looking after the herd... He wasn't ready to retire, was he? Ballington Hall. Bloody Hell. She'd never really thought about it like this. Not so soon, anyway.

* * *

There were six of them in the dining room. The lovely burr walnut table covered by a thick protector to prevent any marks. It seemed to go on for ever. Just when one set of papers had been properly dealt with, Paul, with his pencil-straight back and pencil-straight manner, fished out more. All needed signatures: transfers, changes of title, powers of attorney, assignments. Deeds, certificates, forms, declarations.

The young couple had been given time to read everything beforehand. 'If we can't trust each other, we're all screwed,' Jason had said, giving the papers a cursory once-over. 'I didn't understand it all anyway. Graham has explained the basics,' he admitted.

Mr Doughty from the bank, thin-faced and unsmiling, was there to sign as a witness – Paul was not allowed to because of his role as a professional advisor.

When it was over, and Mr Doughty had been seen out, the champagne flowed. 'You just need to live for another eight years, don't you, Dad?' Susan joked. The rule meant that the tax liabilities decreased to zero by then.

'That's why Jason is not going to get me mixed up with a pheasant during a shoot, purely by accident, of course,' he quipped back.

Driving to their farmhouse afterwards, too much alcohol inside him to be entirely safe or legal, Jason observed, 'It seems a bit funny to be driving back to Underbank when we now own the Hall.'

'I know what you mean,' Susan replied. 'Makes one think, doesn't it?'

* * *

'You're going to be a grandmother,' Susan said, glowing.

It was another of their Tuesday outings together and they were having an expensive lunch. 'That's why I'm not drinking anything.'

'Oh! Darling, that's wonderful,' Veronica said, not entirely sure that she was ready to be called 'granny'. 'When did you find out?'

'I did a test at the weekend. Then yesterday, I went to see Dr. Rachel at the practice. She confirmed it.'

'That's marvellous news.'

'We're thrilled. It seems like the right time now that things are a bit different.'

'Have you any idea when?'

'Probably early January. Not brilliant timing, but...'

'Oh! I'm so pleased. For you both. How's Jason about it?'

'He's delighted too. Said it was about time! He thinks *he's* done the hardest bit...'

'Men!'

'I know but we might be surprised. I've got a tiny feeling he could turn out to be a great dad.'

'Well, you can never tell. I thought that about your father. He badly wanted children, he said. But it was never the right time. I had to just... well, you know...'

'Oh! Mum. You've never told me that before.'

'He is who he is. He wasn't any different then from how he is now. And he'll never change.'

They certainly agreed on that.

* * *

He slammed the letter down so hard that Veronica thought the table would collapse. His face purple, his language blue. 'What did we agree? What did we fucking agree?'

'Agree what,' Veronica asked timorously.

'Your daughter and her bloody husband. They want to come to live here. In the Hall.'

Veronica looked nonplussed. '*Our* daughter...'

'Well, they can't. They just can't. We have an agreement.'

'I'm sure we can sort this out,' she said.

'Read the letter. Read. The. Bloody. Letter.'

She picked it up. Her daughter's handwriting. She'd gone to a good school: it showed. She read it quietly, her husband glowering. They wanted to start their family here in the Hall. It was theirs, after all. Grandparents-to-be could move into the East Wing. They could make it self-contained. Or they could swap houses. Move to Underbank Farm.

'The cheek. Well, they can't. I'll tell them. Kick us out? Not likely.'

Veronica said nothing.

'I didn't spend my life building this place back up just to clear off when some yokel who has married my daughter feels like taking over.'

Veronica stayed silent.

'An agreement is an agreement. That's all there is to it!' He grasped the letter in his fist, rose from the breakfast table and swept out, car keys in hand.

Veronica thought for a few moments before she picked up the 'phone.

'Your father is on the way over,' she warned. 'He's in a rage. You know why.'

Susan did.

'Is this all Jason's doing?' Veronica asked.

'No, Mother. It is not. It doesn't feel right. You two in that great mansion, us in this farmhouse, starting a family. We own the Hall, legally.'

'I suppose you do, dear, but there's an agreement, isn't there?'

'Well, words were said, Mum, but there's nothing in writing.'

'Isn't there? Are you sure?'

'We've been into this with Mr Doughty, you know, from the bank.'

'And…?'

'And he explained that it was a verbal exchange at the time. An understanding. There couldn't be any more or it would have broken the rules. Seen as a tax dodge.'

'Yes, darling, but if there was an understanding…'

'Well, that was before we knew we were starting a family. Circumstances change. You wouldn't mind moving into the East Wing, or coming here, would you?'

'I'm not sure, dear. I'd need time to think about that.'

'Hang on, there's someone coming. It might be him. I'll ring you later.'

* * *

Matthew put his arms around his mother and they hugged. Hard. For a long time. Her tears silently flowing.

'It's so good to see you. I wasn't sure you'd come.'

'Of course I was coming. I've only one father, haven't I? Or did have.'

'Yes, but you two didn't get on. Never did.'

'Well, that's all in the past now, isn't it?'

She looked older and black had never suited her.

'The car's parked on Level Five. I hope you are still allowed to drive over here.' He said he was and drove them back from the airport. His mother talked almost all of the way. Out it poured. The grief, the hurt, the last twelve years of misery, first in the East Wing, then in Underbank. She'd lost her new conservatory.

He'd heard much of it before. From her and from Susie. Two sides of the coin. Quite different. Almost no similarities. It was going to be a big funeral. Hundreds. Graham had been well liked, especially earlier. And the Ballingtons... Not many were likely to miss this one.

Heads turned as the family came into St Andrew's. Sympathy for the grieving widow and for her sun-tanned son few of them barely remembered. A definite murmur as Susan entered with the twins and carrying her youngest. Last of all, Jason with twelve-year-old Oliver, now the spitting image of his grandfather, striding down the aisle, ignoring the glances and growing whispers, taking their place on the front pew.

HOUSE CALL

Beryl St James was a short woman of uncertain middle age with the kind of stout appearance which made one doubt that she'd ever been young. Her newly-dyed ginger hair was clearly not as naturally wavy as it was now presented and her complexion, even before eight in the morning, had been created with compliments to Max Factor. She was wearing an unflattering brown skirt and a pale blue twinset and she had pearl-coloured clips on her ears the size of mint imperials. Her none-too-dainty feet were deep inside a pair of pink fur mule slippers that all but still purred or squeaked.

'Come in, he'll be down in a minute,' she said, standing back from the front door to let me in and then leading me through to the large lounge,' which looked like a furniture showroom, empty of customers. I stopped in the doorway, sensing that the pale carpet had never been insulted by the pressure of outdoor shoes.

'I'd better take these off,' I said, looking down at my wet, worn footwear, now embarrassed that I had even crossed the threshold with shoes on. She left me to do just that while she crossed back to the bottom of the stairs.

'Kenneth,' she shouted. 'He's here – and on time.' I took the comment to be a dig at him, for he was rarely punctual. I think I could hear movement upstairs but it might have been the plumbing.

'Would you like coffee?' Beryl asked, sidling towards the open kitchen door. 'I'm sure you've got time.' If any food had ever been prepared in that kitchen, it had left no trace. The sink had an empty plastic bowl in it, perched on its side, and the JCloth still had original creases. I declined the offer. I didn't want her to have to think about throwing away the kettle because it had now been used.

'Do sit down, Alan,' she said, 'I'll take your coat,' and she reached out a slightly pudgy hand with a red-nail manicure to take my crumpled khaki parka. She held it like one might a poo-bag and I wondered if she had a special space where she could store such highly contaminated items... Cloakroom or incinerator? I couldn't be sure.

I looked round the room. The only ornament was a slim, stylised grey-and-white china greyhound sitting on its haunches on the shelf above the low gas fire. I suspected it had been given obedience training. Above it, The Chinese Girl with her tell-tale green skin frowned at me from her frame on the wall and I frowned back, sticking my tongue out.

'Kenneth,' Beryl screeched again from the foot of the stairs before coming back into the lounge, to find me almost hovering on the very edge of the dark-brown leather sofa.

'We still have some time,' I said, trying to diffuse the situation, although we'd have to get a move on to catch the 8.22.

'So, tell me, Alan, how are you settling in?' she asked. I'd been working with her husband for five months now. She had seen me several times in the office when for some reason she needed to come in with Ken. It had usually been when she was on her way to or from the hospital. 'Waterworks,' Ken had told me once, using a whispered voice that came with a suitable facial expression.

'Well, I think we've found a house,' I told her. 'It's rather stressful. There's a chain, of course. We've sold at the other end, but they are pressing us for completion. You know how it is.' She clearly didn't. I worked out later that she was possibly stuck with the mental image of a metal chain across the end of a long sweeping driveway.

At last, there was a noise from the top of the stairs and Kenneth descended noisily: the chief executive of Yorkshire Oil & Gas, wearing a well-tailored pinstripe suit, crisp white shirt, elegant silk tie and nonchalantly sporting a pair of novelty Big-Foot hairy monster slippers.

'Sorry to have kept you, Alan,' he said, smiling warmly at us both. 'Late night, you know. Shall we go?' I wondered if he was going to rush for the train still wearing those slippers.

'You haven't had any breakfast,' Beryl chided. Or anything else eaten in the never sullied kitchen, I mused…

'I'll be OK,' he said. 'Come on, let's go.' And he went out into the hallway where he swapped the silly slippers for a pair of polished black brogues. My parka was saved from the disposal unit and handed back to me with Beryl's reverse dog-poo gesture and Ken put on an only-worn-once-before trench coat as I fiddled with my scruffy shoes.

'See you later, love, don't wait up. It'll be a long one,' he said as he bent to offer a dutiful kiss to his wife's proffered cheek, and we were out of the door, up the drive on to the pavement before he spoke again.

'Sod the 8.22,' he said. 'Let's have a fry up at the station and catch the 9.22 instead.'

BEFORE CHRISTMAS

From the diary of Bernard, recently relocated to Missoula, Montana, USA

Wednesday November 23rd

More snow this morning. Dorothy next door says it started back in October, about a week earlier than normal, which means a hard winter. I wonder if she's right. I love snow.

She asked Glenys and me in for cherry pie and coffee. We've only been here since Monday but she's already been so nice. I'm glad we're here and not back in Milton Keynes. We hardly knew our neighbours there. Earl, her husband, works for a local car dealership. And it is something called Thanksgiving tomorrow. All her family are coming – she called them her folks. I said they should park on our drive; she says over here, it's a drive*way*.

Thanksgiving: Thursday November 24th

I love snow. That's partly why we moved here, but of course, mainly to be near our daughter, Gail, who's expecting her first. Chuck, our son-in-law, has a good job here in Missoula. I haven't really gathered exactly what he does, but whatever it is, Gail says he is doing really well.

About six inches of snow fell overnight and I spent the morning shovelling the 'driveway' and I also cleared the pavement outside – I suppose I should learn to call it the sidewalk now. At about lunchtime, a big street-maintenance truck came along and blew snow off the road, onto the sidewalk and across the end of the driveway – I had to clear it again so that Dorothy's folks could park. I wonder if it'll snow again tonight.

Friday November 25th

Exactly a month to go before Christmas and I spent the morning shovelling overnight snow from the driveway. I didn't clear the sidewalk in case the truck came past again but it didn't. Dorothy came round to say thank you for allowing people to park on our side. There were several of them, all with what we used to call a pickup. She seemed amused by the small car we have and suggested that we talk to Earl about trading it in for something bigger. They're such nice people.

Saturday November 26th

Great, still more snow. It is our first weekend here in Montana near our daughter. I'm glad we sold up and moved out here. We're never going back! After I had cleared the driveway and the sidewalk, I put on skis and slid into town. It only took me half an hour – and only twice as long to get back. When I got home, Glenys said there was something wrong with the heating. It appears the boiler isn't working: they call it a 'furnace' here. I went and asked Dorothy next door if she knew who could help. She told me Earl's cousin would call round later. They're so friendly here. The snow truck came and blew the snow back on the driveway. Apparently, they come every other day. I wish I'd known...

Later, Earl's cousin, Dean, came round to look at the furnace, even though it is a Saturday. So kind. I made a joke about 'Earl and Dean' but no one laughed. (Maybe they never had Pearl & Dean out here.) He said he could mend it but it might be better to buy a new one. He says the modern ones are more efficient. He also suggested that we might want to buy a different car: he is the second person to have mentioned it.

Sunday November 27th

It seems it snows most nights here through (or should I say thro) the winter – and sometimes in the daytime, too. I cleared the driveway and the sidewalk – no snow truck today: there you go! I've got the hang of it now.

Glenys and I wanted to go into town to meet Gail, our daughter, but I found the car wouldn't start after I had dug it out of the snowdrift. It doesn't seem to like the cold! Glenys rang Gail and rearranged our get-together for tomorrow.

Later the snow truck came past and blew snow off the road and over the driveway. I must ask Dorothy why it came today!

Monday November 28th

Dean called round to fit the new furnace. They do things so quickly here and without any fuss. It seems we've got the first of a brand-new model which has just come out. It is a lot bigger than we really need, but because it is new, it is on offer and we've got it at the same price as a smaller one. Dean is so thoughtful. Everyone seems to like our accent here, though they do confuse us with the Australians. When I told Dean that Glenys and I originally came from Wales, he was even more confused.

I remembered to ask Dorothy why the snow truck had come round yesterday and she said it was because it was the Sunday after Thanksgiving. I wish I'd known. Later, I shovelled about eight inches of fresh snow off the driveway and tried to open the garage door to put the car inside but it was frozen closed. And I didn't manage to start the car… Glenys rang Gail to tell her we couldn't make it into town today, either.

Tuesday November 29th

It was sixteen below last night. The new furnace isn't working too well and we are very cold. I rang Dean first thing this morning and asked him to come round. He said he'd try. There was no snow overnight but it is really icy now and the sidewalk is treacherous. Dorothy invited us in for coffee when she learned that our heating wasn't working well. She says Dean is a bit of a cowboy, much like the rest of Earl's 'kin' as she called them. We can't get the car out because the snow that the truck blew across the end of driveway is now frozen solid. Anyway, the car still doesn't seem to want to start, so we couldn't drive in to town anyway. Glenys rang Gail again to explain. She said not to worry, she'd come out to see us.

Later, after seeing me struggling with the icy blockage at the end of the driveway, Dorothy suggested that instead of digging snow with a shovel, I should buy a 'motorized pedestrian snow blower'. Her cousin, Danny, sells them at a good price. We're lucky to have such a nice 'neighbor'.

Thursday December 1st

A new month and more than a foot of new snow has fallen in two days. Lovely.

I didn't write my diary yesterday. It was not a day to remember. I tried to ring Dean but there was no answer. We were too cold to do much and I still couldn't start the car.

Today, things are looking up. Danny came round with a snow blower and helped me set it up. He's so helpful. It's a great bit of kit! Then he helped open the frozen garage door so we could put it away safely. Unfortunately, that means we can't put the car away but it doesn't really matter because I haven't been doing that anyway.

Luckily, we have plenty of food in the amazing two-door fridge we got with the house. Gail came round for coffee. So good to see her. She suggested that we should get someone else to fix the heating. She doesn't seem to think Dean is up to the job. Perhaps I shouldn't say this because she is our daughter, but she is *so nice*. She said we should trade the car for a 4x4: everyone has them around here apparently. I'll talk to Earl about it tomorrow.

There's fresh snow falling now. Great! I can use the new blower in the morning.

Friday December 2nd

I was trying to open the frozen garage door to get out the snow blower when Dean came round to look at our heating. He said that it needed different fuel to work efficiently. He made some adjustments and said it should now work. Glenys and I are getting warm again after three cold nights!

I wanted to talk to Earl about changing the car for a 4x4 but they are not home next door. Glenys wonders if they have gone away for the weekend. Dorothy did say something about a cabin in the woods but I wasn't really paying full attention.

Saturday December 3rd

The sun came out today and the temperature rose a little. There are icicles everywhere. We went out into the garden: I can't get used to calling it a yard. That is how we met our neighbours on the other side for the first time. They seem so nice too, like everyone here. They had been away. They introduced themselves as Connie and Clyde. I said it sounded like Bonnie and Clyde, but no one laughed. (Maybe they don't remember the film with Warren Beatty and Faye Dunaway.) Clyde helped me get the snow blower out of the garage but between us, we couldn't start it. He said the cheap Chinese engines were not much good in the cold. I said my car was like that too, but it was American. He didn't laugh.

Sunday December 4th

More snow today, on top of the ice. It has made things very slippery. Glenys went down with a crack of the driveway. Earl, who had come back on his own from their cabin in the Blackfoot Valley, asked if she had hurt her fanny. I thought he was being very vulgar until it was explained to me that he meant her backside...

We couldn't get the snow blower going, nor the car. He said that Dorothy's cousin, Danny, was a bit of a cowboy and that all her kin folk were not much better than 'trailer trash'.

Monday, December 5th

Bright but cold today. Several degrees below. I wanted to talk to Earl about changing the car but he'd gone to work early, I presume and Dorothy was still not home. Strange, that. She'd normally been around most of the time.

Glenys rang Gail for a chat but we can't meet up at present 'til I can get the snow-blower going again and the car started. Still, we can walk to the local mall in a few minutes, so we're not short of food and we're going out for a pizza tonight.

Tuesday December 6th

We bumped into Earl at the pizza parlour last night. They only do take-outs so Earl came and had his pizza with us. He does eat a lot. Dorothy is still away but he didn't seem to want to talk about it. He said he'd be happy to sell me a car and I should pop in to his dealership today. He told me not to worry about bringing in my present 'vee-hickle' because he had seen it in our driveway so he knew what it was worth. Helpful as usual. A little more snow today. Still very cold and now the furnace is playing up again.

Thursday, December 8th

Our new car – or should I say truck – arrived today. A Dodge Ram Laramie. Earl says it was almost new and 'the best bargain on the lot'. I quipped that it seemed to cost a 'lot' but no one laughed. The garage sent a man to tow away our old car. The tow truck made short shrift of the snow and ice on our driveway. That's a relief. The driver was so nice. Dean came round and fiddled with the furnace. I don't know what he does in there, but after he'd been, it was working again: such a relief.

Saturday, December 10th

We were due to drive into town today to meet Gail for coffee, but the heating is playing up again so I needed to stay in for when Dean calls. Glenys won't drive over here. She has never driven on the right side of the road – she calls it the wrong side - or an automatic and she hates the big Ram truck. We said we would now meet Gail tomorrow, downtown.

Dean arrived and did something to the furnace. He said it should be OK now.

I couldn't get the snow blower working but I did manage to clear the end of the drive by shovelling. I now leave snow clearing until later in the day in case the snow truck drives past.

Sunday, December 11th

We took a cab into town to meet Gail. I should have thought of that before! I don't really like driving the Dodge either – it is way too big for me. Anyway, the snow-plough was round again and blew snow all over the end of the driveway, blocking it. They must have been clearing the road during the night. That is a new one! We left Dean in the house mending the furnace. When we got home, he had got it working again. He said the filter was clogged from the wrong type of fuel. Helpful and nice.

Monday, December 12th

The heating went off not long after Dean left. I couldn't get him on his cell phone. The cold kept us awake during the night, but perhaps it was just as well since it meant we saw the police car outside Dorothy's house at about 3am. No sign of Dorothy but Earl went off with the police. Later a policeman, Officer Krupczyk, called at our house. (Cat-sick, I called him but no one laughed). He was so nice. Asked a lot of questions but I'm afraid we couldn't give him much help. He wondered why our house was so cold. I told him about the furnace and how helpful Dean had been. He noticed the Dodge Ram as he was leaving and asked me about something called out-of-state vehicle registration. I said I'd talk to Earl about it and he just gave a sort of dry laugh…

Tuesday, December 13th

Gail called round unexpectedly this morning. She'd heard some local gossip and wanted to see if we were OK? She wouldn't say what the gossip was but it had really spooked her. I showed her the Dodge and she said it was too big for us. That's what Glenys thinks too. Women! Still, she admired the driveway. Said it was the clearest she'd seen in Missoula. I felt so proud. Later Dean rang. Said he'd heard we were still having trouble with the furnace. Helpful as always, he said he'd see what he could do.

Wednesday December 14th

Dean called to look at the furnace. He said there's a well-known problem with unreliable fuel supply in our area. Seems that this could be the problem. Dean said he'd change the filter which could be clogged again.

I also managed to get the snow blower working properly. Danny had thought it was his two-stroke model and had filled it with the wrong fuel. It can happen so easily. Now after draining and cleaning the fuel system and renewing the spark plug, it starts on the sixth or seventh pull without fail, which is just as well because there is heavy snow forecast tonight.

Saturday December 17th

The last weekend before Christmas and we finally managed to get out of the house today.

We've been snowbound for three days. I couldn't get the garage door open to use the snow blower until this morning. I'd have used the car but on Thursday, Officer 'Cat-sick' came to say there was some problem with the Ram's paperwork and I'd better not use it for now. Nice and helpful, like all the others. We're hoping that we can go round to have Christmas dinner with Gail and Chuck. Chuck's parents will be there over Christmas, too. We have never met them but they sound so nice.

Sunday December 18th

I wonder when Dorothy and Earl will be back home. I miss them both. Earl hasn't been around for a few days,

Dorothy even longer. Maybe he's snowed under with work. I expect Dorothy's stayed up at their cabin. Our driveway is quite empty now. A police tow-truck took away the Dodge this morning. I'm sure it's all pretty routine. Perhaps Earl screwed up on the paperwork. It is so easy to make a mistake with these complicated forms. He's always trying to help.

The furnace has been working perfectly for four full days now. The house is lovely and warm. We wanted to invite Connie and Clyde in for coffee this morning but they were at their church. Glenys says we should probably join a local church too. Everyone is so nice. We can't decide which one.

I have been kept quite busy with a small problem with the icemaker in the fridge. It won't stop making ice. It is fine as long as we keep a bucket under the door to collect the cubes as they plop out and we top up the reservoir every four hours or so. It only means getting up once or twice in the night. At my age, I have to do that anyway.

Tuesday December 20th

I'm really getting the hang of this snow blower now. First, I unfreeze the garage door. It only takes a few goes with the hot water straight from the coffee percolator. (We do miss an English kettle here, but no one's ever heard of them in Missoula). Once the door is freed, I've got starting the engine down to a fine art. I rarely have to pull the cord more than a couple of dozen times. It is so much easier to clear the driveway now that we don't have a vee-hickle on it. And if the snow plough comes, it is no big deal. After all, without a car, we can't be blocked in, can we?

Thursday December 22nd

We did our last shop at the mall today for Christmas. Glenys says she doesn't want to do any more shopping now until well after Christmas. We were hoping to firm up our Christmas arrangements with Gail, but she's not replying to our cell phone messages. She'll be so busy with such a big party to cater for. Helpful Dean came round and said he'd just check on the furnace. I offered him some of the spare ice from our fridge but he says he's got plenty.

Friday December 23rd

Connie and Clyde visited us today with a Christmas card. Nice to see them again. They brought us a copy of the local newspaper, *The Missoulian*. We were so surprised to see Dorothy's picture on the front page next to that of Earl. There must be some mistake. He's being held in connection with a murder. The paper claims Dorothy disappeared when they went to their cabin in the Blackfoot Valley. Clyde says that the TV reported that police found bloodstains in the snow. I expect it is all a big mistake. Maybe Earl went hunting. They all do that round here all the time. Gun mad really. He can't be a murderer. He's been so nice and helpful.

Later, Officer 'Cat-sick' came round with news. They are keeping our truck for a while longer while they examine it carefully. He said they had found *something* in it but wouldn't say what. It looked fine to me when Earl sold it to me. Perhaps it's just the paperwork. Poor old Earl. Connie from next door said I was being naïve and then clammed up. I'm not sure what she meant. She didn't need any ice cubes either. Shame.

It snowed quite a lot during the late afternoon, but since we're not doing much tomorrow, you know, Christmas Eve, I told Glenys I'd leave it overnight...

Christmas Eve: Saturday December 24th

It was quite cold overnight and snowed some more so I was busy blowing the snow away today when three police vee-hickles drew up outside and several men got out. They were wearing head-to-toe white overalls and wanted to check our furnace. I said it was working fine at last, but they didn't smile. Glenys said they were looking very carefully at stains on the floor of our boiler room and on the furnace itself. I expect someone spilled something in there. I told them that Earl's cousin, Helpful Dean as I call him, has been looking after everything. The police officers also seemed pleasant. They all have guns. They asked me if I had a gun. Of course not, I said, I'm British. They didn't laugh. I don't think they always understand our 'humor' here. They asked us not to go anywhere without telling them. I said that, apart from visiting Gail and Chuck, we were here to stay. I managed to give one of the officers a bucket of ice cubes. I told him we were glad to get rid of them.

Christmas Day: Sunday, December 25th

Glenys and I had an extra lie in this morning. We lay in bed and watched the snow falling outside. Then we got up for breakfast. Glenys eats something they call Granola and drinks 'juice'; eggs 'over easy' for me. We're real Americans now, aren't we... We were just getting dressed to go out when the door chimes went. It was Gail. I thought she'd come to fetch us. But she surprised us and said, 'It's over between Chuck and me.' I think she'd been crying because her eyes were very red. She said that Chuck had another 'girlfriend' who had arrived along with his parents. I was surprised. He always seemed so nice. Lucky that we have a big fridge, even if it does keep making ice, ceaselessly. Glenys said she could easily make lunch for the three of us. It didn't matter that we'd not got a turkey. I opened a bottle of Thunderbird. I've discovered that white wine is quite nice with ice cubes in it.

Over lunch, Gail explained that things hadn't been good between her and Chuck for a while. We couldn't tell. She'd hoped things would change but having a baby on the way had only made things worse. She said she'd asked her employers to transfer her back to Milton Keynes. They said they would see what they could do. I thought she was being a little hasty but I didn't say so.

After lunch, Officer Cat-sick called. He's so good he even works on Christmas Day. He said that they had found 'traces' in our boiler room which seemed to suggest that the furnace had been used to burn something other than fuel… He wouldn't say what but asked a lot of questions about Dean. I told him Dean had been so very helpful to us. When he left, I pressed him to take some ice cubes as a gift.

I know there have been some setbacks and surprises here in Missoula but it's been wonderful to have a white Christmas. Everyone's been so nice. Happy Christmas.

SLEEPLESS

It is late at night and I'm on my own – Mary went to bed about an hour ago. I've had my last swig of whisky and I have made myself put the bottle back on the shelf. I didn't have that much. Not really.

I go through into the kitchen because Rufus is scratching at the back door waiting to be let back in. We sit down together and talk for a while. I let him know what a lovely dog he is. Of course, he already knows that.

Also, he probably knows about the problem with Mary's younger sister, Gail, who isn't living with her husband any more. It is what we were talking about before she went to bed. Gail hasn't told Mary why she has moved out, so we can only speculate. She is now living in a small flat while Alan continues in that big house on his own. She won't ask him for anything. She hasn't taken legal advice. She doesn't seem to talk about it with anyone. We live less than half-an-hour away, but we might as well be on another planet.

Rufus doesn't know what to do about Gail either. Nor has he any idea about what to give Mary for her birthday at the weekend. I think he knows we've both left it too late, really. Maybe just flowers and chocolates again then, we agree.

I watch him lap water from his bowl which reminds me: 'Can you fix the bathroom ceiling where the leak came through?' I ask him. He doesn't seem to think he can. I try not to look too disappointed. I can't either. We are just discussing how to find someone inexpensive to do it when we hear a noise on the stairs.

Mary is coming back down. I put the whisky glass in the sink. She comes into the room, blinking and a bit bleary eyed. Rufus wags his tail. Bright as he is, he doesn't seem to realise that she's not going to take him for a walk when she's only wearing a nightie. I smile and put my finger to my lips, just to remind him not to tell her about the flowers and the chocolates.

'Aren't you coming to bed?' she asks. Neither of us answers. She sits down opposite us and Rufus lays his head in her lap. Traitor.

'You'll be tired for work in the morning,' she warns me.

'I'll be up soon,' I reply.

We all sit in silence for a minute.

'Don't be long,' she says. I'm sure she can sense that something is wrong but she's wise enough not to ask and get evasive answers.

When she's gone, I tell Rufus he might as well be renamed 'Judas' as I put a few more biscuits in his bowl and retrieve my glass from the sink. Just another small one perhaps.

I don't know how to tell Mary that actually I will not be going to work tomorrow. Or the day after. They dropped it on me earlier. Paid for the rest of this month and a month's 'pay in lieu', the boss said.

In lieu of what? A life? I know, Rufus, you can't answer that one either.

Twenty-three years of dedicated work. Gone. Whoosh. His father wouldn't have let me go like that. Not old Mr McKenzie. Knew each of us by name. Not Sonny-Come-Lately. I was the fifth he was 'sorry to have to let go' this afternoon. Have to, Rufus? Have to?

Of course I'm bitter. We all knew it would be bad when they installed those machines, didn't we. Chi Peng Nang, it says on the side. We call them Cheap-And-Nasty. OK, so they are clever, do things a machinist can't. Not even in twice the time. But where's the skill? The variation? An extra small lip for the ones that are going to Seatons? The tabs cut a tad shorter for Waintree? Computers don't work in tads.

Mary saw it all coming, warned me when they put them in. I thought she was being pessimistic. They told us it was because they had more orders than we could manage and needed more production. We thought it was just that they could not find enough good, experienced machinists. Mary said 'Phooey!' and gave me that look she gives when she knows she's right and I'm wrong.

So, you can see why I don't find it easy to tell her now, can't you, Rufus? Mind you, she's probably guessed what's happened already. Waiting for me to say something first.

Oh! Sod it. This is no good. I'm going to bed...

GOING WRONG

'I'm pregnant,' she says as I come through the door. To say that it catches me unawares is a massive understatement. I don't know whether to hug her tightly or prepare for discord. I get no hint from her tone of voice. And anyway, it takes me more than a moment to process the information.

It is not that we are on an even keel. I thought we were until a few months ago but it has been anything but since the summer.

I put down my backpack and take off my jacket, moving closer to her by the sink. Tall and lissom, she stands with her back to me, dressed as usual in a mix of well-worn clothes that still make a stunning impression.

'Did you just find out today?' I ask as neutrally as possible.

'Of course, and you're the first to know,' she almost snaps back, half turning now.

We hadn't planned to start a family together. I'm not sure now that we were even planning to stay together much longer. We oscillate between the cold indifference of hurt and the fragile tenderness of desperation.

'Are you pleased?' I ask her cagily. I should be able to tell but I can't.

'I did a home test this morning and saw Dr Symons this afternoon. She confirmed it,' she says, not answering my question.

My mind is racing at breakneck speed and I can't slow it down. I'm not even sure that the baby is mine, but I can't very well go there, can I? Not now, just at this moment. I know she's been seeing someone else. I'm pretty sure she doesn't know that I know. This is not the time for all that, is it? Perhaps it is! I know I'll get it wrong, whatever I say.

'When is it due?'

'Sometime in June probably.' Matter of fact. Withdrawn. Here we go. I've blundered, obviously.

'How are you feeling? Are you sick or anything?' I really am trying hard.

'Don't be daft. You don't get morning sickness right at the start. Don't you know anything?'

Apparently not.

'Let's go into the other room and talk. I'll make us a cup of tea.'

'Cup-of-tea' she mimics. 'That's your answer to everything, isn't it?'

'Janine, I've just come in from work, you've hit me with a bombshell and, well…'

'Well what?' she jumps in. 'It's what you wanted, isn't it? Play happy families. Your mum asks '*when?*' every time we go round.'

She crosses her arms in front of her chest. 'Well, now we're going to have to. Don't make tea for me, I'm going to have a gin… and don't you dare ask if I should!'

She flounces out, leaving me open-mouthed and completely at sea. I make myself a cup and go through to the other room where she's spread herself on the sofa, a glass tumbler in front of her on the coffee table next to a large box of chocolates.

'I bought myself these,' she says through a mouthful, 'I know you'd not buy any for me. Not now…'

I let that one go.

'I'd love to be a father. But I'm not sure we're ready for it yet as a couple. Are you? You know…'

I'm trying.

'Bit late now, isn't it…' It is not a question.

'Well, I guess you could still, you know, terminate…' The word hangs there.

'Yes, I could, couldn't I?' she says after quite a while, but I don't get the impression that idea has gone down well, either.

She swigs down the last of her drink, gets up and, over her shoulder, tells me: 'I'm going round to Julie's.' Moments later, I hear the angry sound of the front door closing.

I sit on my own, sipping my tea, trying to make some sense of what I'm feeling. This year has not been good for us as a couple. Too much time together during lockdown didn't help. Or at least, showed up fault lines I hadn't seen before. I went back to work while she still worked from home through the summer.

It was August when I saw her with Lance. On his motorbike, arms tightly round his waist. It didn't look like it was just to hold on. She wouldn't have expected me to be anywhere close, but that was the nearest library that had a copy of the book I wanted.

'What kind of a day have you had?' I had asked her when I got home. She told me she'd been home all day working on a proposal. I said nothing but after that, I started checking... and I didn't like what I found out. I shied away from confrontation, which was probably the wrong thing to do. Either way, it changed everything.

I go back into the kitchen, wash out my lunchbox, and look in the fridge for anything to nibble on. I'm not really hungry.

In my head, I'm working back from next June. Is it 39 or 40 weeks? Doesn't that mean...? I can't be sure but maybe the baby isn't mine. I feel sick, no, really.

We are going to have to have that bruising discussion I have been avoiding. As soon as she gets back from Julie's. It may not be the best time but now I can't put things off any longer.

I think I hear her at the door and get up. There in the dark on the other side of the frosted glass is a figure but it's too big to be...

I open the door just as he's about to turn and walk away.

'Lance! What the fuck are you doing here?'

'I... I... How d'you know my name?'

'Oh! I know much more than your name, mate,' I say. He's bigger than me, even without all that motorcycle clobber. Trimmed red beard. Large hands.

'I didn't know...'

I don't let him finish. 'You'll have to come in. We need to talk.'

He looks very sheepish but also, perhaps, slightly relieved. He's younger than me. Perhaps not much.

'You can put your stuff there,' meaning his huge boots and a full-face helmet. 'Come through into the kitchen.'

He does what he is told, by which time the kettle is on again. Perhaps she's right. Perhaps tea is my answer to everything.

'Sit down,' I tell him. 'I know you've been seeing Janine.'

'Did she tell you?' he asks.

'No, I've been playing detective.'

Neither of us knows quite what to say next.

'She texted me this evening,' he says quietly after a long silence. 'Says she's pregnant.'

This is not what I had expected.

'And...?' I ask.

'I was hoping to see her about it. It was only when I got here that I thought...'

'You're the father, aren't you? It's not me, is it?' I spit out the words.

'I don't really know...' he struggles. 'I'm sorry. I didn't know at first that she was living with someone. She said...'

'So we both only found out this evening that she was pregnant,' I say. 'Now she's gone over to Julie's. I haven't had a chance... Why am I telling you this?'

We sip our tea. He takes two sugars.

'She has told you you're the father, hasn't she? That's why you came.'

He looks down into his cup, avoiding my eyes. 'I needed to have it out with her,' he says quietly. 'You see, it can't be mine...'

'Why not?' I snap back.

He is still avoiding eye contact. 'I was ill as a child, mumps. I...'

'Are you sure?' I say, understanding the mumps link.

78

'Pretty.'

We sit a while longer. Eventually I tell him: 'You see, Lance, I am pretty sure it's yours because... Well, it's private, but if it is due in June as she says, then it...' I don't finish. We are not going to find common ground.

'I'd better be off,' he says. 'I'm sorry for...'

'No, I think you'd better stay here until she gets back. We need to sort this out between the three of us. Tonight. You're not going anywhere.' I am not usually as forceful as this.

'Well...'

'I was really angry with you when I saw her on your bike. I knew straight away you were not just giving her a lift.'

'What can I say?'

'You don't have to say anything. I should have had it out with her straight away. That way, we would all be better off now. I felt like coming over and clocking you one. I'm going to ring Julie and ask her to get Janine to come home now. She can't run off like this. Just wait, it won't take long.' And I leave him in the kitchen and go to the hallway to use the landline.

A minute later, I am back. 'She's not there. Hasn't been all evening. Julie didn't know why I was ringing, said I sounded odd. Have you any idea where else she might be? Could she have gone round to yours?'

'I s'pose we might have crossed,' he admits. 'She didn't say in her text she was coming round.'

'I've tried ringing her mobile, but I think it's switched off,' I tell him.

We sit looking at each other, an uneasy bond growing between us fuelled by mutual concern.

Now it is getting quite late and I don't really know what to do. I try ringing a couple of her other girlfriends but they know nothing. It's too late to call a colleague from her office. I'm certainly not going to alarm her stepmother – the only family member she's ever in touch with.

I realise I haven't eaten and ask Lance if he wants a mushroom omelette but he tells me he's a vegan. Funny: he had milk in his tea.

It is well after 11, almost midnight, when the doorbell rings. I jump up, wondering if Janine stormed out without her key, but it is not her. It's a policeman, with a female officer a step behind.

'Mr Carlisle?' he asks.

'Yes.'

'Can we come in?'

I let them through into the kitchen, asking 'What's this about?' over my shoulder and feeling quite alarmed.

'Is this a relative?' the woman asks me, looking over at Lance.

'Not really… It's compli…' I start to reply.

'Well, I'm sorry to have to tell you that Ms Pennant has been in an accident,' the policeman butts in.

'What kind of accident?'

'She was knocked down,' the woman says. 'She died at the scene.'

Both Lance and I have turned white.

They used that special language to describe what happened…

In response, I feebly tell them that Lance knew her too.

'You're her next of kin,' the policewoman says. 'Sorry to have to ask this but could you come to identify her... when you're ready?'

* * *

We are a small, disparate group at the crematorium. Janine's step-mother and two cousins I have not met before. A few colleagues from her work. Julie and two other girlfriends, who come over to stand with me. An older woman who stands on her own, a bit back from everyone. My mother and my older brother, who doesn't really want to be there. And Lance. It is the first time I have seen him since that night and I nod an acknowledgement to him after which he stands at the edge of our little cluster.

There's a short ceremony inside, led by a celebrant who I suppose is trying her best. Afterwards, we go to a small community centre where we have arranged a meagre buffet. We are all very subdued. The woman on her own, it turns out, was the driver who hit Janine. She has left.

An open verdict had been recorded at Janine's inquest. She stepped out into the road without looking. It was nowhere near our flat, nor apparently anywhere close to Julie's. The post mortem found no evidence that she was pregnant nor, apparently, had she visited Dr Symons on the day she died.

There was a time, for more than a year, when I thought Janine and I were made for each other. Now I am left with too many questions and I wonder if I ever really knew her at all.

TIME

Tick   Tick   Tick   Tick

Ehhh! This is a new one on me. Like Semtex but bright green. Not seen this before. Where's the detonator? Or perhaps detonators?

At least I'm staying calm. It is what I do, that's not the problem. Dirty business this. The bastard knows something about plastique, that's obvious...

Tick   Tick   Tick   Tick

Stuffing so much into this little space... must have been here for quite a bit. It'll take out the whole hospital, the neighbouring buildings. Mind you, green! Is that new stuff, EPX1? *Command Control... Have you seen bright green plastique before? Yeh... That's what I wondered. Could it be EPX1?... Thought so. Shit! Blast velocity twice that of Semtex if I... Yes, OK. I'm still looking for the circuit... OK...*

Tick   Tick   Tick   Tick

Three batteries - bad news. Probably means three detonators. Up here at chest level. Can't get the robot in here. Can't put a blast bag over... Nasty one. Glad they have cordoned the place off. No one asking questions, giving opinions, demanding answers. Nothing to co-ordinate. Just one task. Quite zen really. Got to find if this one's got a timer or a remote trigger. Can't see all of the circuit. Might be a little transmitter behind this... Got you, you bugger... Timer. Good.

Tick   Tick   Tick   Tick

Not like the movies. No red LED display counting to zero. Might find a timer controller. Not always. Wiring looks a bit crude. Hope this bloke knew what he was doing. There it is. Come on... that's it. Got you. What have we here? Oh! Bloody Hell! Two of 'em in parallel. Not seen that before.

Doug, there are two controllers, look to be in parallel.... Yes, that's what I thought. Meant business whoever did this. Yep... No, not yet... Yes, three PP9s... Duracell... OK... Will do... No, I don't want to wait for that. Might go off any time. Can't tell... No, it could take the whole bloody block out. I've read about EPX1. Nasty stuff and this lot looks sweaty; not a good sign... Yeh... OK...

Tick   Tick   Tick   Tick

Where's this red wire going? That's confusing. Guess I have to follow the loop. Hope I've got time. Take this cover off. Looks familiar. A Mukeswar! Done these many times. Reliable as hell. Indian quarrying, that's where they came from. Plenty about. Knows what he's doing, this guy. Knows how to modify it for two timer controllers. Why did he do that? They never fail. He's testing me. The sod.

Tick   Tick   Tick   Tick

This is one of the older boards. Got the relay on the top, capacitor underneath. Should be able to clip this one. Err... need to check something.

Doug, me again. Just checking -- can you clip off the solenoid controller if there are two... No, I don't either.... Yes, three... All coming from the microprocessor side... Yes, it's Chinese... IC4... I know, used in almost everything. Got one in my lad's toy car... Can sometimes blow if there's a current spike. OK, I

don't either. Have to try something else... Ta... Yes, do that...
Cheers...

Tick Tick Tick Tick

Let's take out the whole timer section. Risky but usually works. Must be a contact breaker somewhere here. This it? Looks a bit like it. Need a better light. This'll have to do. OK, two of these leads need clipping. Positive first, then neutral. Never the other way. It is usually the one on the far left. Can't see that. Hope it hasn't been put on upside down. Mustn't clip neutral first...

Ti...

CLEARANCE

This will now be the sixth time I have met my sister, Kathy, at the house and I am determined not to cry again.

It has taken us many months to get even this far and it feels to me that we are still a long way off finishing.

Part of the problem is that neither of us lives very near. She is less far away, actually, but I guess my journey is more straight-forward because I don't have to cross the city.

We have always had a lot of affection for each other, but since she is five years older than me, even now when we are both grown up, I can't help deferring to her. Not that this has ever really been a problem.

She still says I was Dad's favourite. I tell her not to be silly. 'He loved us both equally.'

But now, going through his things, she keeps coming back to it. 'He never wore this once,' she says as she finds a cashmere scarf still in tissue paper in the drawer. 'He would have if *you'd* given it to him.'

'I don't think he often wore a scarf,' I say, trying to placate her but now I sense that she may have taken that the wrong way, too, as if I'm saying that I knew him better.

I don't really want to be here at all. After the funeral, I suggested that we went once to the house together, took a couple of things to remember him by, and called in a house clearance firm.

'Don't be silly, Shar,' she said. 'There's some valuable stuff there.' She's the only one who calls me Shar – has done since I was very little and Charlotte is a bit of a mouthful, I suppose.

She was right, of course. I didn't know it but the third time we met at No. 14, she came with a dealer and he offered us quite a lot for the bureau and a couple of other things I wouldn't have picked out.

It was the same all those years earlier with Mum's jewellery. All carefully valued. Not sure why really. I didn't want any of it. I was happy with the bangle they gave me for my fortieth.

Of course, Kathy is super-organised. No wonder she's a senior partner.

Four piles every time: Sell, Keep, Give Away, Throw Out. I rarely disagree with her decisions, although I did quietly put a small item in my bag last time from the Give Away pile, which I thought Tom might like to remember his grandad by. Fortunately, Kathy never noticed.

We sit on the sofa side by side and she tells me about the complications of probate. Her firm is handling all that. I quietly nod but it is a bit of a foreign language as far as I am concerned.

Kathy was always good at figures. She did finance as well as law at Uni. I was still at school. She got a double first. There was a framed photo of the four of us at her graduation. Funny, I haven't seen that around now.

I make us a drink with the tea bags and semi-skimmed I brought with me – the kitchen cupboards and fridge have been cleared. I notice that there's a Coronation mug but I make the tea in two others to avoid complications.

'How many more…' I start to say, as I look at the four carefully labelled piles in the hall.

'Two more times,' she says. 'Then I'll get Wilkins & Kings to do the rest.'

I have no idea who Wilkins & Kings are, but I'm relieved that we only need to come again twice.

Kathy gets out her phone and looks at her schedules. 'I can do the nineteenth next month and the seventeenth in July,' she says. 'Both Thursdays, about 2.30 here?'

'That's fine,' I say without needing to look at the dates.

Routinely, she asks me about Christopher and the children. I tell her they are fine. I am about to tell her about the changes at The Medway but she cuts me short.

'Graham is going to have to have an operation,' she tells me. 'Down there…' She doesn't want to elaborate. 'I know you're a nurse and all that but…' and her voice trails off. I don't press her.

We have been in the house now for more than three hours and I help her pack the Sell and Give Away piles into the back of her car. She has already stowed away Keep items. I put the two black bags of Throw items in the boot of mine.

We hug and she goes back in to lock up with the only set of keys as I drive away.

I turn left, then left again out onto the main road, and despite what I promised myself, I start to cry.

<u>FLASHBACK</u>

She is standing in the midst of a small group just outside the crematorium. I'm late and they have just come out. At least I have not missed them completely.

She is dressed in black, of course, but then she often was. Her hair is, as always, long, but now an even silver-grey. Her dark eyes still flash, though today, understandably, they are tear-red. As I approach, I can make out one daughter, Debbie. The spitting image of her mother at that age. She has the trademark jet-black hair, long, straight and shiny. I haven't seen her since she was a toxic teenager. She must be, gosh, almost in her fifties. And there is something familiar about one of the other people in the cluster but nothing immediately comes to mind.

Molly has now seen me approaching. I am embarrassed because in my rush, I didn't even change into something more respectable but I only saw the message this morning, among junk emails. I'm in jeans. Clean but still jeans. She turns slightly from the group and holds out an arm in invitation. 'I'm so pleased you came,' she says, after we have released each other from a long, firm hug.

'You remember Debbie, of course, and Ben, over there...'

Yes, of course, Ben, that's who it is. Like all of us, he looks older. The years have not been kind to him.

I explain why I am late. 'You didn't miss anything,' Debbie says, her mother wincing slightly. 'The celebrant tried her best but she didn't know him. She was only fed the good bits and...'

'You'll come back to the house,' Molly interrupts, halting her daughter's bitterness, still there, even after all these years.

Debbie asks if I know the way. I tell her my phone does.

Now that they have set off ahead of me, I'm fiddling with my mobile, trying to find out where I can buy some flowers. Lush Lilies, Petal Perfect or The Flower Pot. Florists are like hair salons, competing for the corniest name.

I have been reminiscing all the way down in the car and I still am.

I first meet Tony at college. He's been at the grammar school. Able, articulate, attractive. I have exhausted the secondary modern. Average, amiable, acquiescent. Molly is already his girlfriend, and if I'm honest, we have really only stayed friends because of her. I don't always like him that much, but I *always* like her. A lot. A group of us meet most weekends at one of our homes. Quite often Ben's. His parents have that easy-going approach that always makes me feel welcome, if they are still up when we get back from the pub, that is. Music is put on, not too loud, and the girls dance, sometimes boys too. But mostly we play cards.

Three-card brag is a much scaled-down version of poker, simple, easy to learn and harmless enough if you only play for pennies. One of us usually hits a winning streak at some stage and ends up in the small hours a few quid ahead. Never more than a small round of drinks might cost. But now, for the first time, I am wary of Tony. Molly, her dancing over, has bought in to the card session too, a purse-full of coins emptied in front of her. 'Deal me in,' she smiles. And we see it. Tony cheats her out of her winnings. Not a fortune but a decent pot. We all notice it but she seems oblivious. Trusting him when he tells her 'two aces'. We know it is a lie: there are three other aces open on the table. He has lied about his unshown brag. Cheated his own girl. We talk about it later, stunned in disbelief. On the scale of things, it is a small incident perhaps, but my skin creeps with the realisation. Later, Ben tells Molly that we're all sure she'd won that pot. 'That's Tony,' she laughs.

And now I'm off on another daydream. I've recently got a job on a paper. It's my twenty-first. Key-to-the-door and all that stuff. Mum and Dad have stayed at Gran's house to keep out of the way. They've given me a Conway Stewart fountain pen, engraved with my initials to celebrate my birthday. We all dance a lot, talk a lot, drink a lot, smoke. Quite a few are staying over. Tony and Molly are in one of the bedrooms. Most of us are in sleeping bags on the floor. And now it is morning and Molly is cooking a big fry up. Tony's still in bed. We have opened all the windows to clear the air. Ben is here, too. We clean up pretty well. No complaints when my parents get back. I vaguely wonder where my new pen is.

And now their wedding. Molly is already pregnant but only she and Tony know yet. Tony is working for the BBC. He's got this job linking sports reporting with news. We see him on TV. He is very good. Becoming a 'name'.

And what about that time he and I meet at a race-course? Kempton Park. He is recognised by everyone. They make a fuss of him. I think he gambles quite heavily that day.

We've always stayed in touch, the odd get-together, a Christmas card, phone-call out of the blue. Helen and Molly get on OK but she doesn't like Tony much; says he made a pass at her. I wasn't really surprised. I should have warned her.

They have two daughters, same as us. Debbie and Bethany. I used to refer to them as the 'four ees' – Ton-ee, Moll-ee. Get it?

Actually, I haven't seen Beth today. Maybe she'll be at the house. I've got the address but I've not been to where they live now. They were always around this part of Surrey, downsized when the girls left home.

I can tell more or less where no. 85 is when I get there because of the cluster of cars. Gravel drive; generous between-wars semi. I don't need to ring the bell because the front door is ajar. Molly is in the kitchen. I give her the roses and a kiss on the cheek. She is busying herself with some food prep. A woman in a wheelchair comes in after me and says my name. It's Beth. It has to be. In a wheelchair? She catches my confusion as easily as a professional outfielder. 'Didn't Mum tell you about my MS?' she says, making light of it, no hint of reproach. 'Beth, I didn't…' I start, but she knows how to deal with people's embarrassment. 'I have good days and bad days. They're bad at present. Probably won't last.'

I remember Bethany as the able, younger daughter. Tony's features, love of sport, played netball at county level. Married an accountant, if I'm not mistaken. Can't remember anything else, really. Helen probably would have; she was better at that than me. Not anymore. Off with the fairies, poor woman. In a home at 73! Beth asks after Helen – she's heard from Molly about her Alzheimer's. 'It must be awful for you both,' she says. We go through into the lounge which is full of people, a few sitting but most of us standing. I didn't see that many at the crematorium. Maybe they had already left. There are quite a few I recognise from the telly – newsreaders, Jack Hazeldene, who does those popular documentaries, Sally Garner who used to front up everything. Ben is leaning against the bookcase, next to the fireplace, talking to someone I don't recognise. I hover and he smiles at me and introduces me to 'Doug'. I listen in for a minute or two before Doug sidles off for a refill and Ben and I face each other, the bond remembered.

'I couldn't recall your name,' I admit.

'I know. It must be all of forty years,' he says. 'Sad to meet up like this.'

'Molly's looking good, considering,' I offer.

'She always does,' says Ben. We were both in her fan club. Still are.

We chat for a bit. He's still 'keeping one hand in' to a bit of legal work. I wish I'd remembered he was a solicitor. He could have done our wills. Made a better job of it than our local firm.

'Do you remember when we went to watch Liverpool?' he reminds me. It's coming back to me now.

Three of us in the car. Tony gets the tickets. Wimbledon in the FA Cup. First time I've been to Anfield.

'Tony never made it to the match, did he?' I recall.

'Linford Christie broke a world record that day. Tony was on that story.'

But what I remember most is the shock I feel when I see a woman coming out of Tony's room at the Adelphi at night. The way she is dressed and the look on her face tells it all. We've always known he is a terrible flirt but seeing it there in the flesh is different.

I remind Ben of it. He shrugs it off in the way only a lawyer can after he has handled so many divorces. 'That's Tony for you,' he says matter-of-factly. We're talking about him as if he's around.

And now Molly approaches with a serving plate of 'things'. Ben takes a couple. I decline.

Dutifully she offers it around the room, calm, serene, in control. It is as if she's had years to get used to being a widow. Actually, Tony's demise was anything but predicted. His car came off the road at that bend on the hill. The one we all know to take carefully. Nothing wrong with the car. He had just been over-doing it. A case of the Tiger Woods. The similarities don't end there, either. Like Tiger, there had been 'another woman' in his life for quite some time. None of us is really surprised. Perhaps not even Molly.

But this is not how I, we, any of us need to remember Tony. He could be kind and generous. It is he and Molly and the girls who squeeze up in that house and take in a family of Vietnamese refugees. Not for a week or a month. They stay for several years before they get on their feet. Tony pays for the garage and two rooms to be converted. Fights the council when he falls foul of the planners.

Tony who has rung me almost every day, sometimes from abroad, when Helen is first diagnosed. Tony who has sent me a case, a whole case of a dozen bottles of *very* good Pomerol, when he hears I've won a Press award. Tony who buys me a flight and a ticket to the Monaco Grand Prix for my fiftieth, comes with me, gets drunk with me, eats the best food France can offer, and who pours me back on the plane home. Generous with his time as well as his purse.

I have wormed my way out into the garden now where the two sisters are talking under a large tree, still in flower. Debbie's eyes are watery as she talks about 'dad, the love rat'. Beth and I listen quietly, a daughter's pain cascading down like the pink petals of the cherry blossom. I try to offer some words of comfort, but she's not having it. 'He even made a pass at one of my schoolfriends,' she spits. 'Did he think I wouldn't know?'

'Some men…' I start, not quite knowing what I'm going to say next.

'Some men should be castrated,' she says, perhaps unaware of the irony. As often is the case, Bethany is left in limbo, aware of her sister's anger, conflicted with her own more nuanced feelings towards her father and the sadness of the day.

'*You* could have married my mum,' Debbie says accusingly. It is a thought I have quietly harboured and suppressed for half a century now.

Regrets, I have a few…

We wander back inside, Beth's wheels making scars in soft lawn. More scars… Still more.

There's a pile of coats in one of the downstairs rooms and I'm digging through it to find my donkey jacket. Yes, even now, in the twenty-first century, I still wear one – part of the uniform of the 70s and 80s. I find it and put it on, looking for Molly to say my goodbyes.

I'm not the first to leave, but certainly not the last. I have said my bit to both daughters and made a tentative arrangement with Ben… maybe something will happen. Then Molly is behind me, something in her hand. We hug again for a long time before she passes me a metal cigar tube sealed with tape. 'Tony always said you were to have this,' she says. 'It has been in his desk for years.' We hug again. 'I'll be in touch,' I offer. And now, suddenly, the sadness of the day catches me unawares and I fill up, fiddling in my pocket for car keys.

I am in the car, sitting behind the wheel, trying to compose myself. I'm not ready, or safe, to drive yet. I take the cigar tube from my pocket and slowly peel back the tape, brittle and no longer sticky. Carefully, I unscrew the cap and tip out the contents into my other hand, expecting of course a flaking Havana cigar. What is this? A Conway Stewart fountain pen, engraved with my initials…

TRIANGLES...

I noticed them quite by chance that Sunday as I rode through the woods, swooshing into the leaf-filled hollows, whooping as I made my red cycle-steed leap from the top of dry mounds, cracking like I imagined gunshot sounded as the tyres snapped fallen twigs and branches. It was an unusually dry, early autumn, the sun still warm. Me in my perfect playground: Belcher Wood, which started at the end of our garden; the place where sometimes we went foraging for mushrooms or blackberries; where Daddy had tied a rope to a beech-tree branch allowing me to swing far, far out above the long, steep slope so that Mummy gasped and said, 'Oh, do be careful. Is that such a good idea for him, Ken?'

Usually, I stayed near our end of the copse, racing on my trusty cycle around the twisty, worn-smooth, footstep-wide track I'd made for myself. But this time, for no obvious reason, I'd wheel-skidded down the tree-swing slope towards the end of the wooded area and the more open ground.

Something must have caught the corner of my eye as I rode because I stopped, panting, still astride the bike, boy and machine almost hidden under arching, long, berry-laden boughs of elder. Even then, I might not have noticed them at the edge of the grassy field if they had been keeping still.

At first, their movements were lazy but later they gained pace and urgency. When I first started to watch, I didn't recognise either of them, limbs twisted together like tree-roots. The blanket might have given them away for it was the dusty brown tartan one from the boot of our car, but I didn't pick up on that, either. My impression was that they were fighting. But a man and a woman? And those noises...

Something about them told me deep down I shouldn't be watching, but before I could act on the impulse to turn away, I recognised first her... and then him. Him of all people. What was she doing with *him*?

Angry and confused, I stepped forward, out from the shade but even then, they didn't notice me: they were so engrossed in each other and whatever it was they were doing breathlessly together.

It was only when I spoke, my voice trembling and squeaky, that they stopped and looked back to where I was now standing, my cycle abandoned to the brambles and long grass. Then there was a hurried scrambling to adjust clothing and embarrassed, eye-fleeting glances.

'How long have you been watching?' he asked. I didn't answer him. I wouldn't answer him. Not now. Not later.

Then my mother came quickly to me, brushing grass from her now creased, flower-print dress. Gently she put her arm round me but I stiffened. 'We don't need to tell Daddy about this, do we, Simon?' she said. 'Not Daddy.'

The words just hung there. And part of my childhood withered.

Mother took me by the hand and we started to walk back home, the longer way round along the well-worn path and out onto Sowerby Lane. She didn't look back towards him. And we didn't speak: not a word the whole way home. We now shared a secret that neither of us would be able to put words to. Not then.

It was only when we got to our front gate that I remembered my bike, my prized bike, still down there by the field. That place. 'I've got to fetch my bike,' I said, the anger, or hurt, still clear in my voice.

'All right, Boopsie,' she said, using that private, mother-only name; a name that would never again sound right. 'I'm doing your favourite tea, so don't be long – come straight back.' Her sing-song voice was laden with anxiety but still suggesting a kindness to which I was now deaf.

I walked out through the gap I'd made in our garden hedge and back into Belcher Wood, down the steep slope and to the field edge. As I picked up my bike, the sight of *them* together came flooding back and my eyes filled with not-quite tears. I saw the flattened grass where the rug had been and I felt a chill in the air that I'd not noticed before. I don't remember getting back home; putting the bike back in the shed; locking the door; hanging up the key; taking my outdoor shoes off by the back door; washing my hands with the red, kitchen-only soap; sitting down for tea.

It may have been my favourite meal but I ate precious little of it and for once, Mother didn't press me to finish what was on my plate. Silently I skulked off to my room, pointlessly to rearrange *things* on my shelves until bedtime, when I lay, eyes still open but unfocused, unable to sleep or reason or understand… or anything really.

I woke early: another Monday morning. For some reason, I could not adopt the routine of countless other school days. Daddy had called me twice from the bottom of the stairs before he came up, impatient. 'You'll be late if you don't hurry up now,' he said, giving me an awkward, squeezy hug, the giveaway odour of shaving soap still on his cheek and now transferred to mine. He turned and went downstairs again, quietly closing the front door and easing the car out of our short drive into the traffic which nowadays queued back past our house every weekday morning.

I watched him through the diamond-shaped leaded-lights of my bedroom window. He had come back home late on Sunday night, long after I went to bed, but I was still lying awake, wanting the reassurance of his arms round me but afraid of my own emotions. I'd deliberately delayed joining him and Mum at breakfast. I felt awkward with him in front of her; the burden of yesterday's events and her plea for silence lying heavily on me. After he left the house, I tiptoed downstairs, my eyes downcast to avoid contact with Mother who tried to make pleasant conversation. All she got back were grudging grunts and s'pose-sos.

I knew my walk to school was going to be an ordeal. Along Sowerby Lane and right at the lights, down Walcombe Hill and past *his* house on the long bend where the lane was narrow and the pavement only on his side. I broke into a run before I got to his large dark house, Oakdene, set back from the road and with overhanging, dripping trees and a pea-gravel drive. I didn't stop for a breather until I was down on the flat and in what we called the village. I picked my way past numerous school-gate mums, relieved of their darlings so now free to chat to each other, and joined the last clutch of pupils pressing through the school's green double doors. Through the hall, then going our separate ways; me and one other late-comer opening the door to Mrs Allender's classroom, trying not to be noticed. Coat on peg, exercise book on desk, pencil sharp, quietly sitting down facing the front and for once, not busy talking and getting told off for being a chatterbox. Several minutes of this and that; money for a school trip; workbooks handed back; it was all a blur. Then the bell rang and we lined up in the classroom ready for assembly. 'Please, Miss, I'm not feeling too well, can I be excused?' I asked, suddenly hot and scared.

'This is not like you, Simon. Come with me and sit by the window.'

Then we filed out into the hall, to sit cross-legged in neat class-long rows on the polished wood floor. Younger children to the front, older ones at the back. I sat at the side on a seat next to Mrs Allender, trying to make myself small so that I couldn't be seen from the front.

And then he came in. Tall and thin but somehow crooked, rather than straight.

'Good morning children,' his voice clear but rather toneless.

'Good morning, Sir,' 150 school-children sang back almost as one. But not this school-child. I froze and shrunk further into my chair. There was the customary reading, a series of announcements, a chosen pupil going up to read the 'daily thought' from a big book, and then

100

back to our classroom. He hadn't seen me. I was quite sure of it.

We got back to our form-room and I was sitting back in the safety of the third row when the school secretary arrived, looking at me while saying something to Mrs Allender.

'Simon, would you go with Mrs Snaith now. Mr Tebbutt wants a word with you.'

The whole class turned to stare at me. You were only called to see him if you'd done wrong. I reddened. Naughty Simon. Scared Simon. Ashamed Simon. Out of the door and along the wood-block-floor corridor, a pace behind Mrs Snaith. Eyes downcast.

She knocked on his door once, didn't wait for the reply – 'come' – and showed me into his study. 'Thank you, Mrs Snaith. I'll not be needing you for this,' he said.

The door closed behind her. Coming round from behind his desk, perhaps trying to appear friendly but in fact now even more menacing. 'Things are not always what they at first seem, Simon. I hope we can be friends. In time, you must regard me as someone you can talk to if you are troubled by anything, anything at all, Simon.' More silence. He probably said other things, too, but I don't remember. 'Back to your class then,' he said, closing our 'discussion'. Through the outer office past Mrs Snaith who looked at me, puzzled, and back to the class, hoping to sneak back behind my desk unnoticed but in fact, once again being tracked by every other pupil; friends and enemies alike. All of them suspecting I'd at least had a good telling off.

* * *

Later that week, it must have been Thursday, it was all over school. I knew as soon as I arrived. My best pal, Robbie, came up to me grinning. Mr Tebbutt and my mum. Mr Tebbutt and my dad. My mum and my dad. It seemed that everyone in the whole school knew something. Teasing, confiding, staring. Seeming to know more than me about my home, my parents, and always that man, Mr Tebbutt.

Then Mrs Snaith took me to the head-teacher's study again.

'Try not to be troubled by the things they are saying, Simon. People say hurtful things but they don't really want to hurt you. They just don't know any better,' Mr Tebbutt said, showing a strange warmness and consideration towards me I'd not expected. I looked back at him silent, perturbed, confused...

'Your mum is coming for you now. You can wait in Mrs Snaith's office if you like.' Still not a word from me. I sat on one of the empty chairs, back to the wall like in a doctor's waiting room, the leather-cloth seat sticking to my trousers. Mother arrived and took me firmly by the hand. 'We're going home,' she said, and we walked out though the school hall, across the yard and out onto the road, the air heavy with that smell of recent rain. Not another word between either of us. My hand still held rather too firmly. Finally, as we walked briskly up Walcombe Hill, getting near Oakdene, she spoke: 'How does everyone at school know these horrible things, Simon? What have you been saying?' I hadn't been saying or doing anything. Things were happening that I didn't understand but I sensed they were important. Was I being punished? Was it because I'd seen her with him?

102

Or because I wouldn't answer him? I hung my head, guilty of something. I didn't know what.

When we got home, Daddy was there. Briefly his arm round my shoulders while he gave Mum a cold stare. 'Go to your bedroom, now, Simon. We'll have a good chat later,' she said. The atmosphere in our home had somehow changed. Tones of voice heard indistinctly were different; doors closed with a different sound. Why was I home now and not in school? What was going on? Why was Daddy home in the middle of the morning?

My bedroom door opened and Dad walked in crouched down, knees bent, to look me in the face, eyeball to eyeball and he put both his hands on my shoulders. 'I'm going away for a few days, Simon,' he said, an unsettling seriousness in his tone. 'Your mother can get hold of me anytime if you need me, and I'll see you very soon.' His voice trailed off, eyes avoiding me.

'Why? Where are you going?'

'There's a lot on at my work, so I'm going to stay near the factory for now,' he said. 'Perhaps I'll ring you this evening. We can talk then.' He stood up, ruffled my hair with his fingers and was out of the door. I heard the front door open, then close rather loudly, not quite a slam. Car engine starting, car reversing. Then he was gone and the house was quiet, too quiet. Later, I heard the 'phone ring, just one ring; answered almost immediately. A while later, the stairs creaked and Mum came into the bedroom.

'What have you been saying about me, about any of us, at school, Simon?' Standing in front of me as if barring my way, hands on hips, elbows out, filling the room.

'Nothing.'

'What did you say about Brian Tebbutt?' It took me a moment to realise she meant him. I don't think I'd ever heard his first name before.

'Nothing.'

'Then how, Simon, how are these stories about me all over the village? Someone's been saying something. Who have you spoken to? What did I tell you? "Not a word". Who have you been talking to?'

I had no answers. 'Dunno. I haven't told anyone. You told me not to tell Daddy. I haven't said anything. Not to anybody.'

'Well, whatever you've said, it's all a mess now. A terrible mess. Everyone's talking about us. About me and Daddy and Brian and about you, Simon. And about you, too.' A hard stare. I looked down at the floor, the guilt back. Guilty of being accused? Guilty of seeing too much? Guilty of not understanding? 'We are going to visit Granny for a few days. Think about what you'd like to take. Not too much now, we're going to get a taxi to Frambourne station and we'll go by train from there. Daddy's taken the car.' All matter-of-fact. No sing-song kindness in her voice now.

* * *

Granny's house smelled. The dominant odour in the lounge was created by Bella, her old Persian cat who never seemed to move far from the lumpy, loose-covered sofa and glared at all visitors, clearly showing her dislike of their unwelcome presence, perhaps a challenge to the near-monopoly she held on Granny's affections. Down the hall, the smell in the poorly ventilated kitchen betrayed what Granny had cooked the night before, including, it usually seemed, cabbage boiled to death. The other downstairs room was now hardly ever used: the parlour, as Granny called it, was more like an over-filled junk shop, the depository for all the paraphernalia of long lives, and had a musty, mothy, mouldy smell, fragranced only by the tiniest hit of lavender furniture polish. The room seemed to say 'keep out' – which I did! Each of the upstairs bedrooms also had their own signatures: mothballs, strong disinfectant, a leaky gas fire.

I liked Granny. She seemed to understand me when parents were less accommodating and I knew I had earned a special place in her heart, possibly just by being her only grandchild. She gave me a whiskery kiss when we arrived and I tried my best not to shrink away from it. 'You know where you'll be sleeping, don't you, Simon?'

I did. I thought of it as the 'hospital room', partly because of its smell and partly because of the contents: an assortment of now useless and redundant medical equipment. Grandad had been dead for years now. Still the machinery of his long-term illness lived on. It was a large room with a high wooden bed, made even higher by the excess of blankets under a candlewick bedspread: it was the same humped shape as the roof of a bus.

I could hear Granny and Mum talking downstairs as I clicked open the spring-locks on my small rectangular suitcase. I took out the few things I'd brought and placed them in neat piles on the glass-topped dressing table which had greying lace sandwiched underneath. Socks and underwear. Shirts, a jumper and trousers. Washing things and my treasured torch which could shine in three colours when you slid the little levers. Facing the bed was that slightly eerie picture: an oil-print of a boy with ruddy cheeks and a smiling face, holding something long and off-white in one hand. The picture was a little too large for its wonky frame and it bulged out here and there, making the boy appear to have a squint. I'd talked to him before and might be confiding in him again tonight.

'Simon dearie, come and have some cake,' Granny called from downstairs. I bounded down, two stairs at a time, rattling the stair-rods. Whatever one's troubles, Granny's cake was not to be resisted.

There they were in the kitchen, at the scrubbed wooden table on which was one of Gran's moist, rich fruit cakes on a doily. Lemonade for me, strong tea for Mum and Granny.

'I'm going back home,' Mum said almost immediately. 'I've got things I need to sort out. Granny will look after you and I'll come back on Sunday afternoon. You've got everything you need here.'

'We'll have a lovely time, won't we, Simon?' Granny said. She was clearly trying to take the sting out of Mum's no-frills announcement.

'OK,' I said but I was flabbergasted: we'd only just arrived. They drank their tea in silence. I sipped the lemonade and dabbed at the last crumbs of cake on my plate. Then Mum gave me a cursory kiss, told me to be a good boy, and was gone.

Granny was brilliant… No sooner had the door closed behind my mother than she laid out a series of small tasks I was to help her with. Take the ashes out of the fire grate. Lay a new fire 'with some of that over there', pointing to a spare kitchen chair piled high with newspapers, kindling in a box on the floor next to it, coal in the scuttle. 'I bet you can make a really good fire: just the sort of thing you always do well.' Hands washed afterwards. She showed me how to make pastry. Flour on the floor, in my hair; my inexperienced-but-flexible fingers making a worse job of it than Granny's gnarled hands with lumpy red fingers the size of chipolatas. Pie in the oven, we sat down together and looked through old family photos. Grandad in his uniform and tin helmet; Mum as a young girl, complete with toy pram and dolls; Granny, her hair rolled under a scarf, smiling with a cigarette in one hand and a banana in the other. Granny told me the story about that. There were pictures of relatives I knew nothing of, holidays in places Granny hardly remembered: 'I think that was the year we went to Frinton when your mother was about seven.' I marvelled at the old cars, the stiff expressions and strange hats, and the horses and carts in some of the pictures.

'Was Mum a good girl when she was little?'

'Mostly,' said Granny, 'mostly…' My question had set her deep in recollections that would never be turned into words, for my ears at least. My question made Granny decide that the trip into the past was over. 'We'll put the albums away now, shall we? Let's put the tea on and have a look at what's happening to the pie.'

And so the hours and days passed. I learned a little about a lot of things: the rudiments of cookery, how to iron a shirt, to lay a table. We called on Granny's neighbours next-door-but-one, a large, loud woman with a small, quiet husband. They'd had no children of their own so Mrs Butcher made a big fuss of me, and I began to forget about why I was staying with Granny or to worry about what was happening at home…

* * *

It was teatime on Sunday before Mum arrived to pick me up. And then she was in a rush to get home with me. In the train, she fidgeted and asked if I'd been a good boy… 'Yes, of course.' Then, just as we getting into Frambourne station, she said that there'd be some changes, and I had to keep my room extra tidy. She was clearly uncomfortable while she told me, eyes darting here and there. And home didn't feel quite the same when we got inside. Quite a few of the things which were normally around had been put away and the furniture in the lounge had been rearranged. Mum asked me what I had done at Granny's but she wasn't really listening when I recounted the details of my stay away. I went to my room and fiddled about with some of my toys. In some ways it was nicer at Granny's, I decided.

I was relieved to find that at school, unlike the previous week, I did not appear to be the centre of attention and while I did attract some sly sideways glances, there were no chants or teasing. I thought that Mrs Allender was being particularly nice to me for some reason but maybe I was imagining it.

Unusually, Mum was waiting for me when we came out of school and we set off for home together, still an awkwardness between us. As we walked up Walcombe Hill, past *his* house, she broke the silence. 'Simon, when you get home, you'll see a For Sale board outside. We're going to live somewhere else as soon as we can sell our house. There are going to be quite a few other changes.'

'Why, Mum, why?'

'Simon, it's not easy to tell you this, but Daddy and I are not going to live together any more. We both love you. But we can't all live together, the three of us, in the same family.'

I started crying and slowed to a halt. Mother hugged me. Hard. Then she started sobbing too. There in the street. Both of us. Crying.

'These things happen, Simon, it's no one's fault really. They just happen. It'll be just you and me now. Your father will be moving away.'

We walked on in silence, heads bowed.

Then, when we got home, Mum sat me down in the front room, the room we kept for best. Her face was pale, eyes still red. 'Simon, this is hard for me to explain but when we sell the house, we are going to live with Brian, you know, Mr Tebbutt.'

'No, Mum, no.'

'I'm sorry, Simon, but the decision has been made. When we sell this house, I won't be able to buy another. Not round here.'

I didn't understand.

'It's complicated. We haven't got much money and your father and I are going to have to share it out.'

I pulled a face.

'I'm your mother and I have had to make some hard choices. I'm looking out for both of us. You'll soon...'

'I won't. I'm not going to live with him. I'll go and live with Daddy.'

'Don't make things hard for me, Simon. It's not been an easy time for any of us. But we'll be happy there – just you wait and see. Mr Tebbutt's really kind and he wants you there, too.'

'I want to live here. Why can't we live here?'

'I've just told you, Simon. Listen to me, will you?'

But I wasn't listening – or taking anything in. 'If we can't stay here, I'll go and live with Daddy or Granny - she'll have me. I'm not going to live in *his* house.'

'Sorry, Simon, but Granny can't look after you, not all the time.'

'Then I'll live with Dad.'

'That's not going to happen, Simon. Your father is working all day and his factory is a long way away and anyway...'

'I don't care. I'll go far away with Dad. I don't care. I won't go and live with that man. I hate him.'

'Simon, calm down, we'll talk about this again another time when you're not so upset. I know it's a lot for you to take in.'

'I'm not going to live with him. You can't make me.'

'That's enough now, Simon. Just drop it.'

'Why do you want us to go and live with him?'

'He's kind, you'll see, he's generous and Simon, listen to me, I love him.'

'You love him, love him? What about me and Daddy? Why don't you love us? If you did, you wouldn't be doing this... I hate you, I hate you.' I ran to my room and slammed the door.

Moments later, the door opened swiftly and Mum came in, her face flushed. 'Don't – You – Dare – Speak – To – Me – Like – That – Simon. Ever Again. I'll not have it. No one speaks to me like that and you're not going to be the first. Do you understand?'

Silence, tears flowing down my cheeks.

'Do you understand, Simon?'

I screwed up my face and stuck out my tongue.

'You'll learn that you can't have everything your own way, Simon. That's not how it is in real life. Whether you like it or not, we're going to live in Oakdene with Brian. You will soon get used to it. Anyway, that's how it's going to be. Now stay in your room until you are ready to come downstairs and say sorry,' and she closed the door, firmly.

I opened it immediately. 'I hate you, I hate you, I hate you.' More tears.

She spun round and I thought she was going to hit me – her hand went up for what looked like a slap. 'I've had quite enough of this, Simon. You have been told. You'll do what I tell you. And when we live with Brian, you'll do what he tells you, too. You'll have to because he's your dad.'

We looked at each other. I didn't know what she meant but somehow, I did know she hadn't intended to say those words; words that now could never be unsaid.

* * *

My father and I sat side by side on the bench seat in an almost empty railway carriage and looked out over the scruffy back gardens of rail-side houses. Neither of us knew what to say. We'd never had to talk much; Mum had done most of the talking for all of us. But she wasn't here now, was she?

'Are you doing OK at school?'

'I s'pose so.'

More silence.

I'd been really looking forward to going away with him... but now it was happening, it was unexpectedly uncomfortable. There was so much we might have been saying to each other, but neither of us was saying any of it.

Mother had taken me to the station because he wouldn't come up the hill to Oakdene. There was an awkward space between them as I was reluctantly handed over.

'He's got everything he needs for the weekend.'

'If you've forgotten anything, it won't matter. I'll get it for him.' As if I wasn't there.

'I'll be waiting here for the 5.25 on Sunday, then.' No warmth between them at all now.

By contrast, she made a great show of kissing me goodbye. 'Now be a good boy, won't you...?'

She stood, waving to me a bit nervously until the train pulled out.

Now we had been on the train for more than fifteen minutes but it still felt really awkward.

Several times, he'd tried to break the ice but he was out of his depth, too. Finally, he put his hand in the pocket of his raincoat and pulled out a loosely rolled comic. 'Here, I bought this at the station. I hope it's one of your favourites.' It wasn't.

'Thanks, Dad.' And I shuffled through the unfamiliar pages while he gazed out at the suburbs, light rain now marking the grubby glass in slanting lines.

A tidy walk from the station at the other end, his bedsit was on the first floor of a terraced house. It consisted of a small bedroom at the back which was completely filled by a double bed, a lounge overlooking the street, and a small kitchen with a bathroom off it. It all seemed slightly tatty and he'd not brought anything familiar from our house in Sowerby Lane before it was sold a fortnight before. We sat and watched Saturday afternoon TV – in colour! Still a novelty.

Eventually, he left me to it and went into the kitchen to make my tea: steak pie, peas and mash. He sat down at the kitchen table when it was ready, but not to eat with me.

'Granny taught me how to cook,' I said, blowing on a piece of meat.

'Bet your mother doesn't let you do anything in the kitchen.'

He was right, of course, but I wasn't going to let on.

And this how it continued. Me, out of my depth, not knowing what to say to the father I actually found I hardly knew. He, badly bruised by the dissolution of his marriage, not able to reach out to me without snide comments about Mum. Confused and angry with her as I was, I was not going to conspire with him against her. No way.

Later, he made up a bed for me in the front room, using the cushions from the sofa, drew the thin curtains and said goodnight. I lay there wide awake, alert to the unfamiliar noises of his makeshift home and very aware of the uncomfortable sleeping arrangements. He clattered around in the kitchen and bathroom for a little, then I heard the bedroom door close and I must have drifted off to sleep.

In the morning, there were Cornflakes and thin toast for breakfast, then a trip round the corner to the newsagent. The *Sunday Post* for him, another comic for me. The day was as drizzly and grey as the previous one, or maybe it was just my mood. Mid-morning, he suggested a trip to the park and we trudged round in the damp air, watching the occasional dog-walker and struggling to make conversation or any real contact. He was no better at this than I was. We walked past a few shops and looked in the windows but time was hanging heavily over us. Eventually, we made our way back to his bedsit and he flicked on the telly in desperation. Horse racing from somewhere. Meat paste sandwiches on the same thin white bread for lunch; something else on the telly, and eventually, it was time for him to accompany me back on the train to Frambourne. She was waiting on the platform for me as the train drew in. 'See you in a fortnight,' he said as we stepped down and he fumbled an awkward hug, his only attempt at affection the whole weekend really. He turned to avoid any eye-contact with Mum and walked away.

'I hope you've been good,' she said a little too loudly. And then they spilled out of me: the tears I had not been able to shed. Anger, frustration, confusion, hurt.

'What's wrong, Simon? Didn't you have a nice time with Ken?'

Ken now, not Daddy?

I didn't answer her. Just as I had not wanted to say anything bad about her to him, now I didn't want to spill the beans on my time away with him, however uncomfortable it had been.

* * *

114

By contrast, Brian Tebbutt knew exactly how to draw out a confused and largely truculent child. We'd been living in Oakdene for the last four weeks and the time had been peppered with my tearful outbursts, tantrums and what mother called 'moods'. She'd been variously sharp, embarrassed and over-protective. Brian, as I now had just started to call him (when I was not in school), had been unfailingly patient, kind and resourceful: his skills as a primary school headmaster were evident.

My bedroom was a large, square, corner room with three windows, two of them looking out over the large back garden, which, unlike the front, was light and open. A sizeable lawn led down to a wooden summer house, which had obviously seen many winters, too. It had now been designated as my 'den' and was the store for my treasured bicycle.

My bedroom had been adapted with consideration for its new occupant. While the rest of the house was furnished with dark-wood heirlooms, my room had a new suite comprising of brightly coloured furniture and a cheerful carpet with a modern geometric pattern. Compared to my small bedroom at Sowerby Lane, it was unbelievably luxurious. Even at my age, I could sense the quality. When I 'took occupancy', the few treasures that came with me seemed lost in the extensive storage options of my new HQ. But not for long: several generous outings to the town shops had filled quite a few gaps.

The large bedroom at the front of the house was occupied by my mother and Brian. At first, I'd regarded this as a no-go area, although nothing had ever been said to induce such a reaction. But later, I'd wandered in on a couple of occasions to ask Mum something and was getting used to the fact that she was sharing the room with Brian. They had their own ensuite bathroom with a special shower cubicle and just one tap that could make the water either hot or cold. Amazing. I was secretly intrigued by my new home, but also longed for the familiarity of my previous one, complete with two parents. Brian might have been resourceful and kind but he was not my dad, whatever my mother had said. And my awkward, uncomfortable weekends with my father were surely their fault: no large bedroom with new playthings could obscure that.

But I was not left alone for long periods to dwell on the unfairness of it all. Whereas, before we moved, I'd made my own entertainment to a large extent, now weekends and even evenings were filled with a series of outings and diversions. It was swimming on Tuesdays, judo on Friday and at least one day out every weekend with Brian and Mum, sometimes even with an overnight stay. And there had been some discussion about France in the school holidays. In Sowerby Lane, Mum and I would have eaten high tea together at about 5.30pm because it seemed she never quite knew what time, or even day, Dad would come back. Now the three of us sat down together to a proper meal: serious stuff because there was always a tablecloth *and* a pudding. And there was conversation. That was new. Often Mum and Brian would chat about something they had heard on the radio or had been told – but my questions were always answered carefully and thoughtfully, never brushed aside as irrelevant interruptions. I guess, overall, we'd not only moved house but also mood, from childish and a bit lonely to considered and more companionable. Is that what they called 'growing up'?

* * *

My father killed himself at the beginning of August in circumstances which were never talked about. We'd just started camping in sunny France when the news came about Dad and we had to set off for home immediately. His funeral was about a week later, attended by very few: the three of us plus Granny, Dad's sister Vera, an elderly couple who I recognised as former neighbours from Sowerby Lane, and two men I didn't know. Mum told me they worked with my father at the factory.

I hadn't known what to say to him when he was alive and I certainly didn't know how to react as we stood by the graveside looking down at his light-coloured wood coffin. It was a warm day but overcast and humid, threatening rain. Mum and Granny both stood close to me, each holding one of my hands; Brian was a little further away on his own. Aunty Vera stood well apart from all of us and glared. Later she wept quietly into her handkerchief. I think she was the only one who did, although Mum's eyes were red. I heard Vera raise her voice talking to Mum and she didn't come to the church hall after, where we all stood around. I ate crisps and a sausage roll. No one talked that much.

It took me some time to realise that I would never be able to ask my Dad anything again, and that actually, I knew so little about him. In the weeks that followed, I started to talk to Mum about him, usually when Brian was not around. How had she met him? What did he do at the factory? Why was he so often away? Why did he move out so suddenly? It was during one such grilling that Mother repeated the words she had blurted out months before. This time, she chose her words with more care: Ken, as she now always called him, had not been my real father, Brian was.

Now that I was that bit older, I suppose she felt able to tell me. She and Brian had met several years before I was born and had had what she called a romance. She said he was then a young teacher, she was the school secretary. Then he had got a new teaching job somewhere else but Mum had stayed at the school. She said it was her big mistake. I didn't really know what she meant.

She said that a little later, she had met Ken and they had 'a whirlwind romance', whatever that was. I was born about a year later. She told me that Ken had played the role of my father but he was not really my biological dad. They been together but then things really changed again when Brian came back to Frambourne as headmaster. I didn't understand how she decided who my 'real' father was, but she brushed that aside with 'I just knew, didn't I?'

To say I was bewildered by the story and its implications is an understatement. I'd just lost the man who was my father but now I had a new dad, who was my headmaster and who had really been my father all along… I was at sea.

Granny came to visit a couple of days later and I took her out into the garden to see my den.

'Who was Daddy if he wasn't my daddy?' I asked her, she who was so wise and often on my side.

'Oh! Simon, it's so difficult to explain. You'll understand it better when you're older.'

She went on to talk about 'Daddies and real daddies' but it didn't actually help. She told me that Ken-Daddy loved me as if he was my father and that Brian-Daddy loved me just as much. 'Ken was a good man, really,' she told me. 'Brian thinks you're pretty special, too and you're my wonderful Simon.' Well-meant but it was as clear as mud.

Before school restarted, we went away again for several days, this time to the seaside. We stayed in a boarding-house with another family who had a daughter about the same age as me and we all went together to the beach several times. She and I were building a sand-bank sea defence against the incoming tide when she said something about 'your dad'. 'That's Brian,' I told her and tried to explain that my dad had died so that now Brian had become my dad. I don't think it made any sense to her, either. 'Is that your real mum, then?' she asked.

A few months later, during the half-term holiday, Mum and Brian got married and I became Simon Tebbutt. There were five of us at the brief ceremony, us three, Granny and Brian's brother, Alan. Mum wore a smart dress and had flowers. We went to a hotel for lunch afterwards and there was fizzy champagne. Then I went to stay with Granny for a few days while Mum and Brian went to Paris by train. As usual, Granny made a fuss of me and we went round to see Mr and Mrs Butcher again. She gave me a not very nice, slightly cloudy drink called elderflower and burdock and asked me how I was getting on with my new dad. 'OK,' I said and I suppose it was true enough.

* * *

It was a warm day in late summer and I'd just started in the third year at secondary school. As usual, I was walking up the steep bit of Walcombe Hill when Brian caught up with me, panting.

'Come on, Simon, we need to get home right now,' the imperative in his voice quite clear and we both broke into a run.

An ambulance was standing in the Oakdene drive and the crew member was helping Mum into the back of it. She looked pale. We both got into the ambulance with her and, with bells ringing, sped off towards the district hospital. As the medic put a needle into Mum's hand and connected a tube, Brian told me that my mother was pregnant. 'We were going to tell you this weekend,' he said. 'She'd only just found out herself.' When we got to the hospital, Mum was rushed off somewhere and Brian and I sat quietly worrying in a drab waiting area that did nothing to lighten the way we felt.

'I'm sure Jean is going to be OK,' he said. 'These things sometimes happen when someone is expecting a baby.' But Mum wasn't expecting a baby now. She'd started losing blood earlier that day and eventually had rung Brian and an ambulance in short succession. We waited at the hospital until a doctor came and told Brian that Mum was comfortable but sedated. He confirmed that she'd lost the baby but said that because it was so early in the pregnancy, she'd be fine and that we should come back in the morning. All routine stuff.

She was far from fine. By the morning, she had a raging temperature, a serious infection and other unspecified complications. Over the next few days, Brian and I sat together at her bedside in the hospital, worrying about her. She was weak and not getting better. Each day, the doctors had a slightly different story to tell. None of it inspired confidence in husband or son. On one visit, Brian had insisted on talking to a senior consultant, and a specialist doctor eventually arrived and took him off to a side room to explain things. When he came back into the ward, Brian looked exasperated and shrugged his shoulders. 'I hope Jean's going to be OK, but they don't inspire very much confidence. She's caught an infection here in the hospital. Typical!'

Maybe he was a bit too frank in talking to a 13-year-old like that but he and I now had a quite comfortable relationship, into which we had both eased ourselves with care. He'd always been sensitive about my loss of a father, as I still regarded Ken. I had come to appreciate the obvious warmth between Brian, me and him and my mother; warmth which somehow filled the whole house. While I had never regarded my mother as an unhappy woman, looking back on our time in Sowerby Lane, I could see how different she was then, not gay and carefree as she'd been more recently. And Brian and I had made connections I would probably not have made before. I'd performed well in the judo club and aspired to emulate him, a black belt, when I was older and would be allowed to join the seniors. I'd got a taste for the outdoors and was a keen member of my local scouts, something that Brian had also done in his youth. My schoolwork had also flourished. I'd been pretty average at Frambourne Primary, but now at Woodland 'Comp', I was getting better marks all round. It was just as well. With a headmaster as a proxy dad, it certainly helped ease tensions at home if one did OK at school, didn't it?

But now we had something less pleasurable to share. Our worry about Mum. Far from being swift and simple, her recovery from the miscarriage was uncertain and protracted. Understandably, she was miserable as well, which didn't help, and she was not nearly well enough to come home. Brian and I were both worried in our separate ways. After several days away from our respective schools, we both slipped into a longer-term routine. Brian managed to fit in a hospital visit during the morning; both of us saw Mum in the early evening. Sometimes she seemed to be getting better, sitting in a chair in the ward and not lying in bed. But on the next visit, she might be back in bed.

Then she was taken back into intensive care and the tubes and monitors returned. She'd got another type of infection and was not responding to her drugs. Brian tried to put a brave face on it but I knew things were serious. We came home together in a sombre mood, the space between us somehow shrinking.

No-one had said anything definite but things being what they were, I had started to think about how I would cope without Mum, too. As Brian started to prepare our delayed evening meal, I joined him in the kitchen and leaned against the fridge as he started melting lard in the frying pan. 'Do you think you're my real dad?'

He turned to look at me over the top of his spectacles. 'I don't know, Simon. That's what your mother says. Jean says she knows for sure.'

'So why did she let him, you know, Ken, be my dad for all those years?'

'It's a good question, Simon, you'll have to ask her – when she's better.'

'Is she going to get better?'

'Oh! I'm sure she will, soon,' he said, turning the gas lower on the frying pan which was now spitting away like fury. 'I know it's worrying to see her like this, but she'll be OK. It's just taking its time.'

We sat down to our bacon and eggs.

'I know it's not easy to get used to the sort of changes you've had,' he said. 'My brother and I never had to cope with anything like that...'

'I wasn't given much choice, was I?' It came out sharper than I'd intended.

'Well, you're doing really well, Simon. I'm proud of you.'

My eyes became wet and I looked down, intently spreading butter on my bread so that I could hide my face from his gaze. 'We're going to be OK, aren't we?' I asked.

'Yes, Simon, we are.' Long pause. 'We are...' Neither of us was sure we fully believed it.

Mother was in hospital for a further ten days or so, but gradually came out of danger. Apparently, at one stage, it had been very much touch and go, I learned later. When she came home, she was weak, fragile and prone to tears. Granny came over to stay with us for the first week, so that Brian and I could both go to school. It was an awkward time because, although Gran meant well, she irritated her daughter, who found fault where there really was none – or very little. True, within hours of her arriving, Oakdene had the tell-tale smell of cabbage boiled to oblivion. But there was a masterpiece fruit cake to compensate. I'd not seen this side of Mum before, nor felt the tension between her and her mother, who I thought got a rough deal. But for different reasons, we were all glad when the week was up and Granny went home.

Then a woman called Mrs Cleverley came in twice a week to help Mum round the house and Brian and I helped with other household chores, the shopping and the washing. It was well after Christmas before things got to be anything like normal and Mum was back to something resembling her former self. Somehow her mood had changed yet again and that brief period of gaiety had disappeared. It meant that Brian and I spent more time in each other's company and a closeness developed between us; a closeness that, to be honest, I'd never experienced with Dad.

Things were changing. I turned fourteen that spring and my voice was breaking. I was also having a growth spurt and was now taller than Mum. I became self-conscious about some of the changes that were happening to me physically. Brian seemed to understand and respected my privacy, but Mum still treated me as 'her little Boopsie', from which I was beginning to shrink away.

One afternoon, Mum and I were alone together in Oakdene. Brian was due back later than usual; a staff meeting at school or something. And for whatever reason, the two of us started sniping at each other. She said I wasn't keeping my room tidy. I complained that my gym kit hadn't been clean and it smelled. I'd been embarrassed. Back and forth the accusations went until eventually she told me: 'I'm not your bloody slave, you know. You're old enough to do things for yourself.' Then she started crying. Since coming back from hospital, she often cried at the tiniest things. I put my arm round her and gave her a squeeze but she kept on sobbing.

'I'm sorry to be silly and cry,' she said after quite a while, wiping her face with a crumpled tissue. I was sitting next to her on the sofa, aware now of the stillness in the house, only broken by the sound of the mantel clock ticking and the faint noise of an occasional car driving up Walcombe Hill.

'Mum, tell me about you and Ken.'

'There's not much to tell...'

'Yes, there is. Why are you so sure he was not my dad?'

'He just wasn't, Simon. I knew. Can we leave it at that?'

'Didn't you, you know, didn't you sleep with him? Is that how you know?'

'Simon, it's all so long in the past. I just know, OK!'

'Had you done it with Brian? Is that why you are sure?'

She didn't answer but got up off the sofa and walked over to the window, looking out at the gravel drive and the dark overhanging foliage. Then she turned, irritation in her face. 'Drop it, Simon. Now's not the time or the place.' And she walked out into the kitchen. Why wouldn't she tell me more? Couldn't she see that I needed to know who my real father was?

When Brian came back, he could sense the tension between us. He tried to smooth things over by chatting throughout dinner about his meeting but Mum and I were both unusually quiet. Later, I was sitting at my bedroom desk, poring over my homework, when he came up behind me and put his long arms on my shoulders.

'Don't be too hard on your mum, Simon.'

'I just need to know why she's so sure than Ken wasn't my dad. I'm not a baby anymore.'

'I know, son, but your mum's been through a lot recently and when you lose a baby, your hormones are all churned up. She'll come round.'

'Has she told you how she knows for sure?'

'Not in so many words, Simon.'

'Aren't you curious, then?'

'Well, yes, I am really, but in a way, she's very private about what happened between her and Ken. It wasn't a good time for any of us.'

A long pause.

'I don't know if I want Ken not to be my dad,' I said and my eyes started filling…

'I suppose I've got used to the way I feel about you, Simon. You're my son in one way or another.'

I turned in my chair and we hugged each other. 'I s'pose I feel the same,' I said, tears flowing properly now. We stood for a long time close together but not touching, neither of us needing to say much more, the light fading so that my desk lamp was the only thing that lit the room.

That weekend, Brian sidled up to me when we were on our own. 'I've sent off for your birth certificate, Simon. That should settle the matter. Perhaps best not to say anything to Jean just now.'

It took about ten days for it to arrive and it didn't settle anything. The father's details were omitted. 'Why is there only the name of the mother?' I asked him.

'Apparently if a mother registers a birth, she doesn't need to say if she's married or even declare who the father is. It's unusual but not impossible.'

We discussed the implications of our new evidence.

'If Ken *had* been my father, she'd have put his name down, wouldn't she?'

'More than likely. It is all pointing that way but we just don't know for sure. Perhaps we'll need to talk to Jean about it when the time is right, won't we?'

Actually, Brian had already rung the local registrar's office to find out more, but they were unable to shed further light on the fact that on this certificate, no father was identified.

Although he didn't say so in as many words, by now Brian was pretty keen to know the facts, too. But short of confronting Mum, neither of us quite knew how to take things further. I wondered what Aunty Vera might know. She hadn't been in touch since Dad died and didn't even send birthday cards now. But I sneaked a look in Mum's address book, found out where she lived and sent her a letter. She never replied. And of course, by doing this surreptitiously, I had made it all the harder to raise the whole issue with Mum again. I was going behind her back and she wouldn't have liked it, would she?

* * *

Sophie was my first serious girlfriend. She'd been in my year at Frambourne Primary but then had gone on to

Sacred Heart, the nearest Catholic secondary school. We'd met again when I joined a local cycling club when I was almost sixteen. She was already a member. Club outings proved a fertile ground for our relationship to develop, away from the embarrassing gaze of parents. We had been seeing each other at weekends for quite a while before either set of parents knew anything about it. But eventually our secret was out.

There were a couple of hurdles we had to get over. Sophie, of course, remembered her primary school head well, an authority figure she now found it hard to relate to in any other way. I, on the other hand, was quickly at ease with Sophie's mother, well rounded, down-to-earth and never without an apron. Her father ran Ryans, the local, family-owned cycle and motorcycle dealership in the High Street. He was almost never at home when I called round and even if he was, his mind seemed not to have really left his shop. A small, slim man with dark, darting eyes and chiselled cheeks, flushed with tiny thread-like veins. He might have been a jockey when younger. He avoided eye contract and seemed to regard me with suspicion, an unwelcome threat to his daughter's virginity. How little he knew...

Spring was in the air but so was revising for O-levels. Sophie and I rationed ourselves. Only one day off on our cycles at the weekend, and perhaps one after-school ride in the week too, now the evenings were getting lighter. There were plenty of routes to discover with or without club-mates. The pared-back routine met with tacit approval at Oakdene, at least.

The weekend before my sixteenth birthday, the two of us were eating our lunch side by side on a grassy slope, cycles carefully laid flat below us.

'Didn't you used to be called Simon Foster at Frambourne, not Tebbutt?'

And so the whole story came spilling out, though I didn't go into all the details. I told her how my father had left home and died and we'd gone to live with Brian. That's when my name had changed. I told her that now I didn't really know who my real father was, and although Mum had certainly been married to Ken when I was born, I might not really have been his child. Now she wouldn't say. How she'd known Brian before Ken came along. How I had tried to find out the truth, first by asking Mum and, when she was evasive, by detective work but it had led nowhere and I'd had to give up.

'You do look a bit like your mum, I suppose. You don't seem much like Brian,' she said. 'Do you look anything like him, you know, Ken?'

I didn't think I did.

She expressed sympathy and asked a few more questions but we needed to move on. When we got back to Frambourne to go our separate ways, she gave me a soft kiss, more tender than usual. 'See you on Wednesday, Simon No-Name.' And with a cheery wave, she was gone.

Mum had made a special birthday meal for the four of us on Wednesday evening. Prawn cocktails, to show how grown up I was now; then roast chicken, my favourite; followed by profiteroles, which she'd never tried to make before - and to be honest, were not a success. Brian opened a bottle of his 'best red' which he said I was now 'old enough to appreciate'. I felt that it was perhaps not the time to tell him that I preferred beer. The evening went well: Sophie had always got on quite well with Mum and had even started to relax a little in front of *The Head*, as she referred to Brian.

After dinner, the two of us went upstairs, 'to look something up in my schoolbooks' – ha ha. Sophie closed my bedroom door quietly.

'Your dad was Ken Foster, wasn't he?'

'Yes…' Where was she going with this?

She opened her bag and took out an old newspaper cutting.

'I told Dad your story and he came back home the next day with this,' she said, handing over the fragile, slightly yellowed paper.

It was an article from *The Gazette*, written the year before I was born.

Apparently there had been a picture, too, but it had not been clipped out.

Her voice something of a quiver, Sophie said, 'My father remembered the name because Ryans had only

Frambourne man, 24, hurt in crash

A motorcyclist was seriously injured on Friday, when he swerved to avoid a lorry on the Frambourne Industrial Estate.

Kenneth Foster, 24, unmarried, of Minster Way, Frambourne, was taken to Frambourne General Hospital and later transferred to St Mary's, Herendon. According to one report he swerved to avoid a lorry which was moving slowly in the same direction.

His Triumph motorcycle skidded and turned over, apparently pinning Foster underneath as it travelled another 100 feet.

His condition is said to be critical. The driver of the lorry, Charles Oakley, 54, of Winchester, Hampshire, was not hurt in the accident.

Police are appealing for witnesses to the accident which occurred at about 5.15pm. Anyone with information should contact them as soon as possible.

sold the motorcycle to your father the day before. Dad said he and his father wondered at the time if it was too powerful for Ken. They felt a bit to blame.'

That's why they'd kept the cutting, tucked away with some old sales records.

I went downstairs, Sophie close behind me, and showed the cutting to my mother without a word. She looked at me, then at Sophie and back at me.

She turned pale, lost in her thoughts and memories. Finally, as if a great weight had been lifted, she said quietly, 'You'd better come and sit down… Brian, can you come and join us, you better hear this, too.'

And then the full story unfolded.

A friend who knew about Brian's new job had introduced my mother to Ken Foster and Mum had agreed to go out with him to a dance that weekend. 'I wasn't making good decisions, I'd let the man I really loved go off and I'd put my job first. I didn't even like the work that much…'

On the strength of their impending date, Ken had gone out and put down the first instalment on a shiny motorcycle so he could show off to his new girlfriend. She'd only learned about his crash from the friend who introduced the two of them.

'Somehow, I felt responsible for what had happened to Ken because he'd only bought the motorbike to impress me. I went to visit him in hospital and when he recovered, we just kept on seeing each other.'

So, was it misplaced guilt, not real love that bound her to him, I wondered?

'You might as well know it all, Simon, Brian.'

Sophie squeezed my hand. Brian dipped his chin and looked at his wife... the three of us didn't know what was coming next.

'Ken never fully recovered from the crash. Not as a man. He couldn't be a husband in the full sense.'

She chose her words carefully. Ken Foster sustained injuries that rendered him impotent. And by then Jean also knew she was pregnant by the man she'd just forsaken. She and Ken were honest enough with each other... and agreed to get married to try to make a go of things as best they could.

'Ken knew all along that he was not your real dad, that he could never have his own children. He tried to love you as a dad. It wasn't easy for him, either.'

Brian moved across the room and perched beside Jean on the arm of her chair. Solidarity.

'I did my best too, but then, Brian, you came back to Frambourne. I'd never expected to have to deal with that.' Her voice was catching with emotion, but she was determined to go on. 'Brian and I started to see each other again secretly. We both knew it was wrong, but it was right, too.'

I looked across at her and slowly shook my head... it wasn't wrong, not really, was it?

'Then you saw us, you remember, when you were nine. I knew then I couldn't keep it secret for long.'

My mind went back to that late summer's day. 'I never said anything to anyone, Mum. I promise.' I was choking on my words.

'I think I probably knew you didn't, really,' she said, now slightly more composed.

'Even before then, there were starting to be rumours,' said Brian. 'Your mother and I had discussed how we could tell Ken, but we couldn't decide. We knew we wanted to live together but…'

Mum seemed to feel she needed to explain something else.

'I've never told Brian about Ken's injury before now. It was somehow too private. Ken's secret. He felt less of a man. I understood that.'

Brian turned and looked at his wife. None of this was easy.

'I made a mess of telling you any this when you were younger, Simon. I'm sorry,' and she started to weep like I'd never heard anyone weep before, great heaving waves of sorrow pouring out.

Sophie pulled back a little, not sure if she should be witnessing such a private Tebbutt family confession. 'I'll make some tea for us all,' she said and went out into the kitchen.

'So you see, I knew all along that you were Brian's little boy. There was never any doubt,' Mum said. Her face became deadly serious and she leaned closer into Brian next to her.

'I just hadn't got the courage to explain. And I didn't want to make Ken feel, you know…. Then when Ken killed himself, well, in many ways, that only made things more difficult.'

We were in full confession mode now. No more secrets.

'Is that why Dad… Ken, killed himself?'

'I don't know for sure, Simon,' she said. 'There was no note. But he knew about me and Brian. It's why we spilt up when we did. Perhaps it was coming anyway but I've always felt I was to blame for tipping him over the edge. It's been...'

'No, you weren't,' said Brian. 'At least no more than me.'

They told me about the inquest held after Ken killed himself. I'd never known about it at the time: Granny had come over to distract me the day it was held. The inquest had heard evidence that Ken had some history of mental health issues, which Mum hadn't even known about. But that hadn't stopped Mum or Brian feeling responsible. It was not a view shared by the coroner, apparently.

Sophie came back in carrying a tray with mugs of tea and we talked quite a bit more, analysing this, remembering that and getting weary with the emotion of it all.

Not all of it was totally clear to me then. A lot of it took quite a while to sink in. And some of it was not totally clear years later... But that evening, a great burden was lifted and I felt I could cope with whatever came next.

EAVESDROPPING

The walls of my council flat are nearly as thin as the girl across the stairwell in 55b. She's a fashion model and can't be more than about nineteen. I think she's from Serbia or Slovenia or somewhere else I don't really know where to find on a map. I meet her when we are waiting for the lift but I never say more than a couple of words to her because she doesn't really speak much English, and I don't speak any Armani or Versace.

My daughter, Melanie, visits me at weekends. She is about twice model-girl's age – and size – and I think she speaks a little Prada. However, she has never said more than a few words to my neighbour, either. Mel complains that 'girl-with-panda-eyes' never smiles, rarely nods a greeting if they happen to pass each other. Maybe she's not got much to smile about.

Nevertheless, I like to think that, in one sense, me and model-girl are almost friends. You see, much earlier I meet her down by the mail boxes on the ground floor and I smile and say hello. She seems startled behind those enormous sunglasses which she wears summer and winter and she mumbles what I assume is a greeting in her own language. It sounds like 'prepechty'.

Mel tries to look up the word for me on her smartphone so we can find out what she is saying in which language but she says it's Bulgarian for teaspoons so I have probably misheard her. But I have learned her name: "A. Toth" is on the official, brown envelope she is holding. Of course, I don't know what the 'A' stands for – I doubt her English will cope with that kind of question. But even though we don't meet often or share a common language, I know a surprising amount about Ms Toth. For one thing, she marks her territory with scent, like an anxious whippet. Several times a day, I hear the metal grating sound when her door opens onto our narrow, shared balcony. Moments later, I smell the grassy smoke of her thick, lumpy hand-rolled thingy – even now, in early November, with my windows taped-closed 'til the spring so as to keep a bit of heat in. I might as well smoke myself – the odour, which I have to admit I quite like, hangs around for hours.

But it is the sounds I hear through the wall which are the most revealing. Every movement, every creak. Or else she is speaking and laughing on the 'phone using her prepechty words. And when she's off the 'phone, she turns up her weird music and the walls start to tremble. It is as if you are being buffeted by a convoy of Eddie Stobart lorries. Up here on the fifth! Late, late into the night. Every. Single. Night.

The first time it happens, right after she moves in, I want to duck under the table, the way we were taught to survive a nuclear attack. Eventually, I find out she's dancing, prancing, stretching because one Sunday, Mel sees her from the balcony and tells me she's doing exercises to music.

"I don't understand," I say. "Why does she need to do exercises? And at night? All bloody night. She needs to put on weight, not lose it."

Mel, who has what they nowadays call a fuller figure, sniffs. "Catwalk models. All they ever do is prance."

Actually, I think A. Toth does more than just the catwalk. I'm pretty sure it's her I happen to see in a magazine advertisement for very expensive Swiss watches. She is sitting, legs coiled demurely under her with her back facing the camera, wearing nothing but a wristwatch, her head turned to one side and her lips slightly parted in a deliberately provocative way. My first reaction is to be outraged: how disgusting to use a sepia image of a naked, emaciated teenager in an advert. But naturally I look again and my breath catches: the hint of a breast, the curve of her hips and the downward glance of her eye are, of course, erotic. Then the thought strikes me. The photo must have been altered in the sly way they do nowadays. It is impossible for those sensuous hips to belong to the tall, brittle, bony thing I see struggling up the stairs in improbable platform shoes and skinny jeans, carrying a lumpy supermarket shopping bag. And that's where there is another mystery. The bag reveals that she does buy food from the shop around the corner. But I never hear or smell any cooking. I will know if she ever turns on her electric cooker because the light on my ceiling will dim and my TV will go funny. Same thing if she even boils a kettle. They say they are rewiring the whole of Shepherds Court, but they've certainly not got to our floor yet. So, I know Ms. Toth doesn't cook or even make coffee, which perhaps explains why she is too thin for a size 8. Can anyone live on salad alone?

Then today, unusually, she's been out the whole time and comes in long after six: the party-wall shakes when she shuts her door too firmly. And almost immediately there is that grassy, citrus, smoke-smell. Extra strong now. But no music, no prancing, no prepechty 'phone call. Do I hear her choke, sob? Then it really starts, a dull, trembling, braying noise which becomes a deep moan so loud and terrible that I am ashamed to be hearing it and heartbroken for her pain. It is one-hundred-per-cent pure grief. I sit on my couch and pull up my knees to my chest, wrapping my arms around them. I really should put my hands over my ears, but I don't. I listen to her wail and I, too, become miserable and alone. I just sit, frozen-still in my grey cardigan and corduroy slippers. It is now dark but I have no lights on and the heating's gone off. But I don't want to move.

Eventually, I hear a second voice, slightly deeper. She has company. A man? A sound I have not heard before. The sobbing stops. Instead, there's lots of prepechty. Then some quieter music. Certainly not Eddie Stobart.

I am still very sad for her. But perhaps, just perhaps, tonight I will get some sleep without being disturbed by round-the-clock prancing.

DESERTED

For most of the night, I had not been able to sleep, the wind howling round the tent, accompanied by the flap, flap, flapping of the fabric and the mournful hum of taut guy ropes. It must have been almost dawn when, eventually, I fell into a heavy slumber.

Now, only a few hours later, the sun was already high. Still weary, I rose, slipped on a crumpled shirt and far-from-clean, light trousers, and unfastened the ties on the tent door. 'Good morning, all,' I called, straining at a gaiety I didn't feel and blinking as I emerged into the harsh, blinding light. Only the two leaders might have understood the English-language greeting but in fact, there was no one to hear it at all.

Our encampment was gone. Where were all the others? Five large tents and another small one used by the two Berber guides. Gone. No tents, no camels, none of the large camel-bags with essential supplies and the precious canteens of drinking water.

My first thought was that they must have re-made camp a little way off to find shelter from the wind and I trudged up the slope behind our encampment, newly decorated in fine blown sand, my shoes slipping backwards into the soft surface. But even when I gained height, I saw nothing. 'Hello,' I bellowed, apparently to no one, fright tightening my chest. I ran back down towards my lone tent and tripped over something half buried, sprawling full length. Spitting out grit, I saw I had caught my foot in the shoulder strap of the large canvas-and-leather satchel used by Jibrail, the party leader. The day before, I had seen him dip into it to pull out maps, money, documents and who knows what else. Now it was empty. Maybe the contents were underneath or had been scattered by the gale? But I found nothing at all.

Back in the tent, I bundled-up the few items I'd taken out of my kit bag the night before and stuffed them back in, taking care to keep the lone water flask upright and at the top. What had happened to the rest of the party? Twenty-seven of them, Africans, three of them women, one with a baby, plus Jibrail and Rafiq. Where were they now? Why had they gone in the night or at dawn, leaving just me behind?

I now realised it had been a huge mistake to trust, and pay, Jibrail, and sat in the tent, glad of the shade it offered and opened up the flaps. The day was heating up. I was alone, apparently abandoned and all-but lost. The sandstorm had obscured much of the rock-strewn track and Abala, the first real settlement on this side of the Mali/Niger border, seemed impossibly far away. The last straw was having to clip the remaining power pack into the satellite phone to ring base, cursing the tedious 'all our lines are busy, please leave a message after the tone'.

'It's Tom, Carl, call me, it's urgent.' I'd have to leave the phone on for his reply, using some of the precious battery. The solar charger, a life-saver in this part of the world, had been in one of the camel bags.

The GPS showed exactly where I was. Under ideal circumstances, it would have been a very strenuous day's hike to Abala. Under these conditions? No longer a clear track? Rocky and sandy underfoot? One flask of water?

I started to take a few decisions. If I was to try to walk there, it would not be through the worst heat of the Sahara day. Slowly now, I unpacked the kit bag I'd hurriedly stuffed earlier, making a careful inventory of what I found. Clothes, a wash bag, travel towel, and, right at the bottom, the little zippered 'survival kit' I always carried. Half a roll of peppermints, a muesli chewy-bar (several months out of date), a compass, spare shoelaces, a couple of sticking plasters, a 17-in-one DiY blade thingy and, neatly folded, a foil survival blanket. Survival. Ha, bloody ha.

I lifted the sides of the tent higher and tied them up, turning it into a sun shelter, more or less. I was hoping to catch a little breeze as the day wore on. Breeze? What breeze? My late breakfast was a tiny sip of precious water and a peppermint to take away some of the dryness in my mouth. Then I re-organised. One pile of things to take on my journey, another of things I would have to leave, together with the tent. Carry as little as possible. Water, bits and pieces, a very light jacket: never really cold in this part of the desert at night, even in February. And my thick notebook: two months of detailed nature notes from the trip so far. I tore off the stiff black cover and most of the blank pages to make it lighter, careful not to lose anything I'd recorded in my own practised notation about breeding pairs of the endangered shikra, the little banded goshawk, for which I had been searching over the border in the nature reserve.

I made tight knots in the legs of my spare pair of trousers and, using the straps from Jibrail's empty bag, I made a rudimentary rucksack, much smaller and lighter than my waterproofed kit bag. The sun was probably at its hottest by the time I had finished assembling and packing the essentials. Certainly not yet the time to set off to find the others, or a night trek to Abala.

As a distraction, I turned to the loose pages of my notes, checking what I had written so far. Copious detail of ornithological sightings but nothing in there about my Land Rover giving up the ghost in a dry river wadi. No mention that I had seen the camel train and paid in US dollars to join Jibrail and the others, allegedly just two days away from safety and fresh supplies.

I must have dozed off because I was woken by the buzzing vibration of my phone. 'Tom, it's Carl. Are you all right? Sorry, I've only just picked up your message. Where are you?' Good question. Middle of nowhere with one battery and no charger was the polite way to put it, but I wasn't so delicate. 'We will get help to you. I can get an exact fix on where you are from the phone signal. Stay put. Don't wander off.' A few sentences more and he was gone, leaving me reassured.

I neatly folded the things I thought I'd be abandoning and packed them back in the kit bag. Anything to pass the time. We'd agreed I would turn on my phone for five minutes at the beginning of every hour and at one-minute past four, he rang again. 'A man called Yusef from the IRC is coming for you. He's got a white Land Cruiser. He knows where you are. He's in Abala now so

142

only about an hour away. He'll get to you long before dark.'

Good news indeed. With the sun now lower, I reclimbed the slope so I could see Yusef as soon as he was anywhere near. It was after five when I heard the distinct drone of a vehicle and I might even have seen dust thrown up by movement. I couldn't be sure. It was away to the south-east, roughly from where I expected Yusef to arrive. But that was all. The sun was reddening, illuminating growing cloud cover when I switched on my phone and talked to Carl at six. 'He had entered the wrong co-ordinates,' Carl told me. 'He's got them right now. I've just triple checked them with him.'

'It's almost dusk here,' I reminded Carl. I'm sure anxiety was clear in my voice. Finding someone in the Sahara is hard enough in daylight; in the dark, it is almost impossible. We agreed that I would turn on my phone's torch app and shine it round during the five-minute sessions, to make me a bit of a beacon.

'It won't be necessary,' Carl tried to reassure me. 'He'll be with you long before seven.' I spent all of the next hour up the slope again, the day's heat now dropping to comfortable, but I was in no mood to appreciate it.

At seven, as the short desert dusk turned quickly darker, I was still up on the top and turned on the phone and the torch app, waving it around for anyone to see. Where was Yusef? No sight nor sound of him or his vehicle. Carl rang again. 'Don't worry,' he told me unconvincingly. 'The road out of Abala was closed, there was a long detour. But it won't take him too much

longer. He knows where you are. He's got your number.'
He rang off.

And then it started to rain. In February! Almost two months before the monsoon. Unheard of here in the Tillabéri region of western Niger. Not the light pitter-patter of a freak shower. This was a downpour. A deluge. A storm of a different kind. Within minutes, all I could see were a myriad of rivulets, streams and mud-patches. I tried as best I could to protect the phone from the rain as I scrambled back towards my tent. But with the rain came a strong wind, howling almost as loudly as in the night. And because the tent had been remodelled during the day as a sun shade, the wind got under it, ripping it off one pole, then the other and it was gone, sailing like a mad witch up into the night sky. The rain lashed down on my back and I cradled the phone beneath me. It seemed to go on for an age but in fact, it was less than half an hour. It stopped almost as abruptly as it had begun. I had possibly saved the phone but in doing so, I had sacrificed the vital contents of the makeshift rucksack.

Switching on the sat-phone again to check it was still working, I saw I had a voice message. Yusef, beaten back by rain-damage to the unmetalled road. He told me he'd no choice but to wait until dawn. Fuck, fuck, fuck!

The stiff breeze and warm night air were doing the best to dry out my sodden possessions but my notebook was a mess of glued-together pages which would need careful handling if I was ever to recover my jottings.

I tried as best I could to get some rest, without much luck. I might have dozed off once or twice through sheer exhaustion, but I was miserable, uncomfortable, hungry and thirsty. I'd drunk half my flask of water during the day, never daring to swig the last of it. My bed roll had not dried out and the ground, now surprisingly dry again, was stony and hard. It was a long night.

The first light of dawn lit up the long strip of higher ground to the east with breath-taking beauty. Shades of light and colour changing every few minutes. And now I spotted my enamelled metal cup on the ground, partially hidden by the bed roll. It was half full of rainwater and I put it to my dry lips, tentatively tasting the only slightly dusty water. That was a real bonus, and I tucked into half of the muesli-bar taking tiny bites and chewing what was in my mouth for as long as I could manage.

As it grew lighter still, I thought I could make out the track we had been on two days ago, which had been partly obscured by the sandstorm. The rain had served to outline the rocky edges again and although criss-crossed with newly formed gullies and small ravines, it was now quite traceable. That's where Yusef would be coming from, I was sure. I was tempted to set off to meet him, but it would have meant abandoning my kit bag and bed-roll and carrying only the small home-made rucksack, which was still very damp.

At seven, I turned on the phone and Carl rang almost immediately. He was concerned and very apologetic, though none of what had happened had been his fault. 'The IRC regional director is now coming with Yusef. He's called Tim Blakemore. I spoke to him just now. They'll be...'

And nothing! The last of my phone's battery drained away and the call was disconnected. I was alone and vulnerable. Needing to stay put and dying to move on.

Somehow trapped in the open wilderness, small scrub, no trees. It is at times like this that one needs to stay focused. A test of character.

Without a phone, how could they find me? How accurate was the satellite locator? I set about making a signal flag, crudely fixing one tentpole on top of the other with a tightly bound t-shirt. Back up the slope, I erected the rudimentary flagpole, steadied by what remained of the tent's guy-ropes. Then I attached the whitest piece of clothing I had found, a thin cotton shirt, sleeves knotted so that it would billow in the breeze. I walked a little way down the track and looked back. Anyone within a reasonable distance of me couldn't fail to see it. That had taken me the best part of an hour and the day was already warming significantly. Now without my tent-cum sunshade, I was very exposed and I scoured the area around, looking for anything that might offer some shade if really necessary. Surely Tim and Yusef would be with me soon.

I spent a while sitting by the flagpole facing the track to the south-east and carefully unpeeling pages of my notebook letting one dry in the sun and then working loose the next. At least since my notes were in pencil, there was no ink to run. I was so engrossed that I never heard them approaching, but then there was a louder noise and turned to see a figure crouched over my kit bag, back where the tent had been, his flowing jilbab robe and turban flashing in the bright sun.

'Hey! Are you Yusef?' I called and he turned to me, as startled as I was. I ran down the slope towards him but stopped short as two more men appeared, one significantly shorter and fatter. It was he who fished out

146

a gun and pointed it towards me, a rusty pistol with a piece of cord dangling from the trigger guard. If he tried to fire it, we might both be badly hurt. He called out something in a language I couldn't fathom. It certainly wasn't French, Arabic or English. I put up my hands. I meant it to say 'hold on there' but it was also the gesture of 'don't shoot, I surrender': perhaps no bad thing. The short man continued to wave his antique firearm in my general direction while the two others went through my belongings, finding the makeshift rucksack and the sat-phone. They found my passport and showed it to the pistol waver.

'Engleesh,' he said. It was a statement rather than a question. Scottish actually, but this wasn't the time or place. They found my wallet, of course, with a little local money, but not my stash of dollars which were in the money belt round my waist.

'Taeal maaeay!', Shorty said, waving the pistol. I'd heard enough Arabic to know he was telling me to come with him and I thought of making a run for it. I was possibly fitter than any of them and trousers were better for running in than their long robes, but it was three against one and at least one gun. Not good odds.

'I'm no use to you,' I said. 'You'll be caught very soon if you take me.' No hint that any of them understood or cared. With a push in the back, they gestured to me to go with them in the direction I had come from with Jibrail and the others two days before. Back along the track towards the border with Mali and away from where Tim and Yusef would be coming. My hands were now tied behind my back with the same strapping I had used to make the rucksack. Tight and uncomfortable. Prod,

prod, prod in the back like a reluctant donkey, along the track, down an incline and into a small gulley where, in the shade of some rocks and low bushes, seven others were sitting, five of them restrained by hands bound behind them like me. They might have been five of the black Africans who had been travelling with Jibrail, I couldn't be sure. I was clearly the prize hostage, for the captors all took turns in checking that my binding was tight and prodding me forward. Shorty, now armed with an automatic rifle, went in front.

We must have been travelling like this for two hours in the blistering sun when our captors all stopped, as one. They looked up in the sky and went into a brief huddle. Then they fled, abandoning us hostages. I wondered what was going on. Then I heard what I guess their keener hearing had already recognised - the faint throb-throb of something mechanical. And it quickly grew louder. Not a car or truck. It was the noise of a helicopter. Louder and louder. Then, deafeningly close and almost overhead, a big, light khaki lump of metal swirling in the sky. It flew by, perhaps only a couple of hundred yards away and very low and travelled away in the direction in which our captors had fled. Then I heard the blast of some weapon being fired, very shortly followed by a huge explosion. A column of black smoke rose into the air from a point much less than a mile away. And there was no further sound of any helicopter.

One of the hostages had managed to free his hands and within no time, we were all untied. A few words of French shared between us. And we started to run. Back south and east. Away from our captors who could well be coming back for their human bounty. We ran until we were well past exhaustion but there was no sign of anyone pursuing us. As I went back past my impromptu flagpole again, the shirt fluttering bravely on top of the slope, I made a brief detour to check if anything of value had been missed. Nothing, only the remains of my precious notebook, which I scooped up and tucked into my waistband. I was still hoping we would be met by the white Land Cruiser of Tim and Yusef, but there was no sign of my IRC rescuers.

What had been a fast pace set by the fittest African, who was some way ahead slowed to a more manageable trot and we sort of regrouped. I was thirsty, hungry and frightened but I guess adrenalin was keeping me going now. The track wound up the low hills in front and, as we crested the rise, I saw a military vehicle coming towards us, a fair way off but closing fast. We all stopped running and started waving our hands and shouting; a mixture of languages and calls. We needn't have bothered because it was on the track we were on and there was nowhere else it could go. As it got nearer, I saw that it was being followed by two larger trucks, also military in style. And at the back by another smaller vehicle. The first three sped past us without slowing, heading towards the area where the helicopter had come down, perhaps to engage our former captors. The last vehicle was like a small pickup truck with a big gun mounted on it. It did stop and a large man with a red beret and a lot of gold braid looping from his epaulettes stepped out of the front of the vehicle.

'Qui êtes-vous?' he demanded and several guns were pointed in our direction. One of the Africans replied. Hostages fleeing from captors summed it up.

'Et lui, le blanc?' Red-beret asked, pointing in my direction. I explained as best I could that I had joined a camel train a few days back, found myself alone, then robbed by the same group of bandits or terrorists who had taken the others.

'J'allais être récouvérée par l'IRC,' I told him. He laughed, either at my awful French or the situation, or both.

'This is a closed military zone now,' he said in good English. 'The only ones who are going to 'recouvérée' you are us, the Niger Army.' He exchanged a few more words with the five others, and then got back in the truck. By then, two of the soldiers had jumped down, their weapons pointing safely at the ground. They took a container of water from the back and led us away to a safer and shadier place as the truck sped off. I have never enjoyed a drink so much. It might not have been the sweetest tasting or the coolest water I'd ever experienced but it was by far the most welcome. We took turns, drinking slowly and carefully. Then we shared our stories, together and at ease for the first time. The five Africans knew nothing of Jibrail or the camel train. They had been travelling north towards Abala when their vehicle engine failed during the heavy rain. Instead of a rescue truck, they had been captured by the terrorists. They said they thought they were connected to Nusrat al-Islam, a militant jihadist organisation. The five of them had been driven out into the wilderness, robbed and had expected to be killed. But then three of the terrorists departed and came back with me. We all knew the rest.

We were tired, and hungry, and uncomfortable. But for the first time for several days, I felt a little elated. I really was going to be rescued now, wasn't I?

At the same time, it was dawning on me now how lucky I was to be alive at all. The more we talked the more I learned that eastern Mali and now this part of Niger was rife with terrorists, people smugglers and common bandits. As a white westerner, I would have been a prime target ever since I arrived three months ago. What the Hell was Birding International doing sending me to this region? Carl must have known, or bloody well should have. And for that matter, why had I not researched it myself, instead concentrating only on habitats of the shikra? I'd been too keen to volunteer for the all-expenses-paid assignment. What a fool!

It took more than ten days to get back home to Britain. After the army rescue, there was the small matter to settle of what I was doing in Niger. Birdwatching among terrorists in Mali? Really? Then crossing the border illegally with thirty others who vanished into thin air? Really?

I have never found out what happened to Jibrail or why I was abandoned that night. People smuggling might have something to do with it, I guess.

I have written up the records on the prevalence of the little banded goshawk in the Asongo-Menarka reserve. They are due to be published in the next quarterly journal. And I am sitting alone in my small flat, pondering a new assignment in northern Iran.

MOTHER & SON

Keith was standing precariously on the stool, reaching as far as he could across the dusty top of the wardrobe. The shoebox was right at the back and his fingertips only managed to push it a little further away, rather than pulling it towards him which is what he was attempting to do. He turned and got down to fetch something, a coat hanger perhaps, he could use to reach it with. Then he heard the front door and he quickly tried to hide the stool down the side of his mother's bed.

'What are you doing in my bedroom?' Edith said suspiciously from the open doorway. She had heard his scuffling upstairs the moment she came in. 'There's nothing for you in here. You'll trap in Micawber if you're not careful.'

'I was just seeing if you still had any of Dad's things to go to the charity shop.'

Her face showed she didn't believe a word of it. She noticed the stool. 'I don't like you in here,' she told him, making him feel like a naughty boy again. 'Anyway, all your father's clothes went years ago - you know that.'

Sullen, he followed her and Micawber downstairs, noticing for the first time how thin her hair was getting. Still, she was eighty-one.

They went into the kitchen, where he'd left his anorak on the back of a chair to drip dry. Two small puddles were now underneath it on the vinyl flooring.

Of course Edith was pleased to see her only child, at least at first. His visits were irregular and always brought problems. Usually, he wanted money. Sometimes, she found that something had gone missing a few days after he came. He had denied removing the antique Staffordshire spaniels from the front room after one visit, but she didn't believe him. Who else could have had them? 'I may be old but I'm not totally stupid,' she had wanted to say, but she had held her tongue.

It had been a lot better when he was still married to Ruth but since their divorce, he had gone back to his old, sly ways.

'Two spoonfuls now we've a visitor,' she muttered to Micawber, who sat expectantly on the table. Every time the fridge was opened, he regarded it as an opportunity.

'Can you get out the biscuit tin, dear? I've bought your favourite fig rolls.'

'I'm not eating those any more, Mum,' he lied, just to be awkward. He was irritated. Why hadn't she talked to her neighbour a bit longer? He could have seen what was in the shoe box then. 'Haven't you got anything else?'

They sat opposite each other at the table. 'It would be nice if you could bring Damien with you next time,' she said. 'I haven't seen him since Christmas. I expect he is growing up quickly, now he's in the comprehensive.'

'I'll see,' Keith said, not wanting to admit that he rarely saw his son.

Ruth made it difficult because he was not keeping up his maintenance payments. Anyway, now Damien had so many of his own friends, he didn't seem bothered about being with his dad. Theirs was an awkward relationship: Damien usually asked his father for things his mother disapproved of, which Keith could not afford anyway. And on the rare occasions when he came to collect his son, there were always 'words' with Ruth before they managed to go off somewhere.

'We might be able to come over at the end of the month,' Keith offered disingenuously. By then, Edith might have forgotten. Otherwise, he would tell her that Ruth wouldn't agree.

'Let's make it the last Sunday, the twenty-ninth,' his mother said, having got up to write on a blank square in the Cute Cat Calendar. 'In the afternoon.'

Fat chance, Keith thought, but he nodded to feign agreement. The end of the month was never good: he was more or less spent up by then. His pay came in to his account on the seventh. By the last week of the month, what hadn't gone on bills and drink had gone to the bookies.

'Can you lend me a twenty to tide me over?' he asked. 'I had some unexpected expenses and, well, you know…'

Actually, she did know. She knew about his gambling, she knew he wasn't contributing to Ruth for the upkeep of his son. She knew exactly when he was 'making things up' as she used to call his lies when he was a boy. She knew then, she still knew now. She went to her purse and took out the lone £10 note. 'That's all I have in the house,' she told him. He took it without comment. 'Lend me' was a euphemism they both understood the true meaning of.

'There's something I've just remembered! I'll have to be getting back now. Mind how you go,' he said, swallowing the remaining bit of chocolate biscuit and before his mother could tell him 'but you've only just got here', he'd let himself out of the front door, swung his foot at Micawber on the path and was gone. Just like that.

Edith trudged back up to her bedroom and brought the kitchen stool back downstairs, putting it where it belonged in the corner. Of course she loved Keith, but his visits were always disturbing, especially when he was on his own without Damien.

She and his father had tried so hard with their son. He'd been a contented baby but had made up for that ever since. He could have done so much better at school if he had concentrated. That's what all his teachers said. When he got a job working at Haskins, they really thought things would change. And at first, they seemed to. Mr Haskins, long gone now, had thought highly of him, she reflected. That's where he met Ruth. He in stores, she in accounts. Then there was that fire. Everything gone. Old Mr Haskins never really got over that, even though the firm started again a few months later in a new building.

Her reverie was broken by a knock at the door. Micawber slipped back in as she opened it to her nosey neighbour, Mary, returning her colander. 'I still haven't found where I have put mine – has Keith gone already?'

The two ladies sat talking. 'I'll make a fresh pot,' Edith offered but Mary told her not to bother. 'I can't stop long.'

'Before you go, can you just hold the steps for me?' Edith asked. 'I have to fetch something from the top of the wardrobe.'

The two women went into her bedroom and Edith climbed the steps. 'Do be careful,' Mary said, certain that her friend should not be up a step ladder. Independent and determined. That she was.

Edith stretched to get the shoe box – noticing that the dust and cobwebs had been disturbed: she had guessed as much.

The box was taken down and put carefully on some old newspaper spread out on the end of the bed. 'Thank you, Mary – my memory box. I need to sort it out.'

'I'll help you,' her friend offered but Edith wanted to do this on her own.

Later, she slowly worked her way through the contents. Several faded postcards. That first one from Robert, on the Isle of Wight, before they really started seriously 'walking out' as they called it back then. 'Yours truly, Robbie' it said at the bottom. A dusty silk rose, from that dress. The handwritten letter from Dr Jenner, explaining why she couldn't have more children. She didn't need to keep that any more, did she? A couple of Keith's school reports. At the bottom, her father's war medals. That was what Keith would have removed. All five of them: *2324092 SGLN. C. Watson. R. SIGNALS.* They would not be worth anything but she was not going to risk them going the same way as the china dogs.

Micawber was up on the bed, where he was not supposed to be. 'We'll send them to Ruth with a note to keep them for Damien, along with the other things,' she told the cat, who carried on licking himself.

DINGHY HIRE

Jilly sat at the front of the boat, her tanned legs dangling down, just her feet in the clear, warm water.

Alan, behind the mast, was busy sorting ropes and God knows what else.

'Pass that sheet through the block and throw it back to me,' he said, the irritation showing on his face and in his voice.

Jilly had no idea what he was talking about, but her idea of a summer holiday in the warm Aegean did not involve hiring dinghies. When he'd suggested a day on a boat, she'd pictured herself spread out on a sun deck wearing the briefest of swimwear. More speedboat or luxury yacht than little sailing dinghy.

'That rope, there by your left hand, darling. Thread it through the pulley, it is called a block, and throw the end back towards me – let's get going while the wind is offshore.'

She did what he asked, but it still wasn't right.

'No, the other way - the rope, the jib sheet, needs to come from the outside to the inside.'

She unthreaded it, did it again and plopped the end as far back as she could reach without actually moving from her perch at the bow.

'Can you do the one on the other side the same, please?' He was getting even more impatient.

She shifted her weight to try to reach the other rope, and the whole boat tipped to one side. This was no fun.

'Are you sure you can't sail this thing on your own?' she asked, feeling less and less sure she should have agreed to share in this diversion. Apparently, he didn't hear: he was leaning far over the back with his hands in the water.

'I've dropped the bloody rudder pin,' he said turning towards her again. 'It should have been tied on. I'll have to ask Ioannis for another.' He got up and stepped onto the quay.

Jilly watched him walk to the hut at the end in his nicely faded red swim shorts and pale green Ralph Lauren polo shirt. She sat back and listened to the clack-clacking of the rigging on the neighbouring boats. That big white one at the end, that was more her cup of tea. Tinted windows, bleached wooden decking, swimming platform at the back, two big Evinrude thingies. None of this sailing nonsense.

It was half-an-hour before Alan came back. 'We had to go to the chandlers, if you can call it that,' he said, holding a bit of metal – she assumed it was the new 'rudder pin', this time with a piece of nylon cord threaded through the loop. 'He's only going to charge us half price for the hire, now.'

Jilly let him get on with it, but he seemed to be taking his time. His muttering suggested it wasn't quite the right size.

'I think that'll do,' he said eventually. 'Can you come back here and hold the tiller while I untie the painter – here, I'll show you.'

She scrambled back, catching a smooth, tanned leg on something rough. But she did what he asked. He clambered up out of the small boat again and fiddled with a rope on the quay. He'd just untied it when a strong gust of wind caught the half-raised sail and blew the boat away from the quayside, the rope slipping out between his hands. 'Push the tiller away from you,' he barked at her, but she was frozen with fear as the dinghy leaned steeply to one side.

'Push it away,' he screamed again. 'Release the main sheet and push the tiller away. It'll come head to wind.' Why couldn't he talk English? 'That rope next to you on the transom. The seat. It's the main sheet, release it. It's caught somewhere,' he shouted, the urgency in his voice very evident as the boat moved further out into the clear green-blue water. 'Push the tiller away from you, Jilly. DO IT NOW.' She was rigid.

'OK, let go of everything. It'll drift, you'll hardly move. You'll be perfectly safe. I'll get someone with a boat to pull you back.' His voice deliberately calm, as if he was talking to an imbecile.

'Where are you going?' she asked, accusing panic in her voice.

'I'll only be a moment, you're quite OK.' She didn't feel it.

She held onto the thing he called the tiller as the boat bobbed about, the steady breeze now taking the little dinghy further out into the bay. Then something came away and she was left holding a piece of wood attached to nothing. She thought about scrambling overboard and swimming back, but the little boat was now quite a way out. There was no sign of Alan on the quay. The sky was clouding, grey. The sail, half way up the mast, was full…

***

It was very late when Alan was woken by a knock on the door. He had dozed off, rather the worse for wear after consoling himself with so much retsina.

He knew it would be Jilly, back to smooth things over after their bitter row. It was all very unfortunate. Couldn't she see that? OK so she'd been scared, but it all turned out safely in the end. She'd still been in the marina actually. Ioannis was used to looking after his dinghies and rescuing the people who hired them. Alan had tried to console her. Typical Jilly. She'd flounced off.

She'd be back. They would make it up. He flung the apartment door wide open with the words 'I really am sorry. All right?' Only it wasn't Jilly. Not even close.

A very large Hells Angel, 6ft tall and almost as wide filled the doorway and stepped into the room as Alan stumbled back in surprise. The visitor had a large, black spider tattoo over one eye, a single-strand plaited beard beneath his double or triple chin, black leather trousers and a black sleeveless vest stretched tight over his huge belly. 'I Alexandros,' he said in heavily accented English. He lifted a bottle into view, filled with some viscous pale-yellow liquid, and stepped into the apartment. 'We drink tsipouro, yes?' Alan was still speechless.

'I sit?' Alexandros said and moved towards the couch.

'I think there is some mistake – what are you doing here? We are on holiday,' Alan managed to gabble out.

Alexandros's face lit up, the spider tattoo moved sideways and two of its legs seemed to wave. 'I should tell,' he said. 'I meet your sister in bar. She say you are lonely… you miss Engleesh boyfriend, no?'

'What?' Alan manged to splutter.

'Is OK, you shy. We drink.' And with that, the visitor pulled two thick glasses from his pocket and put them on the low table, pouring a generous shot of the liquor into each. 'Yia mas.'

Alan was still standing. 'There's a big mistake.' He said quite slowly in his clearest voice, still cracking with fear. 'You have the wrong apartment – I am here on holiday with my wife. Not my sister. She will be back very soon.'

Alexandros was having none of it. 'Try drink,' he said, at the same time patting the cushion next to him. 'We become good friends. You see.'

Alan stood well away from the unwelcome visitor. This can't be happening. 'I want you to leave. Now. Please…'

Alexandros smiled. 'Lady said you very shy. Why I bring tsipouro.'

Alan held one hand up to signal 'stop' and reached for his 'phone.

'What have you done?' he all but screamed into it.

'I guess your visitor has arrived,' Jilly chirped. 'Enjoy the rest of your evening.'

'Aren't you on your way back?'

'I'll see you in the morning. I'll not come too early in case you two are still…'

'Jilly,' he shouted but she had disconnected.

'Your sister, she safe,' Alexandros said. 'She with my friend…'

161

THE BOX

Chapter 1 – Ann

Had the postman known the significance of the small brown box he left at No. 29, he would certainly have had second thoughts. But there was nothing about the parcel to indicate that the contents were anything out of the ordinary. There it stood from mid-morning onwards, propped against the door, protected only from the wind-driven rain by the canopy.

Countless people must have walked along Windermere Avenue during that time and one or two might even have noticed the package. Had any one of them known its contents, he or she might well have chanced the quick incursion to make off with it. But no one knew, so no opportunist struck.

When Ann Cherrington got home, just after six as usual, she too thought little of the unexpected package addressed to her, which she presumed had been left on the mat because it was too big for the letter box. She picked it up and went in, putting it to one side on the hall table. A cup of tea was always her first priority. Phillip came home about half an hour later and, as he hung up his coat, caught sight of the package as he leafed through the irritating unsolicited mail. He noted only that it was addressed to his wife whom he heard in the kitchen. An hour later, they sat down to their evening meal, followed by that night's must-watch item on TV. It was a little after eleven, as she was going up to bed, that Ann caught sight of the brown package again. She guessed from the size it was possibly a free sample of something and detoured into the kitchen for scissors.

When she opened the parcel, she gasped.

Inside, carefully wrapped in tissue paper, was a small, exquisite, antique silver-gilt casket. She had last seen it at her grandmother's house almost half a century earlier. As a child, she had craved the contents – it was where Grandma kept a few small pieces of the finest dark chocolate. If one was good, extra good, one might be allowed to take just a single piece. It had to be the same box for she had never seen another even remotely like it, and she opened it immediately, lifting the small latch on the front edge.

It was empty and now didn't have the tell-tale smell of her grandmother's favourite confectionary. Search as she might, there was no indication at all of who had sent it or even from where. She now vaguely remembered that it was one of the antique items stolen from her grandmother's treasure-trove house all those years ago in that terrible raid. A daring night-time theft, presumably by professionals, from which her grandmother, cowering in her bedroom, never really recovered, and which probably contributed to her death just two years later.

Now here it was on her kitchen table. The box, some tissue paper, a brown stiff-cardboard box the right size to accommodate the antique, brown paper outer wrapping. No note, no sender's name, not even a helpful postmark. Her name and address had been computer-printed on an adhesive label, which is what had made her think it was a sample. No other details or tell-tale markings.

'Phillip, come and see this.' She showed him the casket and explained how and where she had seen it before.

He picked it up, incredulous at her account. 'How do you know it's the same one?'

'It's got to be... who can have sent it and... why?'

'It must be worth thousands,' he said, turning it carefully in his hands, looking at the hallmarks. 'Are you sure there was no note with it?'

'Have a look yourself.'

'Maybe it slipped out in the post – or they forgot to put it in – the senders.'

They sat facing each other across the kitchen table, both perplexed, lost for words.

After a while she picked up the box again and held it close to her face, as if it might tell her something.

* * *

Ann Cherrington did *not* like mysteries or puzzles. She always wanted to be on the safe side, not take risks, to know where she stood at all times. Even as a little girl, she was cautious and reserved. Her mother died when she was not yet ten and she had been brought up by her un-prepared father and a series of housekeepers, some more kind and attentive than others. Ann knew from that early age that the family business came first. It was the largest firm of undertakers in South East London, founded by her great grandfather. It was where her father was most at home, and he worked long hours.

When he was not at work, he was tucked away in some corner of the large, dark family home, reading obscure classic novels of the 19th Century, perhaps his spiritual home. He did not like to be disturbed. As a result, Ann missed out on play and childish things.

She left school with good results, thanks to hard work more than a brilliant mind.

'I don't want you going off to Leeds or Liverpool to do something pointless like sociology,' her father told her. 'You may be a young woman but that doesn't mean we can't find a role for you in Williams Bros.'

She didn't dare protest, and a week after her very last schoolday, she joined the family business as a 'junior'. Two-and-a-half years later, when Mrs Dorcel, the firm's bookkeeper, retired, Ann took her place. And when her father died (he never retired) she took to running the whole firm. She liked to remain in the background, which probably was a good thing. She had an awkwardness about her, the result perhaps of being an only child who had never made many friends. The general manager, Mr Fortescue, was excellent in the front of house role and anyway, clients did not want to deal with a woman undertaker, did they?

Like everything else in her life, Phillip had been a pretty safe bet. They met at the Dulwich Bridge Club when she was in her late twenties. He was her first proper boyfriend, several years older than her. He had a promising position as a clerk at a large London law practice. You might say their courtship was cautious and measured: partners round the bridge table, why not in life too? They got married without too much fuss after four years, with the muted blessing of her father, who did not like the idea of his daughter leaving home. He suggested building an annex for the young couple and Ann would have gone along with the idea just to please him. Too late: Phillip had already put down a deposit on the Windermere Avenue house. He never imagined his new wife would not continue to work and neither could see themselves coping with babies and young children. Instead, they had a succession of Siamese cats, all with names beginning with an 's' – Sasha, Suzie, Suki, Sammy.

* * *

Ann had a disturbed night, at first unable to sleep, turning over in her mind again and again the whys and wherefores of the mystery parcel. She woke before five and reached across the space between the beds to nudge Phillip. Sleepily, he did his best to supply answers. 'If it is from that raid, I suppose it now belongs to the insurance company who paid your grandmother's claim,' he told her in response to her question about the legality of its ownership.

She didn't know who her grandmother's insurers were or how she could find out. And would the police still have any record of a break-in from the previous century, or any interest in the item? It all happened so long ago now, before anything was online. There was not going to be a quick and easy way of finding out anything from the internet. Part of her was delighted to have the casket, for she had very little by which to remember her grandmother. But another part of her was disturbed by the presence of an object she could not lay rightful claim to and the malign mystery its anonymous arrival presented. Whereas it used to hold rewards for good behaviour, now it had sinister overtones. There it was beside her bed. A link to a fond memory from the past and at the same time, representing an entirely unsettling connection to the here and now. She shuddered and asked Phillip if he thought she should take it to the local police station. He suggested that she do nothing immediately: just keep it somewhere safe, together with all the wrapping.

She went in to work as usual and tried to apply herself diligently to administration. But she was tired from lack of sleep and unsettled by the casket sitting there in her house. Uncharacteristically, she drove home in the early afternoon, brewed some tea, took an aspirin and went upstairs to the room they used as an office. The box beside her, she turned on the laptop and started searching the internet, scrolling down through long, long pages of images on various sites, hoping to find a photo of the one now next to her on the desk and some information about a dealer or a saleroom. Thousands of variations on the theme but none was hers. She saw a slightly similar one which had been sold for nearly £16,000 at auction a couple of years before. Submerged, she didn't hear Phillip come home and was startled when he came into the room, bringing her a fresh cup of tea. She showed him what she was doing and they talked about what else she might look for online. But it always came back to this: if the casket had not been sold by someone, it was not likely to show up. And none of that resolved the riddle: why would someone send her a valuable antique? A guilty conscience after all these years? Why her? How did they know of her connection? So many questions. No answers…

So here it was, an item possibly worth as much as a small car, stolen from her grandmother forty-six years before and now sent anonymously in a cardboard box to someone who was just 12 years old at the time of the theft and could not have been known to the thieves. And that led to another thought. She was one of three grandchildren. Her cousin Andrew was a few months younger and lived in Essex, his sister Diane was two years older and lived in Cheshire. 'So why me?' she asked herself out loud. Dorothy Glennon, her grandmother, was her mother's mother so none of the cousins had the family surname. She was a Williams before she became a Cherrington. How did anyone know how to find her?

Phillip was asleep when she crept up to bed at 2am, her eyes still unsettled by the long hours peering at the computer screen. She was physically tired but her mind was everywhere, turning things this way and that. None of it made sense. The casket had been taken along with other things that the thief, or thieves, knew something about, so perhaps they had a buyer in mind. A collector or a crooked dealer perhaps. Could that person be connected to someone who tracked her down and then sent it through the post many, many years later? It didn't begin to add up. If she couldn't work out how it got here, who should she go to for help? The police? Would that mean she'd lose it again? Should she talk to her cousins? Apart from Christmas cards, she'd not been in touch with either Andrew or Diane since her father died more than a decade before. They were not really that kind of family. Eventually, she drifted off to sleep, a myriad of questions unanswered.

Chapter 2 – Oliver

The black Daimler swept through the gates, splashing muddy water from the shallow puddles in the yard. Rear doors opened and two men got out, making their way towards a small group of employees trying to shelter from the light April rain. Oliver Smart, short and rather too stout for someone in their thirties, went first, careful not to dirty his well-polished brogues. The people moved aside as he and another man pushed past them and unlocked the warehouse door. 'Come inside now,' he announced over his shoulder. They filtered in behind him silently, many looking down at the floor so as not to meet his gaze. His reputation was well known.

'I'm now the owner of Argyles and this is your new manager, Mr Thompson. We're going to get this business back on its feet and reopen some of the shops. Those of you who want to work, really work, will have jobs.' It was the end of the Swinging Sixties and the Wilson government had recently published the *In Place of Strife* proposals, trying to curb some of the power of the trade unions.

He spoke for a few minutes longer, failing to reassure anyone. 'Any questions, address them to Mr Thomson,' he said perfunctorily and with that he left, striding back to his large, shiny car.

Argyles was his latest acquisition, one of many which were subject to his talent for asset stripping and what a *Financial Times* columnist had called 'commercial sleight of hand'. (His lawyers were looking into that with a view to suing for defamation.)

169

Overall things were going rather well for him. 'Smart by name, smart by nature - that sums me up,' he was prone to say. Generous donations to the Labour party had helped to buy him time, keeping some of the worst aspects of his business dealings away from the Press and the public.

Oliver Capel Smart (the Capel was a pure affectation – he'd added it himself) liked to regard himself as one of the new breed of British businessmen, coming up the hard way from humble origins. Hard graft, good fortune, a talent for turning risky dealings into profit, some outrageous corner cutting and a few friends in high places had contributed to his success, which had not been without spectacular setbacks. If you charted his business history it might look like an alpine skyline, steep ups but also sharp downs. Generally, though, the mountain peaks were getting higher, a lot higher. This month, he had bought Argyles from the liquidator for 'a song'. It had been a chain of eight high street jewellers' shops, mostly in the East Midlands, and also this small warehouse and workshop. Now he already had his sights on Fergusson & Drake, struggling shoe shops with branches in almost every town in England and Wales. The price was still a bit high for that one but it could well come down. Nicely timed bad publicity might help. He had ways of engineering that now, didn't he?

The light rain just kept falling as he was driven towards Holmeworth, his Grade One listed Norfolk manor house. He sat back and massaged his neck muscles. Tension, why did he always have such tension? Perhaps he should play more golf… 'Take your time,' he told his driver. It was his son's fourth birthday and

Doreen had laid on a party. The last thing he wanted was to catch the tail end of that. She was, he supposed, a good mother. Steady, loyal and reliable but oh so dull. A churchy type. He should have known. Still, when he wanted excitement, he could find it elsewhere, couldn't he? They'd married while he was still a commercial minnow and even back then, they were quite unsuited. She was timid and quiet, everything he was not. They say opposites attract and in those early days, he'd found a certain strength in her reserved calm. But later, the marriage would have ended if he'd had to spend any significant amount of time at home. The thing was he was too busy making a fortune and living the high life that went with it. Doreen seemed quite unperturbed by the fact that he was mostly away on business. Her home was where she belonged, even if it was more lavish than she really wanted.

When little Lennie came along at last, Oliver was, in theory, happy to have a son and heir. But that wasn't going to change him into any kind of a home-bird now, was it? The nearest he came to that were the large parties he threw, showing off the trappings of his wealth and making new, important contacts. Increasingly nowadays, he was on his own at them. They made Doreen uncomfortable and she'd found a way of opting out: so much so that several people wondered if Oliver was still married to 'that quiet, mousy woman'. He didn't really mind. He'd never found it difficult to find someone to play glamorous hostess for the night. I must have another party soon, to show off my new collection, he thought to himself.

* * *

Doreen, the daughter of a vicar, had been an average pupil at High School. Perhaps the most risky thing she had ever done in her life was to go to a Saturday dance with Ollie Smart, one year her senior and even back then, a bit too showy. The boys who went to the church youth club would have been more her type. But her father was always far too much in evidence there. On Oliver's part, he'd been attracted to Doreen's respectability and the fact that she was a grammar school girl – far superior to most of the girls who, like him, went to the local secondary modern. Anyway, he'd had a small wager with his best chum that he could 'pull' the vicar's daughter. Then, the more her father counselled against 'someone like him', the more she was determined to see the best side of a boy who'd not had her advantages in life. Son of a soldier killed in the war, he'd never had much of a chance, had he? Perhaps she was that chance. After a short engagement, they were married, by her father, who did very little to conceal his distaste for his new, far-too-flash son-in-law, and from a family of Catholics!

Now, a decade later, Doreen was much more likely to agree with her father's initial assessment. As her husband gained more and more swagger, climbing the greasy pole without any scruples, she shrank back into the conventional shell she'd never really left. She certainly did not want to flaunt the vulgar trappings of wealth which were now surrounding her; she did not feel at ease with his new friends in high places and their ambitious wives. Holmeworth might have eight bedrooms; a lodge for the chauffeur and his wife, who was their housekeeper; and a cottage where the gardener now lived. But Doreen would have been more at home in a three-bed semi in Beckenham where she grew up. So, in keeping with her modest outlook, little Lennie's birthday party was actually a very small affair. Just three little boys of a similar age from the village, along with their mothers, whom she was slightly embarrassed to invite to the manor with its undisguised lavish style. To avoid appearing to flaunt her advantages, they all sat round the scrubbed wooden kitchen table and played sensible party games. Then they would have neatly cut paste sandwiches and a slice of Lennie's birthday cake. She would not inflict on them the costly furnishings of the large lounge or the extravagance of the sun room, let alone the library, which in any case was a bit of a mess at present. It was in the library where Oliver had just started to unpack and catalogue a collection of antique silver which had been tucked away at the back of a warehouse he'd recently bought.

* * *

It was very late on a Sunday night in November when Oliver heard the bell. Doreen was long in bed and he was just about to turn in himself. Shoeless, he padded through the hall to the passage: the indicator box showed that someone was at the back door. Don't tell me my driver can't make my 7am start, he thought to himself as he went through the scullery and cracked open the heavy door. Someone, largely in the shadows, stepped out so that he was more or less under the outside light. Oliver did not recognise the man, who was wearing a long grey coat and a dark trilby which shaded his face.

'I've something 'ere what might interest you,' the man said, revealing a large cardboard box.

Oliver's immediate thought was that the stranger was a poacher. 'I doubt we want anything you've got,' he said and started to close the door.

'Just 'ave a look, guvnor. No harm done if youse not interested.'

Oliver, still slightly wary, unchained the door and let the man step inside. The caller was surprisingly neatly dressed under his open coat, with dark clothes, but had a rather gaunt face, hollow cheeks and red-ringed watery eyes. His accent was London, not Norfolk. Without being asked, the man went over to the table and quite carefully took out about a dozen awkwardly shaped items wrapped in newspaper. ''ave a little look at these.'

Oliver picked up one of the largest ones. Inside the wrapping was an engraved silver coffee pot. Since he'd obtained the Argyle antique silver collection a few months earlier, he'd learned quite a lot about antique silver. Not enough to be any kind of expert, but he was developing a bit of an eye for the good stuff. 'Where did you get this?'

The man avoided the question. 'Word is youse a new collector. I can give you a special price fer some or all of this lot.'

The workmanship on the coffee pot was extraordinarily fine. This was not jumble-sale junk. Oliver unwrapped two other pieces. A sugar bowl and a small oval platter. In the inadequate light of the scullery, he could not properly make out the hallmarks but he was pretty sure this was fine antique silver. If asked, he might suggest it was George II.

'A grand fer the lot,' the man said, clearly sensing Oliver's interest.

'I don't have that kind of money in the house,' Oliver lied. 'And I'm pretty sure you wouldn't take a cheque…'

''ow much 'ave yer got?'

'I might find a couple of hundred in cash, that's all. I'd have to check my wallet.'

'Make it a monkey – that's my best offer.'

'Wait there and I'll see what I've got,' Oliver said. A minute or two later, he came back with £440 in tenners.

The man carefully counted the money and then shot Oliver a glance, and with an expression on his face of reluctant acceptance, put the notes in his pocket and, without another word, slipped out of the door into the cold night air. Oliver did not hear the sound of a vehicle driving away, if indeed there was one.

In the scullery, he quietly unwrapped all the items. As with the coffee pot, the workmanship was outstanding. He rewrapped the items in the crumpled newspaper for now, put them in a clean, dry box which he bundled round with a dust-sheet and put the whole thing at the back of an out-of-the-way cupboard. No one would look in there for anything any time soon, he was sure. Further examination would have to wait until he had his magnifying glass, reference books and better light.

He knew he had got a real bargain, albeit a dodgy one. Sold in a respected auction, each item alone could fetch at least what he'd paid for the whole lot. The items would not be able to go to an honest dealer, but they could be added carefully to his private collection. He bolted the back door, turned out the lights and went upstairs. I need to think very carefully about this, he said to himself, almost aloud. Very carefully indeed.

Chapter 3 – Lennie

There were those who appeared to find Leonard Capel Smart amusing but perhaps what they really liked most was his money. Hard to tell sometimes. Increasingly his wife, Ebony, was not one of those who was amused by him. There was a coolness about the couple these days that was impossible to ignore when they were together, something of a rarity.

Casual observers might think that Lennie had had an easy life, born into money. But he never bonded with his father and his devoted, quiet, sensitive mother had died of cancer when he was nine. Boarding schools and housekeepers were the answer, his father decided.

Lennie left school with a clutch of O-levels – no one had suggested he should stay on into the Sixth, least of all he himself. His father, something of a stranger to the lad really, tried to immerse him in commerce, hoping he would one day take over running the whole of SmartBusinessCorp. All Lennie really wanted to do was race cars. His father's wealth bought him cars and a support team which would probably have propelled a more talented driver to the very top. Unfortunately, the only place Lennie was going fast was nowhere. When he didn't crash, he was too slow. Lennie-the-Last they called him behind his back. He blamed his mechanics, the track conditions, his tyres, the fuel, anything really. The truth was he lacked the required lightning-fast reactions and fluent coordination. He was impetuous and showed poor judgement. After a while, even he came to realise he was not cut out to be a successful racing driver. It didn't stop him from having his red Ferrari, L3NNY, and enough points on his licence to almost disqualify him from driving on public roads.

In a desperate bid to get him focused on business, his father put him in nominal charge of a chain of shoe shops but he was not interested and paid no attention to the role. Mr Smart senior had to rescue the business after several crazy decisions and the inability to file required returns. Father and son did not see eye to eye over anything and Lennie drifted in and out of one hair-brained scheme after another. A nightclub called Liquor-Ice held his attention for a while and to be fair, it did well at first but eventually the trendy set moved on and his interest waned. Truth was he didn't need the money and lacked motivation. It was while Liquor-Ice was briefly doing well that he met Ebony, a member of The Rock Crystals girl band. As a couple, they were soon in the tabloids. *Hello* magazine covered their wedding with a spread of several pages and minor royals were guests. Later coverage in the papers was less favourable. The Rock Crystals broke up amid some unsavoury allegations and both Ebony and Lennie were pictured arm in arm with other partners looking much the worse for wear.

Oliver Smart died in January 2000, aged just sixty-six, after catching a rare strain of pneumonia which his doctors struggled to identify. Lennie, no stranger to remarks made in bad taste, quipped it was the millennium bug. The funeral was large and conspicuous with several politicians rubbing shoulders with business moguls, several of them of the less savoury type. Lennie was pictured at least looking sad, holding the arm of Ebony, who behind her veil really was tearful.

Shrewd tax lawyers and accountants minimised the death duties and Lennie inherited a very large fortune. He had no intention of trying to run the SmartBusinessCorp empire, and for once, made a shrewd choice of a CEO – actually a person his father might have chosen if he had lived. For a short period after his father's death, it seemed that Lennie might make something of himself. Greenpeace in Britain had been de-railed by the McLibel case and he and Ebony became involved in one of the eco-protest groups formed in its place. Positive press coverage came from a rock concert at Holmeworth and involvement in road extension protests in Scotland. Briefly the couple were regarded as wealthy do-gooders, getting more favourable Press coverage.

All that ended very abruptly when anti-hunting protesters were very roughly dealt with on the Holmeworth estate. Lennie's big mouth got him into further trouble with the media and even the pro-hunting lobby distanced themselves from him when he suggested that protestors deserved what they got as their vehicles were trashed and limbs broken by hooded vigilantes wielding clubs.

Lennie started spending time abroad, anywhere that was sunny. He and Ebony went their separate ways – he didn't much care. He had a new all-consuming interest in a former American air-hostess with the most amazing body…

Chapter 4 – Florence

Quite out of character, Florence Barker went to work for the Smarts as a housekeeper in 2007, well aware of the celeb reputation of her employers. By contrast, they had required exemplary references from her, which an exclusive Mayfair service agency had no trouble in providing.

Her previous employer, an hereditary peer, had died and she had been promised a modest bequest. She'd thought of the new position as something a bit different: for the first time in her career in service, she was working for 'new money' rather than those with long, titled histories. Anyway, she saw it as a stop-gap. Then she learned that her last employer's will was being challenged and, in the end, the expected windfall never materialised. So she stayed on at Holmeworth rather longer than she had at first expected. Her employers moved in separate circles.

Mrs. Smart ('call me Ebony') was emotional, flighty, a bit scatter-brained but underneath kind enough. She was rather awkward in Florence's presence, uncomfortable in dealing with servants. Mr. Smart was quite different. Fortunately, he was not usually interested in what went on in the house and had little to do with staff, apart from occasional outbursts of annoyance. If he had any positive sides to his personality, she was yet to find them. Sometimes she would overhear angry exchanges between the couple which always seemed to end the same way. Ebony running from the room in tears, Mr. Smart shouting after her in a rage, using four-letter words.

Later, he might try to make amends but Ebony did not thaw easily.

Now Florence was on the point of going back to the agency to ask them to find her a new position. She had been happy to take instruction from Ebony but recently, he'd been the one telling her what to do. Barking at Barker, she secretly mouthed to herself.

'Come to my study,' he demanded, shouting in the hall so loudly she could have heard him almost wherever she was. She came downstairs and entered his room. He was standing, stiff, his face reddened with anger. 'Here's your notice, one month's pay. I want you gone from the lodge by tonight.'

'Have I done something wrong?' she calmly inquired, professional and determined not to be browbeaten.

'You know bloody well what you've been doing. Probably for some time. Did you think I wouldn't notice?'

She had no idea what he was talking about. It showed on her face.

'Don't come that 'Miss Bloody Innocent' with me. I've seen the gaps. I know where items are missing.'

'I'm sorry, Sir, I don't...'

'Got to fucking well spell it out for you, have I?' She winced.

'OK. I know you have been taking my silver. You're the only one apart from me who has the keys to the bookcase. Not a very clever thief, are you? Now get out.'

She froze in confusion.

'GET OUT,' he yelled and raised his hand as if to strike her.

She shrunk back, dumbfounded, and they looked at each other for several seconds.

Then, only a bit louder than a whisper, she said: 'I have not taken anything from you, Mr Smart. I never have and I never would.' And with as much of her dignity as she could muster, she turned and left him standing by the door, which was slammed shut behind her a few seconds later.

She knew exactly what he was referring to, of course. One of the glass-fronted bookcases in the library, which appeared to be filled with leather-bound volumes of great age, was in fact a front. The spines were all there was of the books and concealed behind them was the large collection of antique silver, probably of great value. The collection had been made by Mr Smart's father, she'd been told. One of her duties was to dust the shelves and silver and to check that the de-humidifier was working in the cupboard, which was always to be kept locked, contents hidden, presumably as a precaution against thieves.

As she had told her employer, Florence would never steal even a cup of flour or a pencil. If silver was missing, it was not of her doing. Now she would phone the agency. They would know what to do. She would pack straight away. It was all big mistake, of course, but she wasn't going to stay at Holmeworth for a minute longer.

* * *

From the age of about eight, all Florence had ever wanted was to be a ballerina. And she had the right ingredients. Demure, lissom and pretty with a perfectly oval face. She practised and practised. Her parents saved hard to pay for lessons and her dance teacher told them Florence showed great promise and could go all the way. Then disaster struck. She started gaining weight, her hair started falling out, and she became easily tired. She was diagnosed with an under-active thyroid gland. She felt unwell and became depressed. Despite some effective treatment, she was sure that she would never dance professionally and gave up her quest. She was partially rescued by the dance teacher who at least helped her to regain some confidence, and she worked at the dance school for a time as a helper, occasionally teaching younger girls when one of the qualified teachers was away.

Then she was approached by Maurice McMaster Esq., personal assistant to Lord and Lady De Clos. 'We have been advised that you might be a suitable person to give dance lessons to Miss Camilla De Clos, their only daughter,' he wrote on crested notepaper. It was her entry to what became a life in service, working for members of the aristocracy. Florence's slim figure and elegant posture meant she fitted in gracefully to some of the finest homes in the land, working diligently and with intelligence. Naturally, her references were impeccable.

Now she was not going to tolerate even the hint of scandal caused by entirely false allegations. It was her own fault in a way. She should have known better than to accept a position from a rich, shallow playboy and his flibbertigibbet of a showbiz wife. If anyone was dishonest, it was the Smarts. She vowed to herself that they would not be allowed to leave any kind of stain on her lilywhite reputation.

Chapter 5 – Ebony

Earlene Rayhelle Precious Grant also liked to dance. The granddaughter of Jamaican immigrants, she had rhythm coursing through her veins and a powerful singing voice. In the clubs and pubs of South London, she went by the name of Ebony Grant. That changed to just Ebony when she became a founder member of the four-girl band, The Rock Crystals. She was bright and cheeky, with a good dose of street cred, fed to her in bite-sized chunks by her two older brothers.

You need special powers to emerge unscathed from the Angell Town estate in Brixton and Ebony almost made it. The girls convinced their promoter that they had kicked the habit, a claim that they all sort of believed themselves back then. Their first tour was something of a slow burn but they started to get large audiences after they were given a great write up in *Melody Maker*, mentioned in the same breath as Supergrass and Radiohead. Their single, *Kiss Me, Kiss Me, Kiss Me*, went high into the charts followed by an album, *Four In A Bed*. The money rolled in. For a while, they were media darlings with a significant teen fan base. Then, one of the four, Cleona, was rushed to hospital and the word was she'd overdosed on heroin. Stories trickled out about self-harm. Only a week later, the *Sun* alleged that they had a video showing another band member, Saychelle, taking the album title far too literally with three white men. The group tried to carry on through the scandals but their own chemistry was no longer there, nor were all their young fans.

That was around the time that Ebony met Lennie. It was her second visit to Liquor-Ice and someone in her crowd said she knew the owner. He was rich, quite good looking and fun. They were spotted together by the paparazzi and she felt good about being back in the magazines without the negative comments of the previous six months. One of the leading fashion mags wanted to feature her as a model in their special 'black is beautiful' edition, exploiting the connection between her name, Ebony, and Liquor-Ice. As the girl band crumbled, Ebony's new life with the rich and well-connected took shape. No one in Lennie's set cared one jot that she didn't come from their privileged background. The fact that she was street-wise had a lot more traction.

Caribbean honeymoon over, she and Lennie went to live off the Kings Road, without a thought about what either of them might do next. She tried a bit more modelling, had a half-hearted poke at a solo singing career, but generally had round-the-clock fun. Motivation changes when you don't really need the money, doesn't it?

When the older Mr Smart died, her new husband changed, and not for the better. Before Oliver died, the couple were spending his father's money and Lennie was as carefree as could be. Now suddenly, it was *his* own money and he put on the brakes. He sold the flat in London and they went to live in Holmeworth.

She hated it. Rural and remote, it seemed a million miles from the London she grew up in. A few of her friends came to stay for a weekend, but they too felt ill at ease in the period mansion far from anywhere. Ebony was never going to play lady of the manor. She was a street girl from Brixton, that's who she was. Lennie didn't understand, or didn't want to.

She went back to London as often as she could, her pink Audi drophead, E8ONY, easily spotted by social columnists and bloggers. She went back to some of her old ways with drugs, and slightly more discreetly, took up with one of her old boyfriends. Darley was seriously into the eco-protest movement and saw Ebony as a way to access funds. The two of them worked out how to press the right buttons to get Lennie involved and financially committed. So, for a while, Ebony spent a little more time at Holmeworth and without too much difficulty, talked Lennie into holding a rock concert on the estate.

'With my music industry contacts, it could become the new Glastonbury,' she told him.

Darley came down for the weekend occasionally, always with a partner so as not to cause suspicion and his enthusiasm for green issues started to chime a little with Lennie, in a receptive mood for once. For the first time in years, Ebony felt that she might just find a way to make more of a life for herself in rural Norfolk. The rock concert was a qualified success. No challenge to Glastonbury, of course, but it was only the first year. There might be more to come later. It was a watershed moment and some of Ebony's former friends were a little more willing to making the tiresome journey to north Norfolk. For a while, Ebony and Lennie appeared to be something of a couple again.

It didn't last. At the same time as he was alluding to green credentials, Lennie was trying to ingratiate himself with the Norfolk country set. Typically, he hadn't thought very deeply about anything. When he announced that the Harriers would be holding their Boxing Day meet on the Holmeworth estate, Ebony was appalled.

'Whatever gave you that idea?' she asked him. He waffled on about being someone in the local community.

'I thought we were green, not posh...' she said. 'Go ahead with this and I'll get Darley to alert every animal rights group he can think of. You won't be able to move for protest banners.'

'It's not the yoghurt weavers I want to mix with. It's people with more taste and stature. They're our natural partners here,' he told her.

There was no common ground and they both said things they would regret later. Ebony packed her bags, this time, she said, for good.

She spent that Christmas in Brixton with her family. They were delighted to have her and to share the new, slightly larger house they'd been able to buy, thanks to their upwardly mobile daughter. Mr Grant was not in the least upset – or surprised – that she wasn't having Christmas with Lennie.

Her family was even more relieved when they watched the evening news on TV on Boxing Day. Hunt saboteurs and animal rights supporters were kicked and punched by pro-hunting vigilantes and charged by horses. One woman was shown being smacked on the head by hooded man wielding a baseball bat. Police were out in numbers, struggling to keep the groups apart. Then someone thrust a microphone in front of Holmeworth landowner Mr Lennie Smart. 'They've got what was coming to them,' he said live on air. 'People have no right to come onto my land and try to disrupt a traditional way of life.

'Any of them who have been hurt only got what they deserved.'

'But don't you think that some of those supporting hunting have gone too far today?' the reporter asked.

'If they have any brains, they deserve to have them caved in,' he replied, looking straight into the TV camera. Over the next few days, a clip of this response was played time and time again. It became a seminal moment in the history of British blood sports. Even those who came from the pro-hunting lobby distanced themselves from his graphic comment.

Among those with their heads caved in was Darley, in an acute trauma ward in Norwich. It was not known how much of a recovery, if any, he would ever make. Two days later, Ebony moved in with Saychelle, 'at least for now,' she told her family.

Over New Year, the two girls went clubbing and the fun went on and on into January. Their old habits came back all too easily, and money became a problem. Lennie, shunned and beleaguered, cut off Ebony's funds and by then, the remnants of The Rock Crystals money had gone, too.

It was a low point for both Ebony and Lennie, for different reasons. For her part, Ebony was making poor decisions, desperate for the next fix more than anything else. Her self-respect absent, she crept back to Holmeworth, always checking first that Lennie was not around. She had one thing in mind and one thing only: to get her hands on some money. Lennie did not make that easy.

* * *

Hidden away in the library was any amount of antique silver, lovingly collected by her late father-in-law. There was something a bit dodgy about it, she believed. Lennie had never really discussed it but it appeared that it had not been properly declared to the tax authorities when Oliver Smart died. Except for that, she thought Lennie might well have sold the lot of it. As it was, it was kept under lock and key and, apart from the occasional dusting, never saw the light of day. Who would ever notice if just one or two small pieces went missing? And so it was that a few items found their way into the hands of antique dealers. One in particular who knew not to ask many questions. She might have got paid more elsewhere, but well, what-the-hell?

Her raids on the silverware were made easier because Oliver was often away nowadays. He had developed a particular interest for St Lucia and a certain female with long legs and blonde hair. Bloody fool. 'Is he around just now?' she would ask their housekeeper on the phone. 'He says he'll be back at the weekend,' Florence replied, knowing full well that her answer would most likely prompt another flying visit from 'the lady of the house'. So Ebony could return to Holmeworth for a couple of hours and, with no questions asked, leave again – with a little more treasure as a top up.

Oliver didn't know and didn't care how Ebony was managing. As long as their paths did not cross, that was fine by him. They had no such foolish thing as a joint account so it would not be his money she was spending, wherever she was.

But this time, Ebony had got things wrong. She'd seen a picture of Oliver on the page of some magazine 'partying' with his blonde air hostess who was wearing a tight sequinned number that emphasised her curves. The caption gave the impression that the picture was current. In fact, it was taken a fortnight before. So rather than ring the house, this time Ebony just jumped in the Audi and drove the 130 miles from London, arriving in the late afternoon. Her tyres were just crunching over the gravel drive when the housekeeper came out of the huge front door, looking unusually flustered.

Ebony had grown to like Florence, not merely because she helped her check when the coast was clear. 'It's not easy to get used to having staff when you come from a background like mine,' Ebony told her on one occasion. She couldn't remember exactly what Florence had said in return, but, always the consummate professional, she had put Ebony at ease.

What was wrong now? Why was the housekeeper so unsettled?

She parked round the side out of the way and crept inside. She froze when she heard Oliver, not in the Caribbean, after all! She crept carefully up the wide oak staircase, wincing as the boards creaked under her feet. He didn't seem to hear. Into what had been her dressing room. Door tightly shut. Oh! God, how I need something now to help me relax. Every sinew tense.

A little while later, she heard the front door close and she guessed, rightly, Oliver had gone out. I hope he doesn't look round the side and see my car, she thought and waited for a few minutes, fearing that he might storm back in looking for her. But the house was strangely quiet. She picked up a small overnight case from her room, plenty big enough for a piece of antique silver. Tiptoeing downstairs, she went to the butler's pantry to collect the key to that special library bookcase. It was not on the hook. Panic. 'He's on to me,' she thought. This was bad, very bad. But as she passed the library door, she noticed that, for once, the bookcase was open, the false cover removed and the silver clearly visible. It has never been left like that before, she was sure. Creeping in, she reached out for the first piece that came to hand, slipped it into the case and crept through to the hall… to be met by Oliver bounding back in.

'Your fucking housekeeper has been stealing my silver,' he said. 'I've just sacked her. What are you doing back here anyway? I've just seen your car.'

Startled, Ebony did not know where to look. 'I've just come back for a few things – I'm going back now,' holding the pink case to her chest as if it were a shield.

He said nothing but gave her a filthy look and stomped off towards the library.

Ebony could not get out of the door fast enough. Round to the side to her car. She threw the case across the passenger seat and got in. Then she was off down the drive, her mind a blur. As she passed the lodge, she noticed the light was on inside. What had Oliver said about sacking the housekeeper? It was only then that it dawned on her what was happening.

Despite her keenness to get away, she pulled up beside the lodge, her legs still trembling, and knocked on the door. She noticed Florence looking through a window. Then the door opened.

Chapter 6 – Phillip

Overall, life had been a disappointment for Phillip Cherrington. Cricket mad, all he had ever really wanted was to open the batting for England. A small ask, really. The thing was that from an early age he needed glasses. Bad but not hopeless, you'd have thought. Geoffrey Boycott had managed with less than perfect eyesight; why couldn't he? The real obstacle was that Phillip wasn't much good at either batting or bowling. He didn't make the school cricket team. So instead of playing, he became a cricket encyclopaedia, memorising Wisden page after page. Later, he used the same powerful memory to become a bridge player, representing his club and county. People still talked about some of his games. He's the Cherrington of the negative double which still bears his name. This prodigious memory also made him a first-class senior clerk in the large City law practice for whom he worked. He was fastidious, industrious and loyal. But notwithstanding the high regard in which he was held in his firm, and a generous salary, he felt little sense of achievement. Reflecting on his life, he would certainly have settled instead for being a largely forgotten middle order batsman for Kent, his home county. It was not to be.

Unlike Ann, who came from a family with plenty of money, his background was modest. His parents had managed financially, but there was not too much going spare and, rather than money, he had inherited a careful approach life. He was tall, very tall, one would almost say ungainly. Oddly, it seemed as if his clothes had been chosen for an even taller man, for they hung on him badly. Although now in his sixties, he had no hint of grey in his light brown, slightly frizzy hair which he found impossible to keep tidy. His long face suited a tall man but was mainly without what one might call character.

Perhaps a little surprisingly for such an introvert, the silver casket presented him with a challenge he relished. What could he quietly find out about it? Ann, who was saying that she was sorry the 'damned thing ever turned up', believed that it was stolen from her grandmother when she was twelve. That would make it 1969. No internet back then, of course. He had developed a good working relationship with several members of the police but no one in the Surrey force who would be of help. Ann's grandmother lived in Purley, near Croydon, so it was on their patch. Most police forces had some sort of records of crimes reported in the 1960s but he drew a complete blank with Surrey.

The local paper, a weekly called the *Croydon Advertiser*, was his next quest but he'd have to go to the National Archives in Kew for relevant copies.

In his lunchtime, he slipped into the office of Eleanor Broakes, the senior partner who specialised in criminal law. She listened quietly while he explained about his dilemma with the box. 'Go and see Erdislan LaTrobe, he might be a good place to start,' she told him. 'You can mention my name – he'll be wary of you, of course. He's unique - he can walk on both sides of the street, legally speaking, but he's not totally safe on either.' She laughed at her own comment. Then she also gave Phillip the name of a retired Surrey Police Superintendent who had been helpful to the chambers in the past. 'He's good, but he's a bit past his sell-by date now,' she said.

Erdislan LaTrobe agreed to meet him 'away from prying eyes in the Bow Bells' after work a couple of days later after Phillip mentioned his connection to Eleanor. And Colin Milton, the former superintendent on the Surrey force, tried to be helpful. 'Trouble is, I'm hopelessly out of touch. It has all changed,' he admitted.

Phillip said nothing to Ann about his inquiries. He didn't want to raise her expectations and need not tell her anything until something helpful emerged, if it ever did! He merely told her he'd got a meeting after work in two days and wouldn't be home at the usual time.

Erdislan was sitting on his own in the corner of the pub when Phillip went in. He'd put his black homburg next to his beer glass as the agreed sign so Phillip could find him. He was a small man with a pasty complexion: wouldn't do him any harm to get some fresh air, Phillip thought to himself. He spoke with the hint of an accent which was hard to identify. Regional? Foreign? Phillip wasn't sure. He described himself as a dealer - 'almost anything, mate, except drugs. Never touch them. Nasty things.' Preliminaries over, Phillip described the little he knew about what had happened in the theft from his wife's grandmother and the fact that one item, the casket, had now turned up.

LaTrobe looked back at him blankly. 'I can't be of any help. It is all far too long ago. South of the river was home to the Richardsons in those days, nasty bastards. If they'd been behind the robbery, granny would have probably ended up dead, or nailed to the floor!'

They talked a bit more. The Richardsons, like the Krays, were the stuff of legend. Easy to talk about now, not so funny if it was your toes being severed by bolt cutters!

'It just might have been the work of Winky B,' LaTrobe offered. 'Croydon, Purley, round there, might have been a bit too far out for the Richardsons. I don't really know. Winky went to prison in the seventies, I think.'

Phillip spent much of the next Saturday at Kew poring over old newspapers. There were a few articles from the 1970s about Winky B(eevers), so called because he had a tic in one eye which made him appear to be winking at people all the time. It took Phillip longer to find any reference to theft in the *Croydon Advertiser* but eventually he came across a short piece in the edition for Friday, 29 November, 1968 – a few months earlier than Ann had suggested. It added no detail that Phillip thought was any help at all.

Nothing he read shed any light on who might have been behind the theft. Could have been Winky B or the Richardsons or anyone else. The police would have had their theories at the time, but as far as Phillip could tell, no one was ever convicted of anything to do with the silver theft from old Mrs Glennon.

The following week, he talked to Colin Milton again and asked him about Winky B.

'Gosh. There's a name I haven't heard for a long time,' said the retired policeman. 'He was around long before my time, but I knew the force had been accused of fitting him up. We didn't, of course, but that didn't shut him up.' It led to a long reminiscence about the inability of the police to present themselves as a decent, honest force. 'You only need one bad apple and everyone says the whole barrel is rotten,' he complained.

Phillip was getting nowhere. And at the same time, he had been trying to find any information about the insurance company – or broker – which Mrs Glennon had used. But there again, the time line was just a little too long and he couldn't find anything which would lead him to whoever might be the legal owners of the silver box now.

Ann's parents had lived in Dulwich. Her cousins, Diane and Andrew, grew up in Coulsdon, an outer London suburb just around the corner from Granny Glennon in Purley. Phillip wondered if they might have known more about the silver theft. Did he dare ring either of them behind Ann's back, given that they were not a close family? Probably unwise. Should he tell Ann about his somewhat fruitless searches? Same answer. He'd come up with nothing at all which might lead to the discovery of the sender of the parcel, or the rightful owner, or anything in between.

One evening, several weeks later, the phone rang at home. Phillip answered. 'Erdislan LaTrobe here, glad I've caught you.'

He told him that he had heard that Winky B used a fence back then. He didn't have his name. 'If Winky was involved, your silver might have passed through his hands. Can't tell you any more than that.'

Phillip thanked him and he rang off. Another dead end. Far too many 'ifs' and 'maybes'. Then a faint bell rang in Phillip's head... surely not? Could it be? He remembered an appeal court case from around that time to do with a man – what was his name? Carter? Car-something, that was it, Carson – who had been accused of receiving stolen goods. It was a case he had come across when he was studying: it contained a key point of law so had made its way into the text books. He remembered it so clearly because the victim of the theft had been Toby Vickram, then treasurer of Kent County Cricket Club. Gotcha! It only took him moments to look up the case online. There it was: *England and Wales Court of Appeal (Criminal Division) R v Carson*. He quickly scrolled through the transcript. Large as life, the name jumped out at him 'Beevers'. Carson, it was alleged by the prosecution, had received stolen items from Winky B. It was nothing directly to do with the theft from Ann's grandmother but it was the right timeframe so maybe Carson was involved in other thefts, too. The point of law didn't matter now. What he needed to do was track down Carson. Could he still be around today? Unlikely. But at least it was a lead. Albeit a very weak one.

It took him two further days to find out that Reg Carson had spent a reasonable amount of time detained at Her Majesty's pleasure, released for the last time in 1991, when he would have been in his sixties. He didn't find any current address for Mr Carson, but one that kept cropping up in the records placed him at an address in Norwood.

The next weekend, he visited 33 Marple Road, a house like all the others on the same road which had undergone renovation and loft conversions after being bought by tenants from the council. The tiny front garden was now a parking space, occupied by a small car which had been left at an angle so as not to block either the pavement or the front door. He pressed the doorbell, setting off a ghastly rendering of *Jingle Bells*. It brought a child of about ten to the door who opened it wide while a voice from another room called: 'Who is it, Kyle?'

Kyle looked up at Phillip who towered above him, left the door open and fled back into the house. A few seconds later, an overweight woman, untidy in track suit bottoms and a loose-fitting, unflattering top, stepped into the entrance-way, wiping her hands on a none-too-clean tea-towel. 'Can I help you?'

'I'm actually looking for a Mr Carson, Reg Carson,' Phillip said.

'He's not here. Why do you want him?'

'I'm trying to tie up some loose ends and I have come across his name,' Phillip tried for starters. 'Is he a relative?'

Not a good start. It made the large lady seem more suspicious of the unexpected caller. 'I'm his daughter. What sort of loose ends?'

Phillip stumbled. He was not good at this sort of thing.

'You're not from the police, are you?' the woman asked.

He shook his head emphatically. Phillip saw no merit in deceiving the woman and tried to explain the very speculative connection to her father. She clearly did not understand. 'He don't remember things now. He won't be any help.'

'My wife would love to solve this mystery,' Phillip told her. 'Is there any chance I might just visit Mr Carson once?'

* * *

The receptionist at Stoneway Court Care Home told him he'd probably find Mr Carson in the day room. They had just finished their lunch and the whole building smelled strongly of the unmistakeable odour of trolley meals. Three men were slumped, dozing, in large leatherette chairs in front of a flat screen TV which was showing afternoon sport, the sound turned low. Phillip didn't want to wake any of them and looked round the room for somewhere to sit and wait. There did not appear to be a free space. Then a young member of staff came in and pointed to a stack of moulded grey plastic chairs. While Phillip lifted off the topmost chair, the orderly went over to one of the dozing men, wearing a loose-fitting dark-red gravy-stained cardigan.

'You've got a visitor, Reg,' she said to the man who woke with a bit of a jerk and looked blankly round the room.

Phillip pulled his chair nearer. 'Mr Carson? You don't know me. I've been speaking to your daughter.'

The old man, hollow cheeked and unevenly shaved with odd tufts of silver-white stubble, looked blankly back at him.

'I wonder if I could ask you a few questions about someone you might remember from a long time ago?' Still no recognition. 'Do you remember a man called Winky B, a Mr Beevers? He might have given you things to sell?'

'Sell, yes, sell,' said the old man in a way which suggested he understood nothing about what was going on. His daughter was right, this was going to be pointless.

Phillip persisted for several minutes more, getting nowhere. Juventus were playing Bayern on the TV, at which Mr Carson occasionally glanced over Phillip's shoulder.

'You like watching football?' Phillip asked, to be polite. His chances of this leading anywhere had really disappeared. 'I had a season ticket,' Reg told him. 'Never had to pay. Winky bought them for us,' he said, as if it was blindingly obvious.

They talked about football and Winky for another minute or so. Then it seemed the old man was drifting away in his mind.

'You don't remember getting a lot of silver to sell, do you, by any chance?' In at the deep end now.

'We never won the Cup. We was runners up.'

This was not going to work. He knew it now. 'Well, thank you, Mr Carson, Reg. It was nice meeting you.' The old man smiled back at him. Phillip put his chair back on the stack in the corner. As he turned to leave the room, apparently from nowhere Reg said: 'Up the top of Norfolk. Young geezer.'

Phillip stopped. 'What did you say?'

Reg paused, not sure what he'd been asked. 'Three all. Had to play again. They won.'

'No, I mean about Norfolk. What younger man?'

But he could get nothing more. Reg Carson was back re-living some past glories of a cup final.

For several more weeks Phillip tried to make sense of what the elderly man had said, seeing if there was any way to connect it to Mrs Glennon, his wife and the small silver casket. The box itself was now back in tissue paper in the box and pushed to the back of a drawer in the bedroom where Ann kept a couple of silk scarves. He could find out nothing at all about a 'young geezer' in north Norfolk who might have bought silver. There were no known collectors who might have fitted that bill. No silver or antique dealers seemed to be able to help. He knew the chambers' contact in the Norfolk Constabulary himself. He didn't need to bother Eleanor this time, but the contact did not help at all. If Reg Carson's muddled words had any significance, Phillip couldn't find it. Again, he said nothing to Ann about his inquiries. Don't rake up anything without good reason.

Chapter 7 – Ebony and Florence

Where do I start, thought Ebony as she stood by the lodge door, which was opened slowly by Florence.

'Can I come in?' Ebony asked, tremulously.

Florence listened to a few sentences. She needed no more prompting: 'Get straight back in your car now. Don't wait. Drive to the Green Man just on the other side of Fakenham. It's off the main road. Park that thing out of sight – it can be spotted a mile off,' she said. 'Wait for me in the pub. I hope I will not be too long behind you. Go now.' She closed the door.

Stunned, Ebony did as she was told, driving fast and all the while checking her mirrors to see if she was being followed. She used her mobile phone's sat nav to find the pub.

It was just gone six when she got there and parked the Audi around the corner in a cul de sac, just as she had been told. Then she locked the small case with the silver in it in the boot and went into the pub. A noisy crowd of early evening drinkers was at the bar and barely noticed her. She ordered a tonic water and sat down in the quietest corner she could find. She desperately needed a stiff drink - and something more - but now new alarms in her head told her she had better stay as sober as she was. Almost an hour later, Florence came in, said something to the girl behind the bar and went over to Ebony.

'Follow me,' and she led the way to one to the pub's ground-floor bedrooms. They sat down facing each other, Florence perched on the edge of the bed, her face remarkably calm and impassive. Ebony, on the one small chair, was anything but.

'I think you've got a lot of explaining to do,' the housekeeper said.

And so it came spilling out. How Ebony had been taking silver items from the collection. What Lennie had said when he came across her in the hall. How she knew Florence had been wrongly sacked. How she and her husband had been living in different worlds for some time, if not always. How she was struggling without any money despite Lennie's huge wealth. What she knew about the new woman in Lennie's life, all of it jumbled in no sort of order. All the while on the edge of tears.

When she stopped, there was a stillness in the room, a sense of unburdening. Florence allowed a long pause before she said quietly, 'I think I know why you needed to steal the silver but I'd better hear it from you.'

Now, very hesitantly, Ebony talked about her drug habit. 'You've no idea how hard it is growing up in Brixton and staying clean. I did it. My eldest brother started taking drugs and told me never to do the same. He threatened me. I managed fine until we formed the band. Then we were all dabbling. It made our music better.' She explained that even then, she wasn't a heavy user. 'Not like some of the others. I got sucked in again after Lennie and I had our big row. That's when I moved in with Saychelle. It was just around Christmas, if you remember. She's been a good friend, but a bad influence.'

Florence just listened, letting Ebony tell her life's story. She'd guessed at the main theme: after all, she'd seen Ebony start to fall apart. She hadn't known the details or the scale of the problem. After about three quarters of an hour, Ebony was done. Empty. Florence got up and boiled the courtesy kettle, a cup of tea for them both.

'In a way, it should be nothing to do with me,' she said. 'What happened between you and Mr Smart is really none of my business. Trouble is it's become my business because I've been accused of stealing.'

She spelled out what she needed to happen next. The police probably had to be involved because an accusation of theft had been made and Florence needed to clear her name.

'You better stay here in the pub tonight, you look in bad shape. Have you enough on you to pay for this room?'

'I can use my card,' Ebony said and started to cry. Tears rolled down her face and she began shivering. Then she let out a wail, a single cry, so desperate it went right through Florence, who froze. Until then, she'd known exactly where this was going. Now she, too, was at sea. She'd no experience of the effects of any form of drug addiction on anyone. How could she have? She looked at Ebony with a mixture of total confusion, resentment and, yes, pity.

'If you really want to stop using drugs, perhaps I can try to help,' she said, her mouth speaking before her brain was working. Who do I think I am, saying that? What am I getting myself into? Forty-three years old and I've gone mad. Why am I even bothering? This is not me, not me at all.

Ebony just looked back at her, her large, dark eyes filled with tears, and gave her a single, silent nod.

They sat together in the small ground floor bedroom, the light fading, not saying anything more at all. A strange, unlikely tenderness seemed to be growing between them. Drug addict former employer and totally strait-laced servant, their roles first reversed and now completely awry. After quite a while, Florence got up and stretched. 'I'll see if they have another room. I'm getting a bit hungry, too. Wouldn't mind a bit of supper. You too?'

Ebony washed her face and straightened her top. Then they went back through into the bar. Both felt drained.

* * *

'I have to protect my reputation. I just can't allow it to be in the least bit sullied by any of this. That's my starting point.' The two women were together in the day room. They were the only ones in there, but from time to time, someone would pass along the corridor and glance through the glazed double doors. The drug rehabilitation centre was comfortable but far from luxurious. Ebony looked different. Her clothes comfortable rather than fashionable. Her face had somehow changed, too. Florence was her usual neat, professional self, not a thread or hair out of place.

'If we don't involve the police, I will need a glowing reference from you. And written assurances from Mr Smart that he is not going to make trouble or accusations again.'

Florence was back in her 'I'm-in-control' mode. Impressive but coming across as somewhat unsympathetic, she realised.

'Have you got another employer, you know...?' Ebony asked.

'I haven't even started looking. I need to get this sorted out first. I have only spoken to the agency, briefly.' She had told them she was having a break. They didn't know whether this was a personal holiday or something else.

Ebony reached down into the carrier bag beside her chair and pulled out the small silver-gilt casket. 'I want you to have this. You've rescued me. And I cost you your job. It's...'

'I wouldn't dream of it. Not if it was the last piece of silver on the planet.' She paused. 'And I suggest you better not try to sell it either.'

Florence leaned forward in the chair and, in a quiet voice, told Ebony what she knew about the Smart silver collection. Dusting the concealed cupboard, checking that the de-humidifier was preventing tarnishing, she had come across a small loose-leaf book. It appeared to be an inventory of what was on the shelves. Tiny, neat handwriting. One column listed all the items. Another said where they had been bought, a third the price paid. There was a space for notes and other figures too, written by different pens. Florence guessed these were later values. At the back was another much shorter list, fewer than twenty items. The origins of these were not given, nor any indication of a price paid. Instead, there was a yellowed snippet from a newspaper about a house break-in. Florence had carefully put the little notebook back.

The implications were obvious.

'I knew there was something dodgy about that silver,' Ebony said. 'Otherwise, why would it be concealed? I just thought it was death duties.'

They talked about that and then other things.

'I've left him for good,' Ebony said. 'I never want to see him again or have anything to do with that house. I'll just go back and get a few things. I'll do it when I know he's away.'

'Are you going to ask him for a divorce?' Florence inquired. 'You know you would be entitled to half of everything. He'll not like that. You'd better watch out.'

'I've never even thought about any of that. D'you think I should? I'm not a money grabber.'

'Of course you must, you'll need a solicitor. Make sure you get a good one. Mr Smart will have experts. They'll try to tie you in knots.'

They talked some more about this and that, the addiction treatment, timescales, a letter from Saychelle. How Darley was not really recovering.

After a while, Florence got up, preparing to go. 'What am I going to do with this casket?' Ebony asked.

'I'll have a think. I'll see you again soon, anyway.'

* * *

'I went back there two days ago,' Ebony said when they were sitting in the day room again. 'He wasn't there. I never have to go there again. I didn't realise how much I'd come to hate that place.'

Her solicitor had told her it might make sense to make a record of some of the items in the house. She'd taken pictures of every room with her phone.

'Apparently, I signed something called a pre-nup when we got together. Nice Mr Colley, the solicitor you told me about, said it won't stand up in court.'

It had been six weeks since Ebony started her treatment and the results were startling. She was a different woman. 'I don't think I've felt this good since I was a kid, not really,' she said. 'And most of it is down to you.'

'It is not,' said Florence. 'You've had the strength to see it through. That takes some doing. I'm sure it is not easy.'

'But I wouldn't have started if it wasn't for you. You found this place, and you rescued me. You've been my guardian angel.'

'Don't be silly. You were already sure you needed to stop.'

'You have no idea,' Ebony said. 'When you are using, one minute you can appear resolute, the next all you want is another fix.'

Ebony reminded her friend about the watershed moment when they were in the Green Man. 'You said you would help, and you did. You took charge. That's what you do so well.'

Florence blushed. She was not very used to warm personal comments like this. Brisk and efficient, keep things at arm's length: she'd been more used to that. They talked some more about the drug treatment and the centre.

'What about you, now?' Ebony asked. 'Have you found another position?'

The agency had been contacted by both Ms Barker's employers. The lady of the manor had written to them about 'the wonderful housekeeper' in terms which were unusually glowing. Mr Smart had sent a short, formal explanation recording the fact that he had been happy to release Ms Barker after he'd discovered that he had made 'a small mistake in her terms of employment'. It was a weasel letter, written under duress after Ebony's solicitor had intervened, explaining that it was his client, Mrs Smart, who had 'made legitimate use of silver items to supplement the inadequate funds to which she had access'. And while he did not at this stage also represent Ms Barker, he could well foresee circumstances in which she found it prudent to make a significant unspecified claim…

'I'm going to have a real break, perhaps do some travelling. I don't yet really know,' Florence said. She had never paused between appointments before. 'I've given my life to service and now I'm going to do something for me. Does that sound very selfish?'

Ebony told her about some of the places she'd visited with The Rock Crystals. 'Trouble was we never really saw anything of the places we were visiting. I must be one of the few people who has been to New York, Las Vegas and Houston and have never seen anything but the inside of hotels and concert venues.'

She told Florence that Darley had recovered sufficiently to have visitors. 'He's a good friend – will always be. They say he'll probably recover almost fully but I'm not cut out to be a green activist. It needs the kind of commitment I just don't have.'

Their conversation meandered round several topics and issues. Then, taking Florence by surprise, she said, 'I thought I should show you this,' holding up a small notebook which the former housekeeper immediately recognised.

'What does Mr Colley say about this?' Florence asked.

'Well, here's the thing. I haven't told him yet that I have got this. I thought I'd talk to you first. I've had an idea.'

Ebony had been examining the notebook for several days and had identified the small casket as one of the items in the back of the notebook. It had come into the Smarts' possession by dubious means, she was sure. Why else would those items at the back of the book not have prices and sources? Why was there a separate list? And the small newspaper cutting? It all added up.

'In the grand scheme of things, no one will know that it's here with me and has not already been disposed of,' she said. 'Wouldn't it be nice if we could return it to that lady it was stolen from?'

* * *

Ebony was on her iPad, Florence had brought her laptop. They were both on the web. 'I think I have found the other one, in Essex,' Ebony said. That made three of them. Only descendants of Mrs Dorothy Glennon, late of Purley d. 1971. Diane Brown, nee Tudor, b. 1955, now living in Cheshire; Andrew Tudor, b. 1957, now living in Essex and Ann Cherrington, nee Williams, b. 1957, living in Dulwich.

'Who do we send it to?' Ebony asked.

'No idea. I'm not sure we should be doing this,' her former employee said. 'Don't let anyone find out who sent it. That could start a shed-load of trouble.'

'We can send it anonymously – they'll just be pleased to have an heirloom.'

Florence wrote the three names on a piece of paper. 'Close your eyes and choose one of them.'

Ebony's finger landed on the name 'Ann Cherrington'.

Postscript

It was the longest time that Phillip and Ann had ever been away. They had visited almost a dozen England test match grounds, which Ann had accepted bravely. After all, it was his retirement trip. And they had added in more than a dozen of the best stately homes in Britain. Yesterday, they had explored Holkam Hall's excellent collection of art, including paintings by Van Dyck, Rubens and Gainsborough. Then Sandringham. Today, they were making their way back home.

'I'm going to make a very slight detour,' Phillip said slightly mysteriously. Instead of taking the main road from the hotel, they went off towards a small village. On the outskirts they passed a large pair of rather ostentatious wrought iron gates. Phillip stopped the car and they both got out. 'I want you to just have a quick look,' he said. There was a Savills for sale sign on the wall next to the gates.

'Have you gone mad?'

'It's on the market for just under ten million,' Phillip said, teasing.

Then he explained. It was the former home of a late industrialist, a man called Oliver Smart. He'd had a collection of silver which he'd started when he bought a chain of jewellers in the late 1960s. Now most of the collection had come on to the market as result of a divorce settlement. The Inland Revenue was also involved.

'Over the last couple of years, I've been quietly doing some digging about your casket,' he said. 'I'm afraid I've been rather secretive.' He explained why. Then he told her that, without evidence to the contrary, there was a somewhat vague connection between the theft of her grandmother's silver and Smart's silver. 'I can't prove anything but there are several coincidences.'

He told her about Reg Carson, who had died the previous year. 'I think he sold it to Smart. What I can't find out is who insured your grandmother's silver or how or why the casket got to you...' He stopped. She looked at him for a long time.

'Shall we just go home?' she said. They drove in silence for much of the journey, Ann deep in thought again about the little silver box at the back of her drawer.

THE INTERVIEW

'Come in and sit down,' she said, pointing to an office chair that had been twizzled too high to be comfortable. Either her previous victim had been very tall or discomfort was part of her technique. Cynthia Morris was a large lady, possibly nudging fifty, with cupid lips, unnaturally blonde hair and a cleavage as deep as the Rift Valley. Her white blouse and navy-blue two-piece work-suit were clearly designed to show off the full geography.

I perched myself on the seat and, inevitably, it revolved a little so I was no longer directly facing her.

'Why do you want to join Coleman?' she asked, not waiting for me to readjust myself back to a better angle. Her desk was spartan-clear except for a wire tray with two or three manilla folders in it. Mine, of course, was open in front of her and it looked like there were more sheets in it than just my CV and application letter. References, I wondered? I checked that my tie was straight.

'Well, I saw the advertisement and thought I would be ideal for your vacancy judging by...'

'So, you are keen to leave Richards & Langdale, are you? Why is that?' she interrupted. Clearly she didn't have much time for flannel.

'It is not that I'm keen to leave,' I said – which was technically true but entirely misleading. 'I thought I would enjoy some slightly different challenges, building on my experience, of course.' I hoped she couldn't smell the bullshit. (Actually, I had already been told I *was leaving* to use a euphemism for the more brutal process in play.)

'So why have you not put Tim Langdale as a referee?' she asked, immediately getting to the crux of things. She didn't wait for me to splutter an evasive answer. 'They are letting you go, aren't they, Mr Lewis,' she said. It was not a question. Whatever was in that folder?

'Well, the pandemic has completely changed the office environment,' I told her, remembering this bit of my rehearsed script. 'They are reconfiguring.'

She gave a quick snort of disbelief or amusement. 'That's a new one. Try 'cutting out some deadwood' instead.'

'Excuse me,' I blurted and stood up. 'Cramp – sorry. Mind if I lower this seat?' and didn't wait for her agreement. It bought me a bit of thinking time as I twisted the chair around until it was a more normal height. I glanced across at her and she was smiling – or smirking.

'That's unfair,' I reasoned. 'I have been a trusted and valued member of their team for a long time. They are not replacing me.' Technically, this was true and with modern IT systems in play, they didn't need as many bums-on-seats as they once did but, let us put it this way, I was not one of Mr Langdale's favourites.

'Actually, you are not the only member of your firm who is hoping to find a berth with us,' she said, glancing

214

at her wire tray. 'With only one vacancy, why you and not one of the others? Sell yourself.'

I felt this was a bit out of order but I was in no position to point that out. I was pretty sure that Fletcher had also applied but I couldn't think of anyone else. I was a better bet than him but he would be better at puffing himself up. My abilities lie in balancing pages of figures. I can even manage a little creativity when it comes to fine detail. But I have never had to sell anything. Certainly not myself. I have been quietly getting on with money-craft since I joined the firm from school. Day-release first and then learning from others: old Mr Richards was a patient teacher who never cut corners and did it the proper way. That's less common nowadays.

'I am careful, accurate, diligent and' (…I was going to say *loyal* but under the circumstances…) 'adaptable.' Quick thinking sometimes too! 'You might find someone cheaper or a johnny-flash-in-the-pan but they cannot match my experience.' I wondered how I was doing. 'As you know, the regulations change every few years, sometimes more than once a year, but I am one of the first to get to grips with them.' Actually, I had no way of knowing if this was strictly true, but it seemed a good line.

'So why should I take you and not mould my own, cheaper graduate?' she persisted.

'Well, first, that's not what you advertised for,' I said, rather surprised by my new-found pluck. 'And second, even the best graduates can only do so much. You might get away with that approach for a while but sooner or later, you are going to put your firm at risk if you don't invest in experience.'

She changed tack, taking a softer approach, and I felt I had managed to pass one test at least. She told me about some of the Coleman working practices and pointed out where they differed in approach from my current ones. She obviously knew a lot about the inner workings of her main competitor.

She also knew that what she was offering would mean a cut in pay for me. Not a big one, but still a cut. 'How would you be about that?' she asked. In a way, I took it as a good sign.

'I knew the salary band when I applied. I doubt I could find other work at my level in town so I'd have a commute or to move house. I've factored that in,' I admitted.

Our conversation – that's what it was now really – went back and forth for a while before she threw me a bit of a curve-ball. 'So how would you feel about working mainly from home? That's what we are looking at here.'

Our house in Cherry Grove was not large enough to manage a home office and I was sure Denise was not going to want me 'under her feet' all the time... 'That'd be fine,' I stumbled. 'It's only to be expected nowadays.'

There was little more of any exchange before she closed with the customary 'We'll let you know in a day or two.'

I thanked her for her time and made for the door. 'By the way, I hope your cramps get better,' she said as I left.

BEIGE

There's orange and red, blue, green and purple
The rainbow is colourful and bright
But where in the spectrum can you find beige?
It's absent when you split the light.
A shade which is dreary, a code-word for old,
Not cream nor brown nor tan
It's a hue just invented by marketing gurus
To appeal to the 'more mature man'.

STORM WARNING

'What's wrong,' Lizzy asks, looking across the kitchen table at Darren who is clearly flustered.

'Nothing,' he replies quickly, a guarantee that something *is* wrong.

Lizzy picks up on his moods really well, but you'd have had to have the hide of a rhino not to sense this particular storm coming.

She smiles back at him, her best shot at a gentle, warm, understanding reaction; certainly not a cheeky grin...

'So how was your shift today?' she asks, but before the words are out of her mouth, she knows it is the wrong tack.

'How do you think it bloody well went?' he counters. 'You know we can't cope. And I suppose you've had a really good day, haven't you.'

'Come on, Darren, tell me what's wrong. Let's not go through this guessing game bit.'

He tosses his head in defiance and glares back at her, before putting another mouthful of scrambled egg in his mouth and chewing conspicuously.

It is so often the same when they have anything from a bit of a disagreement to a blazing row. He will oscillate between a defiant stare and looking away to avoid eye contact. Occasionally the icy atmosphere will last only few minutes, although that is rare. Usually it takes longer, sometimes even days.

She knows the storm will come sooner or later. It has to before the air can clear.

She has guessed that she has 'done something wrong', at least in his eyes, but she has no idea what. And even after all these years, she still doesn't quite know how to cut through the atmosphere and reach his better side and the sunny uplands of their life together.

In her heart, she knows that they'll sort it out in the end but she hates these sullen interludes.

She is also sure her approach is the better one - more straightforward. Where he will sulk, she will come out with it straight away, cards squarely on the table.

Then he will say she is 'accusing' or something like it and he will become defensive, which is counter-productive.

They have always managed to sort things out between them without too many hiccups, she reminds herself. Most of the time they rub along really well. Especially compared to her sister in Scotland who has never really got on with her husband, Stuart. Mind you, he is a first-class pig. She is better off now they are apart, despite the other problems.

Come to think of it, there were bitter rows her parents had at home when she was little. That has left its scars. No, Darren is nothing like that. Bit moody perhaps. But she thinks to herself: he's put up with me all these years, I'm still his Dizzy Lizzy.

He has finished his supper and pushed the plate away from him across the table. That is the clue if you know where to look. Something wrong with the food?

'How were the eggs,' she asked, faking nonchalance.

'Fine,' he tosses. Monosyllabic.

'Oh! Come on Darren,' she says, still trying to keep it light-hearted.

'You still don't know, do you?' he spits back. 'You have no idea.'

'I won't have if you don't tell me,' she says lightly, desperately trying not to rise to the bait.

'Well, when you got the eggs out of the fridge for supper, you must have seen the bottle of champagne I put in there this morning,' he says, almost shouting, and then, without pausing, he adds, 'Twenty-five years ago today, we walked down the aisle together. And I'm the only one who ever remembers our anniversaries. Scrambled-bloody-eggs-on-toast. It should have been a romantic candlelit supper.'

Lizzy reddens, her lips tremble, then she bursts into tears. She'd remembered a few weeks ago but come the day, it has completely slipped her mind.

Darren gets up from the table and thunders out into the hall, Lizzy's sobs, now unconstrained, following him. Then he is back, carrying a huge bouquet of flowers and something wrapped in gift paper. 'Oh bloody Hell, woman, I wouldn't have you any different,' he says putting his arms round her and pulling her in tight.

And now they are both crying.

THE KISS OF DEATH

It is not easy to kill your husband and get away with it. All along the way, I had to plan, plan, plan. I mean, murder is never straightforward, and if you are certain to be a suspect, as I was, then your problems multiply, many fold.

Choosing the 'how' was really challenging.

I considered interfering with the brakes of his beloved white Lotus. But in the end, I worked out that would only guarantee a crash, not necessarily a fatal one. Shoot the bastard. Untraceable guns are hard to come by. Usually, they involve the underworld, with which I have no connection. I know a bit about poison, and it had its attractions, but I wanted him dead, not so ill he became an invalid and people felt sorry for him.

There were other options I considered in some detail but, to cut to the chase, Raymond Paul Ellis died from a huge dose of a pentobarbital sodium, administered by syringe. Enough to kill a bloody horse. My only regret: it was relatively painless for him.

It meant they knew immediately the 'how', the 'when' and the 'where'. They strongly suspected a 'who' - but they don't have any proof. And they don't know the 'why'.

I appear to have convinced them that it could not have been me who injected him. They haven't found anything to dispute my claim that I was miles away at the time of his death, which they know very precisely.

So, no holes in my carefully planned alibi. And thanks to inside information, no crucially implicating forensic evidence: that's something I know a bit about.

His affair with Candice was a help. She was as much of a potential suspect as me. And the truth is that, long before I killed him, I no longer really cared about Ray's other women. No, honestly.

When I first found out about them, I was angry and hurt. I had been watching the pennies, skilfully managing the budget for our modest home, and all the while, he was buying expensive gifts for other women. But after a while, it no longer really bugged me that much. By then, I'd come to value as a bonus the fact that I had been left to bring up our two children on my own while 'Daddy' was out screwing. Me and the children were all the closer for that. Many wives would have kicked him out. Instead, I'd just given up on him and got on with my own life. I suppose I'm a bit like that: compartmentalising. When we did part, it was because I'd found out too much and I couldn't bear to be near him. Not for a minute longer.

But I suppose I better start at the beginning.

You will have read all about it at the time, even if you are now hazy about the details. Schoolgirl goes missing. Massive manhunt for days and days. Eventually, she's found dead. Her pale body discovered in the dark woods by a dog walker. You'll certainly remember her name, Nicola Mercy. She'd not yet turned sixteen.

Her inquest returned an open verdict. The post mortem report said she died from meningitis but there were too many loose ends for the jury to believe it was natural causes.

Her family don't yet know how she came to be found dead in the woods, not in any detail. The police don't seem to have been able to piece together all the bits. Of course, I know more than both of them.

It was Penny, my oldest, who first alerted me to things. She was still at school in those days and had seen the police cars outside a house on Pyke Road from the top of the bus. The whole street blocked off, she said. Blue lights flashing in the growing gloom. Rumours were all over town. December 11, a Wednesday. Ten years ago tomorrow.

The TV crews showed up before the weekend and then Tewkesbury was awash with reporters, photographers, cameramen. The police called in reinforcements and were doing house-to-house searches down that end of town. Combing the fields, checking both rivers. It was the first item on the national news that Friday.

The girl in the petrol station told me that the police thought it was Nicola's dad. She might have been right because there was a big tent in the Mercys' back garden, lit up inside all night. About ten days later, just when the big papers were starting to lose interest, her body was found twenty-five miles away on the other side of Cheltenham. It had been there for less than 24 hours, they said. I remember the headline in *The Sun*: 'Mercy Killing?'

A few days later, around Christmas Eve, one of the papers, I think it was the *Daily Mail*, reported that she had died from meningitis and that there were no signs of violence on her body. Then it was on the BBC. I don't think there was any official comment at the time, but it turned out to be accurate enough. We learned that the police had no real idea how she got there. I remember the details so well because we'd never had anything like this before. Almost everyone knew someone who knew someone who knew the Mercy family. Tewkesbury's like that. Rumours were rampant. Our own GP even came into the equation, for some reason. Then, when the body was released for burial in January, virtually the whole town turned up at the funeral. Schools closed for the day and of course the Press was back.

The inquest wasn't until early June, but none of us had forgotten about Nicola – something was in the *Echo* almost every week. And even after the inquest, the news didn't fizzle out for several months longer. One madcap theory after another. Some said it was travellers – apparently, a convoy of them had been passing through and you know how rumours start. Someone else had a theory that a big black panther was on the loose and had stolen her body from a stretcher at the hospital when she was being taken to the morgue. Of course they said they had seen the cat. Hazy pictures in the press. Yet another yarn was about witches and ritual rites. I even heard a couple of children in the bus queue claiming it was aliens.

But eventually everything seemed to die down – or at least be replaced by the depressing cycle of news from Iraq, Afghanistan and the elsewhere in the Middle East.

Our kids were growing up. Penny left school and Todd was in the Sixth. I was thinking about getting a job. By contrast, Ray was lukewarm about the idea: we were still sort of together then. He liked the image of his little woman at home ironing his shirts, the misogynist pig. Tough! I'd trained in a lab before and saw an ad. in the paper for a part-time assistant. It set the wheels in motion. I remember being quite sure I'd not got the job after the interview, but I was wrong. Three days a week, receiving samples, logging, tracking and disposing of them and the inevitable entering of data on a computer system. That took some getting used to.

What I hadn't really anticipated was the change it made in my whole outlook. From being the cowed and timid hard-done-to-wife-at-home quietly putting up with things I didn't like, I slowly started to become a real person, with a confidence in my own abilities and opinions on matters outside of childcare and home-making.

Several months into the job and three of us 'lab girls' would have the odd night out together. He didn't like that at all. Once, when I came in just before midnight, Ray started on at me and I think he'd have struck me if he hadn't woken the children with his shouting. Todd, six-foot something by then, stood at the top of the stairs and just glared at his father. 'Go to bed, you,' Ray said but Todd didn't move. I was glad to sleep on my own that night.

Ray and I had met when we were both students at university studying life sciences. He was a year ahead of me and confident. I was away from home for the first time and anything but. I'd never really been out with anyone else. No, seriously. When Ray graduated, he got a job nearby at a forensic science lab, and a year later, I also got a job there. We worked together for about a year before I became pregnant. We got married and Penny was born six months later.

Everything seemed fine back then. He was promoted the same year that Todd was born. We were buying our house.

Forensic science was going through the DNA revolution and Ray was going to conferences in the US and elsewhere. I guess now that is when he started being unfaithful. His success at work went to his head and increasingly, I saw the worst side of his swagger. He was getting used to giving orders in the lab now and expected the same at home. I just let most of it wash over me. I loved being a mum; nothing else really mattered as much, I told myself.

At the time of Nicola's death, it certainly didn't occur to me that Ray could be involved, never mind her killer. Why should it? I just didn't think of him in that way.

But things really began to unravel for him in a big way when the government privatised the forensic science service, closing his lab along with all the others. It was a dreadful government decision, the worst sort of dogmatic action. From being a public sector scientist, Ray suddenly found himself having to compete in the commercial world. He found a new job easily enough; similar pay, different fringe benefits, some loss of status.

I'll tell you what happened as best I can. And I'll tell you how I found out. You'll have to bear with me on this because it's complicated, but I'll try to explain.

Nicola did die from meningitis, but how did she get it, and where was she for those ten days? When she went missing, she seemed well enough, according to her mother. Ten days later, she was dead. Meningitis acts fast, really fast if it's not treated. Hers wasn't treated because she was a runaway with a guilty secret.

Meningitis is usually caught from people who carry the virus or bacteria in their nose or throat but aren't ill themselves. In her case, 15-year-old Nicola caught it from her lover, 38-year-old Ray Ellis. Yes, him. When she went missing on December 11, she was with him, with his flash car and smart suits. He whisked her away to a cabin near Chedworth, ten miles outside Cheltenham. You may have heard of the Roman villa there. It is one of the finest in Britain, owned by the National Trust. The site is closed in winter but Ray was renting a small building nearby which he'd been using as a love-nest.

He and Candice had been using it, though she wasn't the first of his mistresses. And somewhere along the line, he must have started fantasising about schoolgirls. I find it absolutely disgusting. There are porn sites full of young girls doing it with older men. I know because Ray kept a laptop at home which was his window into that world and he was careless about keeping it secret. His password was Candice38D. It was written on a strip of Elastoplast stuck inside his desk drawer, God knows why. Presumably from just watching, he graduated to grooming because I discovered his revolting, disturbing interest in teenage girls. It was horrible. I thought of going to the police about it and rehearsed in my own mind what I'd tell them. But I didn't know then about him and Nicola. In the end I didn't tell anyone, but we were not living together as man and wife by then.

I have not discovered exactly when he started his affair with Nicola, a schoolgirl just a couple of years younger than his own daughter. I can't bear to even think about that. I started to question whether I was partly to blame. Hadn't I been a good enough lover? Did he want more from me than I could or would give?

What I know now is that while police were doing house-to-house hunts in Tewkesbury ten years ago, she was with Ray every evening in this hideaway home. I don't need to spell out what they were doing.

I didn't suspect anything at the time. He told me he was working late because there was a rush of extra forensic work. With what was going on locally, that was not hard to believe. But what I know now is that he wasn't working at the lab those evenings, he was working on her!

I reluctantly have to accept that he probably didn't know he was a benign carrier of the killer bacteria. I'm assuming that she caught it from him and fell ill. But he must have known that something was very wrong, even if he didn't know exactly how or what. Despite the seriousness of her condition, I still cannot get my head round the fact that this man, my husband, kept her there until she died. Too ill to take herself to hospital. Shut up in his love nest, much of the time on her own. He must have taken away her phone. All because he knew his life of freedom would be over if anyone found out what he was doing with an under-age schoolgirl.

When I found that out, he had to die. I couldn't let that go unpunished. It could have been Penny. I just couldn't leave it to the police to mess up. Prison was too good for him.

Nicola died what must had been a horrible death, one he almost certainly cruelly witnessed. Then he knew more than enough about forensic techniques to be able to conceal any evidence of his presence and he left her body in the woods a few miles away. I don't think he expected it to be found quite so soon.

Of course, at the time, I knew nothing about any of this, nor had any suspicions. I don't think I even wondered if he was spending time with Candice rather than me. But as I've said, by then we were going through the motions, he and I.

It was almost two years later when they finally told him his lab was going to close, with the loss of jobs. In those two years, DNA testing had come on by leaps and bounds and I'm pretty sure some of the samples taken from Nicola could have incriminated him. He must have thought so too. You see, his DNA was on file – everyone who works at a lab like that has to have been extensively tested and recorded to identify any possible cross-contamination. He would have known that it might only be a matter of time before his particular DNA footprint showed up in Nicola's samples. And by then, he was too senior to have done any of the actual testing so questions would have been asked about how his DNA came to be involved. That would have taken a Hell of a lot of explaining, wouldn't it?

This is crucial - while he was a senior officer at the public lab, he probably could keep a tab on who wanted what samples and why. But he knew that when the lab closed, he would lose that control. And in the upheaval of the lab closing, he thought he could get hold of the samples and destroy them. If anything ever came up, they'd have been 'lost in transit'. And, to make things less obvious, he got hold of her samples and what was probably a random selection of others, too. He destroyed them and he tried to do it in a way that would make it look as though they were mis-filed. But in fact, he broke all security rules and took them out of the lab, so they could never be found. He brought a large bundle home and set fire to them in the garden incinerator. No one would ever have been the wiser if they had all burned to ash. But whether he was called away or rain put out the fire before it had all burned, some bits of the evidence were not totally destroyed. He didn't realise because, by then, he was over the other side of town with Candice. His attention was probably on her cleavage.

When I got home, I smelled the smoke in the garden. Ray was never a gardener and I went to investigate. It was then that I saw some of the unburned fragments of paper. I immediately recognised the lab's crest on the report forms: after all, I'd been working at the lab myself years before. There wasn't that much left, but enough to reveal that some of the paperwork concerned Nicola Mercy. Blue forms signifying police work. And then two red forms: the colour used to identify staff DNA. It was Friday May 14; the day I knew something far more serious was going on. The last day he ever spent at our family home.

Perhaps I should have rung David Skelton, the outgoing lab director, and told him. Who knows what would have happened then? But it wouldn't have brought Nicola back, would it? Perhaps I should have rung the police. I thought of both but did neither. I suppose I was confused and angry. This was a side of Ray Ellis I didn't expect to see. The love-cheat, yes. An arrogant bully even. This was different... and I needed to find out more myself.

What I did was out of character. I tracked down Candice's address from his mobile phone contacts and I went to see her on Saturday morning. It was before nine. She could have slammed the door in my face. For some reason, she didn't. I asked her if she knew why he would burn forensic records about a girl who died less than two years before. She looked back at me blankly. She obviously didn't have the first clue what I was getting at. Pretty unforthcoming, her front door still only half open to me. After all, I'd taken her by surprise. More out of spite than anything, I told her about his apparent penchant for schoolgirls. While I was saying it, a penny dropped for me. Nicola had been a schoolgirl. I started to wonder what the connection was, my mind racing. Candice said nothing but I'm pretty sure she hadn't known about his use of porn sites, or his taste for teens. While I'd always thought of her as a love-thief, I guess she had seen herself as his true love. Then she came out with a curve ball. 'How's the cancer treatment?' I think she could tell from my expression that I didn't have the faintest idea what she was talking about. Suddenly it hit me. 'Never mind what he's told you, Candice. I. Have. Not. Got. Cancer. I. Have. Never. Had. Cancer.' I can still hear myself saying it. Perhaps that's when it dawned on her that the person she probably had loved until then might not be all that he seemed. 'You better come in,' she said quietly and opened the door wider.

I winced at the whiff of a perfume I now realised I'd smelled on him. I'd have liked to have found her flat rather seedy, fluffy pink cushions and the like: that's what I'd sort of imagined. It wasn't at all. It was neat and tasteful. Quite a few of the books on her shelves were the same ones I'd read, Maya Angelou, Anne Tyler. She made us a cup of tea and we sat and looked at each other. Both of us wondering how to start asking the multitude of questions we had for the other. She was older than I'd imagined and much less tarty in appearance. I'm not meaning to be at all catty when I say I was slightly surprised by how plain she appeared. Down to earth even. A better figure than me, though.

We talked a bit more, neither of us at all at ease. Maybe she was starting to reassess her future with him. She said she knew nothing about Nicola. I guess she was going to ask him some difficult questions later. I was beyond that, way beyond.

He was out when I got home. So were the children. I started emptying his stuff into bin bags, suitcases, boxes. He came back while I was in the middle of it and I'm sure he could tell from my demeanour that I was not being rational. 'I want you gone from here today. Now. Gone for good.'

He tried to ask me why but I was not giving him explanations. He packed some more of his things in silence, loaded his precious car and left. No longer the overbearing bully.

Todd came back from his sports practice at lunchtime and I told him his father wasn't going to be living with us anymore. I tried to give him reasons but I'm not sure what came tumbling out made any real sense. He listened quietly to my emotional rant and then hugged me and asked me if I was OK, bless him. 'Not really,' I said. We looked at each other. Penny came in a couple of hours later; I'm sure Todd had called her back from college. She burst in and put her arms round me. We stood in the hall holding each other for ages, both silent and in tears. It took me a while to calm down. Had I done the right thing?

I left a message for Ray on his mobile telling him when he could pick up the rest of his stuff. It would be packed and left 'out front'. He was never coming into our home again.

It took me several months to start to get a new life on track. I had new locks fitted and looked up the names of local solicitors. I started to wonder what had really happened, why I hadn't seen it coming, why I'd put up with it for so long, what I'd ever seen in him. Had he changed? Had I? Had we both? And in among it all, I couldn't stop wondering why he'd been destroying official records about Nicola Mercy in the back garden. Over that summer, he tried to ring me twice. Both times I put the phone down before he could say anything.

It was autumn when Candice phoned me one evening. Blurted out that he wasn't with her any more. Asked if we could meet. I went round the next evening and we talked for quite a while. I'd been right. She had seen herself as his true love, rescuing him from a terrible wife and an unhappy home. He'd had her on the end of a piece of elastic, promising he'd leave me, then stalling, one last obstacle after the next. He couldn't leave me dying from cancer, he'd told her. They had met some time before when she'd worked in a pub near the forensic lab. Barbara Windsor barmaid you might be thinking, but that wasn't her. Not really. She told me that when I kicked him out, he had expected to move in with her. They had talked, she had not got the truth and his lies didn't add up, either. Now six months later, she had told him it was over between them. If she was looking for sympathy from me, she didn't get much. Sorry and all that. She said he was probably now 'shacked up with someone else at the shack', as she put it: his Chedworth cabin. It was the first I'd heard of that. It didn't occur to me until a little later that it was in the general area where Nicola's body was found. That was another piece in the horrible jigsaw.

Back home things settled down and if the children ever saw their father, they certainly didn't tell me. I saw a solicitor and he told me about divorce, adultery and separation. He would sort out financial affairs, too, but he needed an address for Ray. I gave him his new lab address. He said it would be better if I asked him for his home address, but that would have meant talking to him.

Candice didn't know the cabin's postal address either but told me roughly where it was – I don't think driving directions were her strong point. I went down there one weekday when he'd be away working. I found it eventually, tucked away behind a black barn type building. It was certainly the place: I recognised a couple of his things by looking through a window. Snooping round, I tried the only outside door but the cabin was locked. I wandered round the small building, looking for the house name on a plaque. I did better than that. Next to his recycling bin was a cardboard box, put out with the rubbish. 'R. Ellis Esq., Dove Cottage', and the full postal address. I took a picture of the label with my phone.

A couple of days later, I was at home on my laptop, planning to write an email to my solicitor with Ray's address. There was the photo of the label on the cardboard box – with the full address. What I hadn't noticed at the time was what was written underneath. 'Vanish Gold Oxi Action Stain Remover 850g x3. Parcelforce 24 to be signed for'.

Three large tubs of stain remover are an awful lot for a man who has a small two-room cabin, isn't it? And it had a special significance for me.

Vanish is a good name for the product because it is a type of oxygen bleach. It destroys all but the most persistent DNA evidence. Forensic tests such as luminal tests rely on stains to take up oxygen. Ordinary bleaches and detergents leave a trace. Reckitt Benckiser's Vanish produces oxygen bubbles, which cause residues to degrade, leaving almost no trace. What was going on?

Coupled with the burned records I had found several months earlier, I was now starting to put together the awful truth.

Back at work, I read up about the causes of meningitis. I was horrified. One of the strains, which affects teens and young adults, 'is spread during close contact like kissing'. You can piece together the rest for yourself! Ray was a carrier, Nicola was his victim in so many senses of the word. And the bastard had put his own wife and children at risk and might go on doing so. He had to be stopped.

That's when I knew that telling the police would not be enough for me. One way or another, he had killed Nicola and got away with it. At least, so far. In doing so, it was a small miracle that none of us had gone down with meningitis, too. And how many others had been put at risk? Candice, for certain.

It took me the best part of another three months to work out how I would kill him. Three months during which I had little doubt that what I was going to do had to be done. By me. Whatever the cost. I didn't want to be caught. But if I did, so be it.

I sourced the killer serum from Spain, where it is used by vets to put animals to sleep. There would have been some in the hospital where I worked, too, but I didn't want it traced. And what was more natural than a newly separated woman having some time to think on her own in the hills around Barcelona, enjoying some winter sun? An hour's drive into the hinterland in my hire car, you don't need to know where, I bought exactly what I needed from a pharmacy I had contacted earlier. They thought I was an Englishwoman with a small farm in the neighbourhood, needing to put a few sheep to sleep.

My bomb-proof alibi took a lot more planning. I had to recruit my best friend, Jen, and – the bit I like least – deceive my mother. It was obvious that when I killed Ray, I would be a prime suspect. Candice would be too, probably, but that was her lookout. The police had to believe that it could not have been me because I was miles away at the time. Jen and I discussed everything. She lives close and we have been friends for years. She never liked Ray but didn't want me to kill him, and certainly didn't want to be involved herself. She took a lot of convincing, but I assured her that she would be 'invisible' as far as the police were concerned. And so it has turned out. Eventually, reluctantly, she agreed to help. My mum was easier because she didn't even know that she was part of the plan.

I picked the weekend of my mother's 79th birthday to do the deed. She lived alone in Warrington and was getting quite confused about things, a fact which I'm ashamed to say I used to my advantage. The weekend before her birthday, I went up to see her and stayed the night, parking my blue Fiesta a couple of streets away. It didn't take me too long messing with her wall calendar to convince her that it was her birthday and we took a photo of us together, clearly showing the date. (I even edited the file data in my digital camera to give a date a week later.) The following weekend, Jen picked up my car, took my mobile phone, wore my tell-tale blue cloche hat, and drove to my mother's house in Warrington on Saturday afternoon. She parked in the street in front of Mother's house and took a bus into town, where she checked in to a local hotel, giving a false name and paying cash. On Sunday afternoon, she went back to my mother's house, collected the car and drove back to Tewkesbury. Nosey neighbours would later be asked by police to confirm that I visited that weekend. My car could be tracked by traffic cameras, my phone would record its whereabouts through the cells used to connect to the service provider… Jen went back home, never to be suspected of anything by the police. My mother was convinced I was there for her birthday. Her neighbours saw my car.

Meanwhile, I rented a car and had booked a small weekend cottage about ten miles away from Chedworth in the wrong direction using a false name. I booked the cottage over the phone and arranged to pay cash.

Planning a route from the cottage to Chedworth that would not show up on traffic cameras was not that difficult. The internet will tell you where many cameras are sited and I was going on small roads cross country and not very far.

I didn't like telling the children a blatant lie, but they needed to believe I was in Warrington that weekend, celebrating Mum's birthday. They sent her their love.

I won't bore you with all the other details. If I'd missed something, I certainly couldn't see it myself.

It was dark when I got to his cabin on the Saturday night. I quietly let myself in using a key which had been 'borrowed' from Candice some time back. She hadn't ever known it had been removed from her key ring.

Ray always did sleep soundly. He sort of stirred when the syringe went in, but not for long… I was surprised that I felt no remorse at all.

When he didn't show up for work on Monday, I guess someone must have wondered why but nothing much happened. It was several days before his body was found. They hadn't got the cabin's address at his new work. Someone did ring me to ask if I knew where he was. I said I didn't. Why was I so calm? When they did find him, his body would have been seriously bloated.

Over the course of the next few days, I had several visits from the police, as I had anticipated. I didn't need to pretend I was heartbroken. I told them that our marriage had ended badly after I found out about his affair. Penny and Todd were interviewed too. They were sure I was in Warrington that weekend. They grilled me at the station, trying to break my alibi, but I remained calm. They found a full trace of my blue Fiesta on traffic cameras driving the one hundred miles up the M5 and M6 to Warrington and back the next day. My mum confirmed her birthday visit. Her neighbours had seen my car, so they could confirm I'd been visiting. I showed the police the picture of my mother's birthday celebration. There in the background, unobtrusively, was her wall calendar, open at the 'birthday' date. Other details to confirm the 'visit' came from my real visit the weekend before, which we could both recall accurately enough.

And in the cabin, I'd made sure I left no fingerprints or any other trace anywhere.

They asked me what I knew about Candice and I was almost entirely truthful in my answers. Did I think she might have killed him? No. Had we planned it together? No. Were we friends? No.

I believe Candice was interviewed at length, too. No, she didn't have a key to the cabin. Fortunately for her, she could account for her movements well enough during the critical period. We were both very much under suspicion for some time. But neither of us was ever arrested.

I'm sure they must have gone through his phone records carefully and scanned his laptop. I've no idea what they found out from those but none of it seemed to rebound on me.

A month or two later, someone from a new unit set up by the Home Office came to ask more questions about what had gone on at the lab. By then, it had been closed for some time but they had found some unspecified irregularities. I was unable to help them. That's all seven years ago now.

Todd is married and they are expecting their first. Penny is in Australia: she works as a trainee anaesthetist in a Brisbane hospital. I've been out to see her twice.

My mother became even more confused the following year and died in a home three years ago. Jen and I meet regularly. She is, after all, even more of a special friend now. We don't refer back to that weekend. Not ever.

I don't regret what I have done. I might have done it differently. I sometimes wonder what might have happened if I had gone the legal route and shopped him to the police. I'm sorry for the Mercy family. They lost their daughter and have never found out why. But would they be happier knowing that she died such an ugly death at the hands of a monster? I know one mustn't take the law into one's own hands. As a rule, I don't. But sometimes, there have to be exceptions.

Footnote:

If you are reading this, it almost certainly means only one thing. That I have not got away with murder. I have written my account to get things off my chest. Writing it has helped me enormously. This full and honest account has been safely lodged with my solicitor in a sealed envelope. No one has ever read the contents. It is only to be opened in the event that I am to be charged with a serious crime in respect of Raymond Paul Ellis.

COVID CHRISTMAS!

Well, bless us all, here it comes again. Christmas: the season of financial strain and stressed-out meals involving family tensions, jealousies, lies and nothing of true importance - apart from the outcome of *Strictly Come Dancing*, of course.

Why then do we react annually to the savage perils of Christmas with wounded surprise? Christmas is bound to be appalling. It is, after all, the celebration of a woman giving birth without anaesthetic or even forceps in a draughty shed surrounded by ass poo. A husband who wasn't the father - so we just know where he's going to be coming from. Boiling water and clean towels? I don't think so! He's got a cob on. He sits around looking suspiciously at the endless series of visitors and trying to assess which one is the 'natural' father. She's not giving anything away. If we are to believe the Renaissance painters, she has orb-like breasts almost coming out of her neck, which cannot offer comfortable feeding, despite which the child looks like a toddler already. All this in temporary accommodation in a place occupied by a foreign power. It is a small settlement without even primitive healthcare provision and a chronic shortage of midwives, of course, since they scrapped the training

241

grants. And here she is with a new-born in a shelter-cum-stable. It's almost as bad as a Priti Patel refugee hostel. Holes in the walls, an earthen floor. And there are no curtains, which matters because for the last few nights, a bloody great bright star has taken up residence outside in the night sky. No one's getting any sleep.

Weird strangers turn up: first three posh blokes and some shepherds, who bring lambs. That's just what you need: more livestock defecating where they stand around the cradle. Then come the flock-watchers: completely freaked out and babbling something like: *'Yeah, there was this light and singing and then this herd of bleedin' angels... They were on something like wacky-baccy because they were talking about love and peace and all that hippy stuff. We were bloody terrified. They told us 'be not afraid' in big, boomy voices, which just made it worse. We were thinking they might be the Taliban and just kill us. Some of the sheep fainted and, I mean, it was just really messed up and crazy. Angels dropping in and monkeying with your life. You don't expect that, do you? Oh, by the way! How is the baby, anyway? Not crying – that's a blessing!'*

The three kings bring totally thoughtless Christmas presents, probably from Harrods or Fortnum & Mason – each one heavy on symbolism. Frankincense might make the place smell slightly better, but it has quasi-religious associations. I suppose if the child doesn't make it as a Rabbi, he could make scented candles for a living. Actually, what is needed are carpenters and plumbers. Myrrh! That's nice. It is used in *funeral* rites. Then there's gold. A great big casket of the stuff. How's that going to be kept safe in a stable? They will be burgled once the bright star has gone. Huddled in the dark, knackered and unarmed, in a doorless, windowless, insecure shelter. No video doorbells in those days.

And today is Christmas? A festival made even worse by the pale mountain of slowly thawing turkey. Too big to fit in the oven, it represents the triumph of a mis-applied tradition over common-sense and any form of epicurean discernment. It is surrounded by unnecessary sausages; something else made once a year of sawdust and herbs called stuffing; and 'green mush' which started its culinary journey as a sword-like stalk of Brussel sprouts the day before and has now been boiled to death. Don't even ask about the gravy! Granules of what look like burned toast scrapings taken from a carton found at the back of the cupboard with a picture of a pair of street urchins on it. This is going to be a ghastly feast – actually, a collective exercise in binge-eating. It was bad enough even before niece Millie told everyone she was now a vegan. Be aware: it has nothing to do with any Christian tradition but stretches back far further, even before Pyrex!

Then there is the rest of all the guff. Snow! Don't be silly. Even though it is December, some days you do not need a coat or even a jersey to wear outside.

Be merry? You are joking, of course. What? With this lot in charge?

Hang up a stocking? 'What's a stocking, Mum,' asks little Jaxon, 5. She cannot explain for he is still too young to understand anything about Ann Summers. So it's an easy peeler and a Cadbury's crème egg left over from Easter, tucked down deep inside an M&S viscose, polyamide and elastane calf-length job (hopefully it still benefits from trademarked 'Freshfeet technology').

'Are you ready for Christmas?' the girl at the checkout asked back in November. Well, yes, actually. I am this year. At 11pm tonight - Christmas Eve. On the dot: 'I think I'm coming down with something. I've got a temperature, a cough and I can't taste anything at all.'

That should do it nicely.

CUCKOLD

Dear Mirabelle,

I know you have been 'seeing' Tony for quite some time, but now that he is moving in with you, there are a few things which you might want to know.

As you probably realise, he and I were married for 29 years, so I know him pretty well. But please don't imagine that I am writing this in grief or spite: even before I found out about your 'arrangement', I had known that our marriage wasn't working for me, either. I really do hope you will make each other happy, but I do wonder if that's a bit of a longshot. Perhaps I shouldn't speculate on that, but it's unusual for such an age gap to work to your advantage.

Your 'romance' may continue with the chocolates and flowers you've got used to (and the rest) for a while, who knows? But since he is essentially rather a tight-wad, I think that is a bit unlikely.

I don't know if you are hoping to start a family with him: you're young enough, aren't you? Just don't expect him to be the devoted Dad. It is not just me: Mark and Ellie have no real relationship with him, either. (Ask him if he knows when their birthdays are if you don't believe me!)

Tony probably thinks that 'the sad little shrew' (yes, I saw that note) will accept his terms without question, but you might like to tell him that I have seen a solicitor. I know he told me I should use the 'family solicitor he's always used' but somehow, I thought that might not be the best idea.

I wouldn't be so cynical as to presume that you are counting heavily on his 'wealth', but from my initial discussions with my advisor, his assets may be a bit more depleted than you were expecting. No, I'm sure you aren't in it for the money. But since you both work at Ellison's, you will not need me to tell you about the pension arrangements. It's not that Tony's due to retire very soon but you will find that, in Tony's case, a portion of the accrued benefits will need to be earmarked for me and his children.

A couple more things may be helpful. My advice would be not to let Tony help with DiY, gardening or anything else at all practical. The last time he tried to put up shelves (11 years ago now!) we had to have the wall re-plastered and then the lounge redecorated. Costly business. And the one time he cut the lawn, all he actually managed to cut was the power cord!

I know you have enjoyed a couple of weekends away (Conference! That was so obviously not true) but if you go on holiday, it might be best if you hang on to both the passports and the money yourself. They have been 'lost' in the past... three times actually! And I don't think you will want to be in a hire car if he is driving on what he calls the 'wrong side'. Take out very good insurance, in any case.

By now, you may be wondering why, if all this is true, we stayed together for so long. Well, what I really came to value about my so-called marriage to Mr Tony McIntee was the space I had to be myself. Yes, it was lonely at first, but then I had the children and the freedom to be my own person. Once I got used to the idea of being more or less a single mum, in so many ways it was really quite liberating.

I was hurt when he started playing around – Janet was the first, I think (I hope you knew about her, and the others) Back then, I decided I had a choice – to be the angry wronged woman, or just to get on with bringing up the children and the other things I have been doing. Don't ask Tony about them: he's no idea that I even got an OU degree.

Anyway, I won't go on and on. Mirabelle, genuinely, if you need to know anything, please feel free to give me a ring – you know our number, of course and you may not be surprised to learn that your name pops up on my iphone.

You probably don't know it yourself yet, but it is dawning on me that you have really done me a huge favour. I needed a kick-up-the-arse if I'm honest and you've helped deliver it.

Best of luck,
Kathleen

THE CANE

The stubby red light-bulb above the door had been glowing for what seemed like an age, but in truth it was probably only ten minutes or so. It cast a slightly ghoulish glow over the poorly lit corridor outside the headmaster's office. But like every other pupil, Tom knew what it meant. You could only go in when the red light went out and the green bulb next to it was switched on. He sat trembling on the tubular-metal stacking chair with a canvas seat, fingers fiddling with the hexagonal nuts between chair frame and seat stretcher.

Tom had been sent there by Mr McMaster, his teacher, for making Alice Spencer cry. Usually, Mr McMaster dealt with discipline his own way, with the fast slap of a well-worn plimsol on the upturned hand of the miscreant. It hurt quite a lot and the recipient's hand would be hot and red for a while after. But today, for some reason, the teacher had decided that this troublemaker needed more severe treatment and was taken to the school secretary, to be dealt with by the head when he had time, that was.

And Mr Carpenter had something much more terrifying than an old gym shoe with which to dispense justice. He had a cane. Every pupil knew that. Boys, never girls, were caned by Mr Carpenter regularly, that was for sure. In truth, it was likely that none of the pupils had actually met a boy who had been caned… but that made no difference. Its reputation was legendary and every one of the children at St Cuthberts Primary knew how much it would hurt and how long the welts of red across one's buttock or calves would last, a shameful sign of wrongdoing. Quite how girls were made to behave remained a mystery to Tom, for they didn't experience Mr McMaster's 'slipper' either. Strangely, they seemed to comply with instruction without the threat of violence.

Alice Spencer was a pretty girl with pigtails and light freckles; pretty but sly and spiteful. She'd arrived a bit late that morning so had been told to sit in the only remaining free seat, next to Tom Frost, whom she disliked for no better reason than because he was a boy. They had clashed before, so it was a combination destined to go badly. Behind Mr McMaster's back, she pulled a face at Tom so he pulled one back. She pinched his bare leg at the back behind the knee – boys at St Cuthberts wore short trousers summer and winter. He tugged at a pigtail. True to form, she made a meal of the tug to her hair and cried out, forcing fake tears to her ice-blue eyes.

McMaster wheeled round from the blackboard on which he had been writing the day's spellings. 'What's going on? Alice, why are you crying?'

'Sir, he pulled my hair, Sir.'

Tom looked down.

'Just behave – you won't be told again,' and the teacher returned to the list of words, all ending in 'a-t-i-o-n' – information, explanation, automation, rotation…

'See,' gloated Alice, quietly enough for the teacher not to hear.

Alice was undoubtedly guilty of initiation but Tom now fell into the trap of retaliation and even escalation.

It was not long before one of Alice's piercing squeals got McMaster's attention again. 'What's wrong now?' and Alice held up her right-hand index finger which clearly showed the mark of a tooth. Indentation.

'He bit me, Sir,' she said.

Tom's eye was red from where she'd poked it moments earlier but he said nothing. The teacher had heard enough and Tom was pulled out by one ear.

Now Tom was sitting outside the headmaster office, certain that he would be caned. Almost as bad, the mothers of boys who were caned were called to the school to collect their villains. Pain and shame.

The red light shone on but offered Tom no comfort, even though while it was lit, he was being spared what would happen once it went out.

Then the bell rang. Elevenses. Milk monitors left their classrooms to hand out third-of-a-pint glass milk bottles with silver foil tops and a drinking straw. Tom sat paralysed in the narrow corridor, listening to the bustle in the school hall. Then it died away and all was quiet. He strained to hear what he expected to be the imminent arrival of his mother, angry at being called to the school, disgraced by her only son.

Anticipation. That was the worst and now he could even spell it.

Eventually the red light went out and Tom shifted in the chair. But the green light did not come on. What was he to do? Mrs Dolman came out of her office, glanced across at Tom and went into the headmaster's office. The fear grew in Tom. After a few minutes, she came out again. Then the green bulb lit. The boy was terrified. He got up and knocked quietly on the oak door.

'Come,' he heard from inside.

Mr Carpenter was a tall, thin, spindly man in his late fifties or early sixties who barely filled his clothes. His authority was underpinned not by fear but by experience, good humour and kindness.

'So why are you here?' he asked Tom, a genuine inquiry.

'I was sent by Mr McMaster.'

'And why was that, Tom?'

'I bit Alice Spencer's finger – but she started it.'

'Well, we can't have boys biting girls, can we now?

Tom looked down, scuffed black school shoes, one of the laces untied, grey wool socks, loose round his ankles.

Mr Carpenter got up from his chair and came around to the front of his desk.

'Here goes,' thought Tom, clenching his buttocks in expectation...

Mr Carpenter put his hand on the boy's shoulder and spoke quietly and clearly to him. 'I want you to go back to the classroom and tell Mr McMaster that the matter has been dealt with. Please tell him that Mr Carpenter would like him to move you in the classroom today so that you are not sitting next to Alice Spencer any more. Perhaps it would be best if you sat next to a boy for the rest of today... Oh! And Tom, no more biting from now on, is that clear?'

Tom's eyes reddened and filled with tears of relief.

'Yes,' he all but whispered.

FOOD FOR THOUGHT

Whoever first coins the phrase 'loveable rogue' clearly has Lester Mulrooney in mind. Actually, more rogue than loveable, but let's not split hairs.

Lester sells wallpaper, lots of it. Floral prints, boys' bedroom racing cars, ponies for the girls, stripes for the lounge. All of it is end-of-line stock, remaindered or somehow damaged. Obtained, sometimes for nothing, from the mill. His ex-house-removers-lorry is piled high with the stuff and he tours the South and Midlands, selling seconds and damaged rolls to gullible bargain hunters. From Kettering to Kidderminster, Basildon to Bath, he will book a church hall and stuff flyers though letter boxes promising home décor bargains but delivering disappointment. By the time Mrs Jones discovers that two of her three rolls are badly faded or double printed, Lester is two hundred miles down the road, misleading Mrs Brown.

I know Lester because I have a room in a small house in Highgate which he owns. There's me, Lester and Disney Dave. Short, red-haired Dave, a film-studies student with an India-rubber face he can twist into any expression. He has earned the nickname for his impressions of Donald Duck. Dave studies for a few weeks, then takes a couple of days off to get money for the rent by joining Lester who is already cheating his way round the smaller towns of Britain.

I always know when the pair of them are back from a selling spree. The dark blue lorry is probably parked somewhere near, but if I don't see it before I come in the front door, I must be careful not to trip over the cash box left open on the stairs. It is overflowing with more money than I have ever seen in a bank.

I am not yet twenty and have come to live in London for my first job in a newspaper office. I have only been here a few months and answered an ad in the paper to get the room. Lester doesn't know me from a three-legged donkey but for some reason, he doesn't think I would ever touch his money. He's right but I have no idea how he knows.

He's large, with pale skin, straight black hair and heavy black-frame glasses, worn well down on his nose. His black overcoat open, he bounds downstairs as I come in and he greets me warmly. 'How's life, my man? If you are around on Sunday, come and have lunch at Angelo's,' and he's out though the door and onto the street. The gust of air from the closing door wafts paper money from the cash box onto the stairs themselves.

You get no prizes for guessing that Trattoria D'Angelo in Soho is an Italian restaurant. I find it eventually, halfway along a street where every third door opens to a restaurant. Greek, Italian, even Hungarian. Anything but British.

It is three steps up from the road to Angelo's six-panel wood front door with a small bottle-glass window in the centre of it. It looks very shut.

I ring the bell. Wait and ring again. Eventually elderly Angelo, short and stout, with long, unkempt, greasy grey-yellow hair, which not quite matches his apron, comes to the door, opens it a crack and tells me: 'We shut.' A brusque bad-tempered go away.

'I'm here for Lester,' I say loudly as the door is closing. But I am somewhat hesitant now. Have I understood the invitation?

'Aah, Lester. Issa-differenta-matta.' Gruff now transformed into purring pussycat.

The door opens in a wide welcome and, Angelo leading the way, we immediately descend to a large cellar room, filled by a single long table that can seat more than twenty. Wine bottles galore. It is my first time here. No one knows me or how I come to be invited and I recognise no-one. No Lester, no Disney Dave. Nervously, I plump for an empty chair near one end, next to a girl with a thin blouse, a flyaway skirt and a broad smile, who pours me a generous amount of the dark wine into a large glass. 'I'm Kirsty,' she says with an Australian accent.

I tell her my name in return, and ask, 'How do you know Lester?' I might as well have asked her the Swahili for 'Good morning'. She's never heard of him.

'I'm here with Graeme,' she says. 'He'll be along in a minute.'

We chat about nothing much for a few minutes and I think I am doing just dandy until a stocky man arrives and stands next to me with a stare as cold as a mother-in-law's kiss. 'This is Graeme,' Kirsty says, lightly. 'He'll want to sit here.' I scoop up my glass and shuffle further down the table. I don't dare ask him how *he* knows Lester.

It is now getting on for three and at last, food arrives to soak up all the wine being drunk. Angelo is feeding the thousands. Dishes of succulent meat, rich with luxuriant Mediterranean sauces; bowls of steaming, naked pasta cooked to perfection. Swathes of caprese salad, thick with tomato, mozzarella, fresh basil and green-yellow olive oil. Chunks of sourdough bread torn from a loaf. More meat, more, more. And of course, wine. Thick, so dark it is almost black in this low-light cellar setting.

We toast Lester, who has not arrived, and stories, ripe to become myths, abound. Through the mid-afternoon, a few more people arrive but still not our host. And no one leaves. The estate agent next to me tells me about his troubles with his wife who is a teacher, and adds, 'You are probably too young to understand, mate. Just don't ever get married.'

As the food is consumed and the wine continues to flow, the noise in the cellar rises. Quieter, more reserved guests have now dropped their guard and I pick up disjointed snippets of other confessions. Alan the architect, is there with his 'assistant', Noel, from south of the river, who tells me I am sweet. All have stories to recount, some of them about our absent host. Quite a few people only know each other from earlier feasts in the same cellar.

I feel an outsider, ill at ease among the much more inebriated, alone where others are in pairs or groups. Kirsty is unobtainable.

It is almost evening when I leave, one of the first, the autumn light already almost gone. As I follow Angelo back up the stairs to the entrance, I ask him, nervously, what I owe for my share? Am I going to have to pay a fortune I do not have for the wine excesses of the others? Angelo looks back at me through his watery, drooping grey eyes. Why haven't I understood? The whole feast is being paid for by Lester. Whether he is there or not. They'll settle up with each other sometime.

I conjure up the vision of Lester offering uncounted handfuls of paper money from his cash box to settle an un-itemised bill.

And now I am lying flat on my bed, back in my small room in our shared house, and I feel distinctly uncomfortable. I have eaten and drunk too much. And I have dined off ill-gotten gains.

Lester's invitation is there almost every other Sunday but I never go again.

ADRIFT

I am in Sammy's Convenience Store four miles from home, buying Sea Salt & Crushed Black Pepper Kettle Chips. I really wanted barbecue flavour, but they only have these or cheese and onion.

I'm the only one in the store, apart from the person I take to be Sammy, who is watching something on his phone while also checking the overhead monitor, perhaps to make sure that I am not shoplifting. He doesn't know me: I've been here before, but not for almost a year. I don't really understand why I have chosen to drive for more than ten minutes to buy a £2.29 bag of potato chips. Only Sammy's is still open around here, apart from the pubs, of course. I pay with my card and he hands me the receipt. I wish him a cheery 'Happy New Year', although actually, that is the last thing I am feeling. I move to the door and catch a glimpse of myself, distorted and pale grey on camera. Do I really look like that, I wonder, as I slip out quietly into the winter night, fumbling for keys?

11.35pm

I'm back home, making a cup of tea, two sugars, which tastes odd alongside a mouthful of salty-peppery crisps.

I'm still puzzled by why I felt I had to buy them at this time of night! The radio is playing hit music but I'm not really listening. It is just on for company. Montmorency, my cat, is looking at me strangely, as well he might, since normally I'm in bed at this time. It is as if he can't make up his mind if this means I will fill his bowl with even more GoCat or whether he might as well head out and see what gives. We're in the same boat there.

11.38pm

I pick up my phone with the idea of ringing Curtis, who I know is at home with Janine, just to wish him well for the coming year. But as I am scrolling through the numbers, I think better of it. He will either be in bed or be celebrating with friends. Either way, he will not want to talk to his older brother 'til tomorrow, or perhaps the day after.

This is the first New Year's Eve that I have been on my own since... well, maybe since ever. I have not really got used to it and I don't like it. Shapeless days. Some weeks, I don't meet anyone else, apart from the short lady with the crooked nose in the Spar whom I know by sight but not by name. She looks at me with a small smile of recognition but we hardly speak. I think she knew Megan better.

11.54pm

We are either at war with the Russians or someone's letting off fireworks. I guess it is the latter. So does Montmorency, who comes back in through the cat flap like a greyhound-track-hare.

I go upstairs into the bedroom and peep out round the curtain. I've not put on the light so I hope no one can see me looking out. Yes, it's two houses down. They are letting off fireworks round the back. I know them to speak to but we are not really acquainted so they wouldn't have invited me anyway. I think I can see Graham and Sarah from next door, but it might not be them.

I watch for a while. There are children outside, too. Quite young. They're up late. Megan probably knew all their names. She was good like that. I turn to go back downstairs just as the light from the fireworks illuminates the whole room and I realise how odd our double bed now looks with only pillows on my side. I don't think I'd really noticed that before.

00.11am

The radio is still belting out music, so I don't realise that it is after midnight. I was in the front room, sitting for a while, lost in thought. My tea is cold. Last New Year, Megan and I drank prosecco, or it might even have been champagne. She wasn't well then, but I didn't know it at the time. She did. She'd known for a while. It was February when I found out, and by then, it was too late. She passed in March, three days before her sixty-seventh birthday. A month or two earlier than they predicted. That's no age these days, is it? I still have the silk scarf, all wrapped, that was my present to her. I think she'd have liked it.

The fireworks have just stopped as far as I can tell, and I put the cup in the sink. I leave the door ajar so that Montmorency can come upstairs and join me if he wants.

I consider having a large glass of whisky, but for the last nine months, I have been conscious that this might be a slippery slope to somewhere. Tonight is no different really. New Year resolutions are supposed to work the other way.

00.57am

I am drifting off to sleep when the phone rings. I have left it downstairs, and I put on my dressing gown and slippers and pad down. It stops ringing before I can answer it. The screen tells me I have to put the phone on charge so I plug it into the cable. Now my fingerprint is not recognised so I have to use my pin. Thank you. It tells me that January 1 is a public holiday in Belgium. I don't think I need to know that just now. Thank you again. I manage to negotiate to the list of missed calls and discover that it was Justin in California. We haven't spoken since his mother's funeral. I ring him back.

'I just wanted to get in before your midnight to wish you best of luck for next year,' he says with noise in the background making him hard to hear.

'That's very kind of you. And the same to you, Justin,' I say as an opener. I'm going to tell him he's not quite got the time difference right, but he's rung off. I leave the phone on charge and turn out the kitchen light, noticing that Montmorency is curled up on whatever is in the laundry basket.

I go back to bed, turn on the bedside lamp, and start reading. I often read in the middle of the night now. I couldn't do that before, because the light would disturb Megan.

06.12am

I wake with a start. The lamp is still on beside me and my book has just fallen to the floor with a bang. These days I often fall asleep while reading.

I realise it is still quite early, but I don't think I will go back to sleep now. I turn on the radio and hear Tony Blackburn. I was going to make myself a special breakfast today, scrambled eggs with the bit of smoked salmon left over from a couple of days ago. But not before 7am. I get up, shower and go downstairs. My phone tells me it is 100%, which is a lot more than I am. I give Montmorency the smoked salmon which he sniffs suspiciously before deciding that it is edible. I stick to my usual cornflakes. Megan liked Special K before she fell ill. I go through the ritual of making real coffee in the hissy-thing. That's what she called the stove-top percolator.

Tony Blackburn is still introducing old records. It is not yet light outside and I think it is raining slightly.

It's the first day of a whole New Year and the emptiness of my new calendar fills me with dread.

<u>QUENTIN</u>

From the street, you would never guess that the house had a full-length attic studio, never mind one which housed one of the nation's most revered abstract artists.

I had been browsing in the Riverside Gallery on Wye Street where Cynthia worked. I'd actually walked into town to pick up my shoes from the menders, but I never missed an opportunity to pop into the gallery almost next door when I knew Cynthia was going to be there. We went way back. Tall and slightly too thin, she was arranging some canvasses for her 2011 spring show and purred with pride as she showed me a highly coloured abstract so thick with oil paint that it was three-dimensional. 'It's a Quentin King,' she said. 'He only lives down there,' and she pointed in the direction of Vanbrugh Avenue.

I rarely like modern art and struggle with abstracts, but there was something about this painting which drew me in.

'Should I have heard of him?' I asked.

'Oh, Peter, you're such an uncultured dork,' Cynthia laughed. 'He's only won the Turner Prize! This is quite an early one. It'll go for six figures.'

'That's a bit rich for you, isn't it?' I said, tactlessly.

'I know,' Cynthia admitted, without having taken offence. 'We've had the security upgraded. We wouldn't normally get anything nearly as valuable as this, but he is local and we have actually become friends. He's getting on now.'

She told me not to miss the opening in ten days' time – she'd send me an invitation to what would be a private view. I said I'd do my best.

'If you're going home now, would you be a poppet and drop this in to Quentin – it's almost on your way.'

It was more than a request and she handed me a copy of the exhibition catalogue with the abstract painting prominently displayed on the cover. 'They only arrived from the printers this morning.'

She jotted down his address. 'Just push the door open when you get there – it is never locked, and go up to the top, he will be in the attic. He never goes out,' and I was sent on my way with a dismissive 'mwah' to my cheek.

From the pavement, No. 59 looked like most of the other houses on the Avenue: tan coloured brick with the odd blackened one is still ubiquitous in some areas of the capital. The slate roof gave no indication of any loft studio, and I checked Cynthia's slip of paper a third time before crunching over a few yards of flinty gravel to the paint-peeling front door and, seeing no bell, gave it a bit of a push. It swung in as Cynthia had predicted and I called through the gap. No reply.

I was an intruder, and I felt it as I picked my way up two flights of stairs to a door which was slightly ajar. Again, I called through the narrow opening but still no reply, and gingerly I tiptoed in.

At the far end of the surprisingly large room, an elderly man with a mass of almost white, unruly hair stood with his back to me, leaning over what looked like a saucepan on a two-ring camping stove.

'Hello, Mr King,' I called really loudly and the man turned, his wild hair and dirty smock making a disquieting impression.

'Who the fuck are you?' he barked.

I proffered the catalogue. 'I'm just the delivery boy really. Cynthia asked me to bring this.'

'Put it down there,' he said pointing vaguely towards the large, cluttered table. Then, paying me no more attention, he turned back to the saucepan. I ventured further into the studio and across to the table, reaching out to deposit the catalogue, trying my best not to disturb anything else.

'I'm sorry I interrupted you,' I said, now aware of a strange smell in the room, embarrassed by my intrusion and hoping to slither away harmlessly. But before I could escape, he turned again, this time with the hot saucepan held in both hands in front of him. 'What did you say your name was?'

I hadn't said. 'I'm Peter. Peter Percival. I'm a friend of Cynthia - at the gallery.'

'Do you know anything about French cooking?' he demanded, as if it was a logical follow-up question.

'Not a thing,' I admitted, completely nonplussed.

'Well then, you're no bloody use,' he said as he moved towards me somewhat menacingly, the saucepan out in front.

I now realised that the bizarre smell in the room was a mixture of oil paint, perhaps turps and linseed oil, and whatever was cooking in the pan. I had assumed he was heating up some type of art material, but actually he was cooking what appeared to be a version of bouillabaisse.

He put the none-too-clean saucepan precariously on the newly delivered catalogue, which had become the only flat landing space on the table, and handed me a spoon.

'What does this need more of?' he said, as if I was an established connoisseur of all things French and fishy.

It tasted sublime, and I told him so.

'You're still no fucking use,' he snapped again. 'Sit down there,' and he pointed to the messy table.

It was a strange invitation since there were no chairs or stools anywhere, but I was way out of my comfort zone and not about to disobey what was not an invitation but an ill-tempered order. Anyway, I'd been wrong, for he then pulled from beneath the table a metal-and-wood folding chair of the type one used to see on garden patios. 'Yours is under there,' he said as if talking to an imbecile, It was actually how I felt. By the time I had grovelled under the table and retrieved a second chair, two bowls of steaming fish stew had been placed on the table. Along with two hunks of French bread, they vied for space amid partly-squeezed tubes of oil paint. Hygienic? Forget it.

I wanted to tell him that I couldn't stay; that I'd not long had lunch; that I'd got to get back for... well, for anything I could invent on the spur of the moment. Instead, I meekly sat on the chair without demur and with no further discussion or explanation, we both started to devour the truly delicious stew.

He finished his bowl way ahead of me and mopped it with the bread until not a smear of food was left. I wondered if he'd ever bothered to wash his crockery. Next, he wiped his now red-stained and whiskery mouth on the sleeve of his smock, the bright hue of the food joining the multi-coloured patches of paint and whatever else was already on the garment. Without comment, he got up and fetched a bottle of wine, already uncorked. He poured two glasses, and drank one without pause, giving a small belch.

'That's better,' he said. 'Is Cynthia coming?'

'I don't think so. She did not say anything to me. I was asked because…'

'I bloody well hope not. Can't stand the woman. Can you?' he interrupted.

Not waiting for a reply, he got up and wandered over to a large, empty easel standing on one side of the room.

I could see now why the studio was not visible from the road. The whole length of the roof on this side of the apex had been cantilevered out and a huge window inserted, giving the interior space ample, even north light.

I got up, hoping to slip away with thanks for the unexpected meal, but he wasn't having any of it. 'Aren't you going to drink that?' he said looking at my wine, which remained untouched. Before I could apologise for not wanting alcohol mid-afternoon, he grabbed the glass and, like the first, downed it with a good imitation of someone just back from 24 hours in the Sahara. 'Help me with these,' he demanded and went into the corner where several large canvasses were leaning against each other and the wall.

We moved three of them, so he could extract the fourth which he then needed help holding upright so that he could fix it to the easel. By then I had got oil paint on my hands and a little on my trousers, too.

'I'm not really dressed for this,' I ventured.

'You're not,' said my host-of-few-words, as if I should have known how to dress before calling round. 'Bugger off now.'

I was glad to get away, confused by the contrast of his rude abruptness and unassuming generosity.

Back home, I undressed and treated my chinos and hands to paint remover and then, freshly adorned, looked up Quentin King on Google.

He'd been lauded more than twenty years earlier, compared favourably to other well respected late 20th Century artists, some of whom I had actually heard of, and then, according to Wikipedia, he'd been admitted to hospital with depression. There was also mention of alcohol. I found no information about him since about the millennium, there or elsewhere on the internet. Perhaps his return to active work was recent.

It was quite a lot later that I heard that the Riverside's Spring Show went particularly well, with many more in the gallery than ever before. Someone said Tracey Emin had been at the private view, which I deliberately missed. It was just not my thing.

Then over the next few years, the King name cropped up occasionally in my local newspaper. Whenever he did anything, they made sure we were aware of the art-celeb in our midst.

It must have been several years after that when I read that Quentin had died. There were obituaries in the heavyweight Sundays: Mark Lawson said Quentin King 'painted to make people happy'.

Then the Riverside had a King retrospective, which I'm afraid I also avoided. When we met shortly afterwards, Cynthia told me prices went exceptionally high for his late, large canvasses. Because of it, the Riverside was very much on the art map, so much so that she had re-stocked with items mainly of interest to serious collectors.

It was later that same spring that I had to go to San Francisco to see Craig and Laura, my son and daughter-in-law. It had been a warm April in California, and even in San Francisco, the temperature was in the high seventies. But there was one really wet day, and so we did some culture. By mid-afternoon, we were in the centre of the city and Laura suggested we go to the museum of modern art. I probably screwed up my face, but we went anyway.

We were wandering through the galleries - more slowly that I'd have done on my own. I just don't get installations, particularly when they're a pile of bricks I might have arranged myself. And blank white canvasses? Come on! A case of *emperor's new clothes* as far as I'm concerned. But I was keeping my comments to myself.

One large room, devoted to 'recent acquisitions', seemed particularly bizarre until on one side, filling a large space, was an eerily familiar oil painting. A swirl of oil paint in bright colours. A particular hue of red generously applied and dominant. A painting style I was sure I had seen before. I walked over to the little label:

Quentin King
England, 1939 – 2016
Peter's Bouillabaisse (2011)

THE POET

Ronnie's tea was always brown-orange and already had powdered milk and at least two sugars in it. Tea leaves nestled at the bottom of the mug. He didn't ask first: it was just handed to you in a mug which had not been washed, perhaps ever!

His crib was a kind of shed set back into the high stone embankment on the long straight stretch of road in Archway. It was about the same size as two phone boxes pushed together, and clearly had never been intended to be a domicile. First a workmen's tool shed from the time when the masons were making the walls. More recently, it could have been used to store a road-sweeper's cart.

The single light bulb, dangling dangerously from a twisted cord, was the only source of illumination if the door was closed, which it always was. Before electricity could reach the light fitting, it had to negotiate a brown Bakelite adaptor from which a second, frayed cable descended, at the end of which was a one-cup heating element: half egg-whisk, half instrument of torture. Electrocution was as likely as a hot drink.

There was no toilet or even running water and, apart from Ronnie's roll-ups, the overpowering smell came from a small, round paraffin heater of the type once used to keep a car radiator from freezing in the winter. Now it was also an improvised cooking ring, doing a good line in asphyxiation on the side. There was no room for a bed: Ronnie slept in the curved bamboo number which dominated the space and in which he was always seated. It was variously covered by large, crocheted Afghan rainbow blankets. The nearest thing to a guest's seat was a low metal-and-canvas affair of the type a fisherman might use on a riverbank.

Ronnie's clothing would have been rejected by charity shops. He chose the daywear of a slightly better class of tramp, for which he might easily have been mistaken. The false impression was enhanced by his wispy beard of the style preferred by Muslim clerics.

Inside his hovel, you would find him lost in whatever he was inscribing in a dog-eared school notebook, using a well-chewed pencil, silently mouthing words to himself. On the floor, one would find several of the many monthly or quarterly poetry publications, in which there was occasionally some of his carefully crafted work. Some paid a small sum for submitted work, others offered nothing more than exposure to their readers. But for Ronnie, it was what he did. And he was getting better known; more frequently accepted by the bigger publications.

Ronnie first started writing poetry in Wormwood Scrubs. He carried on when he was transferred to Winchester Prison. It was the moans, screams and shouts, echoing off the hard surfaces, which resonated in the words he wrote.

Superficial conclusions would have it that he had suffered a nervous breakdown somewhere along the line.

As so often, the truth was more complicated. He had never fitted in anywhere, growing up in the rougher areas of north London. His education had not been scholastic but learned from the gutter, from gangs and by guile. A mother in and out of mental institutions; a father, recently de-mobbed, continuing to use the violence the Army had ingrained in him. Ronnie's abilities were shaped by the trauma of tough life-lessons and a natural ability to shape soundscapes into poignant words. Nowadays there might be a three-or-four initial label for his condition.

Mina Lubinska was everything Ronnie was not. The daughter of Russian émigrés, expensively educated, tall, graceful and poised. She spoke the impeccable English of someone who has learned it as a second language from an early age. A good degree from a Russell-group university was a foregone conclusion. Daddy's connections had certainly not hindered her appointment to one of the nation's leading publishing houses, where she was able to rub shoulders with the literati. The current Poet Laureate had become an acquaintance; it might not be long before she would be asked to sit on the Booker prize committee. Papa had hoped she would have married by now. Someone in the City would have been fine.

Yet here she was, getting out of a taxi on an inhospitable, noisy stretch of road that was a major bus route. Surely no one could live along here. Certainly no one the least bit creative... The kind of place where the security cameras needed security cameras to make sure they were not vandalised. Even the taxi driver had been dubious about stopping. And here she was, a few minutes later, perched on the tiny stool, mug of 'Oh! Is that for Me!' in her hand, her five-denier knees together and demurely slanted to one side, as one had been taught.

Ronnie said he could vaguely remember receiving a letter making the appointment for her visit. He was not sure where he'd put it, although in the space of his miniscule abode, the options were not great. What she was suggesting had its attractions. An advance payment which, though modest, was many, many times more than even the most generous of the publications to which he now submitted.

But the effort expected was also far greater. His visitor would need a minimum of forty-five unpublished pieces, preferably fifty. That would more than double his entire published output so far, and while he had several unfinished attempts in his notebook, he had never, ever been rushed and could not begin to imagine what the yoke of a signed agreement would do to his psyche, never mind the quality of his output.

Mina told him that her Executive Publisher (Poetry) had assessed his work. With a degree of reluctance, she passed over the description which was supposed to be flattering. It used language Ronnie entirely failed to understand. Apparently, his poems 'borrow some of the ghosts of TS Eliot to tell stories about splintered realities, where the wasteland is everywhere and nowhere captured in a word-opera of fluent cadences... with expansive forms, often in sequences or variations to stimulate existential confusion.' He was praised 'for continuing the objectivist tradition'. He didn't know he was.

His reaction was quick and blunt. He told Mina to fuck off back to Harper Collins. Undaunted, she told him to think their offer over, and since he was without a phone, she would visit him in a week to see if he had changed his mind. They could 'of course use other language to describe his work' and perhaps discuss better terms.

He did not want to see her ever again.

* * *

Ronnie and Mina Dubbs now live in the Broomhall area of Sheffield. He drives one of the new supertrams. She works in the university library. Without ceremony visitors are offered a (clean) cup of brown-orange, sweet, milky stewed tea from the heirloom samovar which always adorns the small kitchen table.

Ronnie's only published volume, *Roads from Nowhere*, is now out of print. It is a collector's item.

YOUR CAR, MY CAR

Your classic car is faded red
And once went fast – or so it's said.
It's now on blocks, the tyres need air,
It's rarely driven anywhere.
The leather's cracked, something drips,
It can't be used for shopping trips.
The gearbox whines; suspension creaks,
The cooling system often leaks.
A blessing if the engine starts;
A nightmare if you need spare parts.

My car is what a car should be:
So cheap to run, emission free.
A family car (I am no fool),
It always gets the kids to school.
The seats wipe clean, there's lots of room,
Performance wise, its vra-vra-vroom.
You never need to lift the hood,
The ride is smooth, road-holding good.
A perfect choice – there's just one snag:
My car is not *your* E-type Jag…

CHILDHOOD MEMORIES

I was born in Jessops Women's Hospital, Sheffield, just after the end of the Second World War (although you may be surprised to learn that is not *really* why the war ended).

Even though it was mid-March, my father had to dig deep snow away from the garage so that he could take his wife to hospital.

My mother had a relatively easy delivery because I was a very small baby, significantly underweight. Almost immediately, I caught whatever was going round at the hospital at the time. Consequently, when my mother was considered well enough to go home a week later, as was normal in those days, I was kept behind. My mother was warned that her baby son might not survive the night.

I was more than a month-old before I beat the odds, and pneumonia, and made it to the family home in the Sheffield suburb of Millhouses, best known for its child-friendly park with a large, stream-fed paddling pool. (Today this landmark is no more, killed no doubt by the Health & Safety Gestapo).

Home was a large, old semi, which my parents had bought shortly before I was born, to accommodate a growing family: me and my sister Margaret – two years ahead of me in age and light years ahead in everything else – and our long-haired Welsh collie sheepdog called Ajo [*pronounced ah yo*], an Eskimo name which my father had selected because of the dog's likeness to a husky.

Although Ajo didn't know it at the time, he was later to teach me to walk by being a handy mobile device for pulling oneself up with. On second thoughts, maybe he did know it because he was only *slightly* less intelligent than my father, a research physicist, and my mother, also a clever scientist and linguist.

I wonder now whether my anxious mother paid too much attention to her miraculously recovered son because my sister, who had been the lone apple of her eye until then, apparently seemed to resent my presence. It was a feud which Margaret and I successfully managed to keep festering for more than a dozen years, well into our adolescence...

By the time I could walk, Margaret had perfected her technique: find out what the younger sibling was not supposed to do and quietly tell him to do it... 'Don't go off down that side path; you'll get stuck in the mud,' my mother might say to her sensible, obedient daughter. 'Go down that path there and see what you can find,' my sister would then tell her gullible, unruly toddler brother.

But it didn't take me too long to develop my own methods for making trouble in return. I know this because many years later, as two now very devoted adults, my sister and I each have a similar, sneaking guilty feeling that we were the main aggressor.

Actually, my very early memories are entirely unreliable. Are they truly my memories or the mental cinecast of family anecdotes which have been circulating for years?

I think I really do remember the 'pig lady' who came to collect the kitchen waste and add it to the barrel of slops on the cart behind her horse. I can still remember the unique smell.

But I certainly don't *truly* remember the time we lost the dog.

Apart from being a teaching aid, Ajo was also a trusted baby-sitter, the story goes. Our friends the Clarks, who lived quite a way up the road, were often given the task of looking after the two of us along with their own three girls. Ajo came with us, too, perhaps to make sure that when the four girls ganged up on me, the only boy, I didn't lose too much blood!

On one particular occasion, my mother went to collect us, completely forgetting the canine childminder who was happily playing with the Clark children. Several hours later, Mr Clark rang my father to tell him that our dog was still at their house.

'Bring him to the phone,' my father suggested. When handset was to dog's ear, he said: 'Ajo, come home' and the trusty guardian arrived back in minutes.

And I wonder if I also remember the fact that Ajo would dart out of the house a full ten minutes before my father arrived home from work. Apparently, our family pet would meet the car about a mile away down on the main road and run alongside it, in and out of the traffic, until they both got home.

Ah, well! Memories. Best not get me started.

BE CAREFUL, DADDY, IT HURTS

I have always been obsessively inquisitive. At the age of four, I was found in bed surrounded by the cogs and springs of my parents' alarm clock.

'Stephen, what are you doing?' my father asked.

'I'm mending the clock,' I said.

'But there was nothing wrong with it!' (There hadn't been).

But by then, I had already discovered that taking things to pieces was always a lot easier than putting them together again. Springs would leap out as soon as the back of a device was removed. Tiny parts clinked to the floor, never to be found again. Brittle plastic would break as little fingers prised apart that which had been carefully designed not to be opened without special tools, especially by someone aged under five!

But I didn't need a service engineer's toolkit or even a set of screwdrivers because I wasn't mainly motivated by mending. What I *did* need was to see how everything worked.

(Later I developed some of the skills needed to help conceal my destructive voyage into an item's interior, so

I could lie about my fatal interventions. But at four, I showed a little less guile.)

I had learned some of my craft as a would-be mechanic on my own toys. Clockwork trains and small metal cars lasted barely a day before they were forensically examined. I was passionate about these cars with their shiny paint. It made no difference. After a matter of hours, they had to have their tyres removed, and anything else that could be prised off was destructively detached. Quite often, the tyres didn't get put back straight away and then got lost... Years later I discovered that one could buy little boxes of spare tyres but by then, it was much too late.

Other children had shiny new Dinky or Corgi cars which they lovingly placed back in their cardboard boxes, their paintwork unblemished, so that later, they became valuable collectors' items for 'little boys' aged sixty or more.

My cars had chipped paint, wobbly wheels and missing bits like headlamps or bumpers.

It wasn't that I was destructive *per se*. It was just I could not leave things as they were. They needed further investigation. And during that examination, inevitably some part would 'ping!' through the air to slip under the wardrobe or get lost in the bedclothes.

Other toys would be put to a use for which they were not intended... Moving a heavy chest across the floor was so much easier with four cars wedged underneath to act like castors. Sometimes these experiments even worked. But in every case, a plastic windscreen would get crushed or an axle bent.

Curiosity and ingenuity are great virtues but, if only for the sanity of the rest of the family, sometimes they need to be moderated.

My sister, on the other hand, was everything that a nice child should be. She looked after the gifts she was given, and so was entrusted with more and more delicate treasures. Her miniature glass and china horses almost never broke. Only once did one need to be treated for a broken leg at the epoxy glue hospital.

It was a mystery to me why she did not need to 'repair' the portable record player on which she listened to Craig Douglas. Nor unscrew the door handle to the lounge on Christmas Eve to find out what Santa Claus had left. Were we really related?

If there were buttons, they needed to be pushed, knobs certainly had to be twiddled. Radios, which had been lovingly tuned to a needle-fine favourite station, played audible slush when next they were turned on after my intervention. And when the outside toilet froze one winter, it was because 'someone' had *mended* the cistern overflow.

Not *all* this mending went horribly wrong. The door handle was screwed back well enough. Sometimes four matching tyres did get put back on the same toy car. And sometimes – not often perhaps but occasionally – the clockwork motor in the toy train did still work after it had been the subject of invasive examination. Or it would have worked if by then, I had not lost the key to wind it up.

Clearly, I have saved many, many lives by _not_ training to be a surgeon!

My own survival is even more miraculous. For during this formative period my father came to change the bulb in the light hanging above my bed. As he reached up to remove the dud from the electric bayonet socket, I told him: 'Be careful Daddy. If you put your fingers in there, it hurts.'

THE DAYS OF CHARS

I suppose you would describe Mrs Potter as 'plain' if you were trying to be polite: actually, in common parlance she was downright ugly. Heavy features and a lantern jaw which seemed to shape her whole face so it looked a bit like a dark pink example of one of those bean-bag chairs which used to be so trendy. She had two wart-like spots which you could not ignore, one in the fold of a plump nostril and the other, sprouting whiskers, on her chin. Her slightly gingery hair was always drawn back and tied in an untidy bun on the back of her head, kept in place by a coarse hairnet through which errant wisps escaped. Ena Sharples was more becoming.

Normally, I believe you can see someone's personality in their face, but if you tried to read Mrs Potter's you'd come up with the wrong answer. She looked stern and unkind, cruel even. But in reality, she was pleasant and tried to be obliging. She went about her tasks with a helpful air, even if, with her prominent pout, it might have seemed as if she'd just been tricked into performing yet another unacceptable chore.

On Thursdays – that was her day with us – she would be found at some stage, scrubbing brush in hand, on her knees cleaning the scullery floor, working backwards from the passage towards the kitchen. Her un-feminine hands, red from the hot caustic water, were almost the same colour as the scarlet quarry tiles. She scrubbed the floor first, then mopped it only slightly drier with a rag wrapped over an old sweeping brush head and then rinsed out in some dubious water. My mother, provider of the sub-standard equipment, saw nothing wrong with any of this. And if she knew Mrs Potter's first name, I never heard it mentioned. It was always Mrs Potter this, Mrs Potter that. 'Mrs Potter's here tomorrow, so tidy your room,' I'd be told on Wednesday when I got home from school. Or 'Mrs Potter's just scrubbed that floor so take your shoes off.'

Mrs Potter was with us for years, always wearing a printed cotton thingummy over her otherwise dull-coloured clothes which one could never really see. And summer or winter, rain or shine, she would arrive wearing a thick, heavy coat which she'd take off and hang somewhere in the passage: she appeared to think that her coat was not entitled to be hung in the cloakroom under the stairs where all the family's coats were hanging.

At the end of 'her hours', she'd put the money my mother left her in her purse and go back into the passage for her coat. Then tying a triangle of scarf round her head, she'd chime, 'God Bless,' and crunch down the path to the pavement.

As you may have gathered, Mother was not in any way particularly house-proud, so in one sense Mrs Potter had it easy. Much easier than a succession of gardeners, over whom Mother would stand and glower as they did some weeding. For some reason, gardeners were never entitled to be called 'Mr' (not that Mother was a snob) so it was 'Fox, don't touch that, it's a bulb,' or 'Fox, you have pruned that too hard.'

By contrast, I never heard my mother complain to Mrs Potter about the standard of her housework. This was never going to be more than adequate at best, given the tools with which Mrs Potter was expected to work. Typical was our Hoover, which had a dangerously worn flex and a slipping belt so it had about as much suck left in it as a miner's lung.

What our char must have thought of us, I cannot guess. She bravely put up with my mother's 'economy' equipment and materials including stinking dishcloths, smelling of drains and made of torn squares of old towels. Surely, she must have been puzzled by why a household which could afford a char couldn't stretch to hygienic materials.

We never knew because Mrs Potter was not a talker so she didn't ever comment. By the time she'd been coming for a few months, I got over being scared of her and decided she was not really the cruel witch or torturer she resembled. So, I was quite happy when once, just once, she stayed behind after her hours to look after me when my mother had to go off somewhere.

Quite why she stopped coming, I never knew. But stop she did. And from then on, things were very different.

We lived not far from one of those labyrinthine mental hospitals which had been built round many major cities in the late 19th and early 20th centuries. Cane Hill supplied my mother with a succession of char ladies, all of whom cheerfully put up with the wheezy vacuum and my mother's penny-pinching approach to household management. None of them ever had first names, either. And each of them brought their own brand of originality to the job of keeping 'Number 97' clean.

Mrs Wraith, small and slight, lasted for all of two months before she finally decided that the pictures on the walls were moving. She was succeeded by Mrs Littlewhite, who had a hunted look about her. She lasted less long and just stopped coming. Then there was Mrs Gunter (whom I called Grunter but not to her face!) She decided on her fourth or fifth visit that the pebble dash on the outside of the house needed the attention of her mop and bucket. Eventually, I think Mother decided that the Cane Hill recruitment resource had its drawbacks and she probably upped her hourly rate in order to secure cleaners from a less unconventional source.

Eventually she recruited Queenie, small and wiry with jet black eyes and as Irish as they come. Unlike any of the others, she did not appear to have a family name: 'Call me Queenie,' she demanded, even of us children, so Queenie it was. I don't know how good she was at cleaning, but she was everything at communication that reserved Mrs Potter was not. Her hours were either longer or just later than her predecessor's: perhaps that was when she could fit us in. She was there when I got back from school and sometimes when my father got back from the lab. One only had to go into the room in which she was working for Queenie's garrulous nature to take precedence over any cleaning and tidying.

Although she had no connection with any lunatic asylum, she too could be unnervingly unpredictable. I must have been about nine when, in the midst of telling me some complicated story about her family back in

Ireland, she took from her pocket a shiny tin box, opened it and offered me a roll-up cigarette. Then she put another half-smoked one in her mouth, lit it for a few puffs and then stubbed it out on the shiny box. I'd have loved to have accepted her cigarette offer, but children's smoking was strictly to be performed behind the bicycle sheds at school and other similarly discreet places and not in front of adults! Both my parents smoked, as did almost everyone in those days, but not young children (or not officially). I never told anyone about Queenie's amazing 'illegal' offer: it was our secret, I suppose.

Apart from chatting, Queenie loved tidying. While it was no show-home, our house was tidy enough: my bedroom was the big exception to that. That didn't stop Queenie from moving almost everything just slightly on the shelves and mantelpiece in the lounge. Dusting round, she wanted the wooden carved-lady ornament to face the front, not slightly sideways, and the clock to be dead in the middle and not to one side. It annoyed my mother on the few occasions when she noticed these miniscule changes. Not because she didn't like the readjustments (which were hardly noticeable) but perhaps because it meant that Queenie had spent less time scrubbing the scullery floor.

Then there was the occasion when, on getting back from school, I discovered Queenie carefully lining up all the little die-cast cars in the toy garage in my bedroom. These cars were among the most used toys I owned and at least once a day were pushed round on the lino floor along an improvised circuit of chalked roads in races of several laps. But until then, they had never ever been arranged neatly in lines in their box, according to size, colour or anything else. Just piled in together and the lid-cum-roof closed on top of them. My first reaction was to be taken aback by Queenie's intrusion into my private automobile fantasy. But her chatty, forthright approach was disarming and quite quickly, we were discussing whether a Triumph TR2 was better than an MGA in the corners or why I preferred the Austin Healey to the single-seat Ferrari. She clearly knew nothing about cars in reality, but she managed to maintain a conversation by asking questions which got me thinking. 'Why is there a band of yellow on the front of that one (a Vanwall)?' 'Where do those ones come from (a Maserati)?' No adult before – or since – had engaged with me so effectively in my fantasy world of motorsport. I probably would have allowed her to choose cars for her own team – to race against my favourites – if we hadn't been interrupted by the sound of my mother coming upstairs. Queenie was busy wiping windows with her duster by the time my mother was in the doorway, checking on what was taking her so long. 'These windows were really grimy. I've already been over them all once,' she chirruped with staggering ease. I doubt that my mother was taken in but she was at least silenced by the deceit! 'I'm just going to finish the bathroom,' Queenie added promptly and before my mother's jaw had finished dropping, she was out of my room and across the hall. Mother looked at me and then at the garage of cars. Speechless, she turned and went back downstairs, leaving me to luxuriate in the new bond of deceit which Queenie had somehow forged between us.

Like Mrs Potter, Queenie was with us for some years, artfully avoiding confrontation with my mother who continued to be both somewhat dissatisfied and rather suspicious of the sweet-talker. That her blarney cut no ice with my mother was clear, but it gave her an edge that was hard for my mother to blunt.

I'm not sure how or why Queenie stopped coming because she was still with us when I was sent to boarding school, but by the end of the first or second term, when I came home for holidays, Queenie was a thing of the past. In her place was Mrs Balint, a recent refugee, who spoke with a very strong eastern European accent and worked without pausing. I saw her very infrequently because I was only around during school holidays and often Mrs Balint was having her own holidays at a similar time. In any case, not long afterwards, we moved from that house to a modern, new home that seemed to need less cleaning and certainly had no scullery floor. Down a remote rural cul-de-sac, it was not at all conveniently situated for home helps. By then, my mother had probably decided that she could or would manage without outside assistance and our days of chars were over.

CONFUSION

I am starting to wonder what is going on inside my head. (*She* says 'not much' which is possibly true). I cannot count how many times a day I realise that a thought which just passed in and out of my consciousness is now unrecoverable. Who was it I was going to phone? Why have I gone into the kitchen? What is the name of that plant?

Part of my attempt at a remedy is lists. Endless lists, dotted about the house. A list of groceries to buy, a list of jobs to tackle, a list of people to call. Reminders galore. It helps but it isn't fool-proof and they bring with them their own problems. What is written on the list might have made sense when I wrote it down, but now I cannot always remember what it refers to. Perhaps a phone number without a name! A measurement – 21.3cm – but of what? Here's one '3E 2006 63152397'. What was that about – and can I now throw it away?

And then there is also the 'stuff' I have to have on me. So much of it. A pen (actually three different pens and a pencil) and a pad for more reminders. A mobile phone which I can't work out how to use, my Swiss Army penknife (of course). My wallet, keys, a mask, a handkerchief and spectacles. And among all that there is a piece of paper in my pocket which is, of course, a list.

Last week's grocery order and something else scrawled on it: '53 pence golden squid.' Another mystery.

And right now, I am wondering where is that *other* list I need with some items on it which I need to help shape the rest of the afternoon. I had it in my hand a moment ago. Where did I put it? I know, I changed my shoes, perhaps it is upstairs? It is a list of things I was going to do today and tomorrow. Oh! Here is something but it is not the one I am looking for – in this case, two phone numbers and some other stuff written on the same piece of paper. I'm not sure whose number that is. I might have to ring it to find out.

I once worked out that if I had not spent all that time looking for things, I'd still be in my forties because the need to find something takes a significant part of every day. Where did I put it? I remember having it yesterday... I think. Or was it the day before? I can try the method of retracing my steps, but often I forget exactly what I did and when. Where did I go after that?

In the end, whatever it is will turn up in the most unlikely place. Why did I put it there? Spectacles hanging on the washing line! Now I'm rummaging for those screws, the little ones I put somewhere carefully while I was mending the door handle. I put them in a little pot. I'm sure I did. But where is the pot?

Wait a minute. Is that the doorbell? No. It turns out it is not. Perhaps a car hooting on the main road. Now, what was it I was looking for?

Why is the door handle missing? That is it! I was replacing the door handle. So where are the little screws? (Eventually they turn up by the front door. I probably had them in my hand when I went to check if someone had rung the bell.)

And now I spend the best part of another hour trying to find the screwdriver I put down when I was looking for those little screws. Of course, I have *several* other perfectly adequate screwdrivers, but it's the one I was using that I want to find. Nothing else will do, even though the others are exactly the same size. It has to be the missing one. It has a wooden handle and I have used it for years. I don't like that one which came with the flat-pack furniture, but of course I have kept it, just in case I can't find the other ones...

Ah! Just in case! That's another large source of complication... There is that area behind the shed, full of clutter which might at some stage have had a useful purpose if the right opportunity arose. Old fridge shelves, a plastic cover for a tumble drier vent – but we never had a tumble drier. An old clothes-line post which I took out when we got the rotary airer... That was twenty years ago.

And then there are all those cupboards in the house: rather too many of them. Several places for everything so which one is chosen is something of a lottery. Even if I had a standard place for something, it doesn't mean that it will escape the 'four of everything' syndrome, which goes like this: The first one, a jar of whatever, is almost empty so I buy another (No. 3), not remembering that I did that two months ago when they were on special offer (No. 2). In fact, I am still left with the feeling that we are running out of that particular whatever, so it is only when I have bought the No.4 jar that I actually master the fact that we now have a surfeit of whatever.

(By the time we are ready to use the last jar, it will be well past its best-before date, of course – but that is a completely different topic: don't even go there!) And if that wasn't confusing enough, it turns out that the makers of whatever have now a new version which our daughter says we should use because the old one had some E312 in it which is not good for your circulation.

(My uncle once told me that if I needed to get a hard-to-find item, I should buy two so that I'd have one spare, just in case. That was only the two-of-everything syndrome. Pah! Just for beginners! But at least I can blame him. Always a relief!)

I can pretend that all this muddle is only because I am trying to do too many things more or less at the same time. Mending the door handle, watering the tomato plants, ringing the car insurers to tell them about that dent, once I have found who the underwriters are this year...

I can pretend that it is multi-tasking which is causing the confusion. It would be good if it were true, wouldn't it...?

MODERN BIRTH CONTROL

Romance did not come easily to me. If it had been a school subject, I would not have lasted more than one term, just like my lack of prowess with Latin. Amo, amas, amat. That's it? What is the genitive or the ablative, anyway?

I had never had a problem with girls. Hell, my sister was one, wasn't she? And I was quite happy at the age of six, square-dancing with Sarah Cummins at the village hall.

It was not that I didn't have some advantages. At 11, I was sent to a co-educational boarding school and almost everyone at that age 'paired off'. It wasn't entirely stress-free, like stamp collecting. But not that *very* different. It seemed to mean that you asked a girl – at teatime on Friday – if you could be her boyfriend. If she said 'Yes', you gave her a peck on the cheek. Then she danced with you at the house hop that evening. And I suppose you tried to be friendly with her over the weekend and even during the following week, or at least until you, or much more likely she, 'gave you up'. It wasn't too onerous really. You didn't have to sit next to her in class or take her to town. She probably wouldn't write you a love-note and flick it across the classroom - you'd both look foolish if she did that. It was a bit disappointing to be dumped as we called it... But since it happened to most boys most of time, it wasn't a big deal. After all, it wasn't as if you'd put too much emotion into the transaction.

No hormones had clicked in for me at that age so it was purely an issue of status and conformity. If that week's conquest had wanted to take things further, she would have had to make all the running, with a good dose of knowledge enhancement thrown in. Whoever 'she' had been was unlikely to take on that task with the likes of me: she'd have realised that, to start with, she'd have had to attend to the mundane, like asking me why my knees were always dirty and buttons were missing from my clothing.

I probably had one-dance stands with the same six or seven girls that the rest of us amateur boyfriends managed. There were clearly a bunch of us who were very much second division and clearly only there for the mild amusement of those girls who were waiting for a vacancy in the higher leagues.

These were not the days when two girls would quite happily dance all night round their handbags in the middle of the floor. It was top-of-the-pops, rock 'n' roll and jiving. And for that, you needed a boy. In extremis, a grubby one with torn trousers.

I am not hopeless on the dance floor but nor am I a natural. I can hear the music but I don't really respond to most of it and like some of my limbs, I am somewhat disengaged. So, where girls were concerned, I was at best good for a dance or two while they warmed up and hoped for something better to arrive.

The girl whom I most desired was Rosemary. She was as unobtainable as a bed in a hospital. To use an airline analogy, while she travelled first class, I barely made tourist class. Just like on the airlines, I didn't even get to see where she was seated most of the time. Anyway, she was the regular partner of that year's pilot in chief, Michael. Square jawed and already handsome. They were what we now call an item all one term and most of the next. Then one Saturday, all that changed. Word got round that Rosemary and Michael had had a falling out. It was not just gossip. There we were at a school film screening, the venue of first choice for couples, and Michael was with someone else. Rosemary was nowhere to be seen.

The film started and even in tourist class, we could see the screen... I can't remember what the film was about but I must have been reasonably engrossed because I was completely taken by surprise when a warm, slightly moist hand slipped into mine... You've guessed, it was Rosemary. We sat canoodling in the innocent way 12-year-olds did back then during the rest of the film, holding hands, the odd squeeze or two and a peck on the cheek, no more.

I was flattered, puzzled and amazed. Why me? I didn't think Rosemary even knew of my existence. Our 'date' lasted for the rest of the film before we were separated and went back to our respective dormitories. Rosemary asked me not to talk about our little secret, a challenge and a disappointment for me since that was the main point of such liaisons: something to boast about.

The next day, Rosemary and Michael made up their differences and I was history. Other romances came and went, mostly went, but Rosemary's brief encounter remained the most bittersweet.

I think that perhaps by sending me to a co-educational boarding school, my parents had, in their minds, subcontracted out the need for sex education. Apart from my mother's frequent references to not getting a girl 'in trouble' and that sex was meaningless without love (not to me, it wasn't – hadn't she ever met a hormone?), this was clearly a taboo area not to be discussed at home.

Like many children, I could not imagine my parents 'doing it' so was very surprised when ruffling though my father's wardrobe for some reason, I came across a bulk, wholesale consignment of coral-coloured condoms. I was in my teens by then so found the secret hoard most useful. It saved me the embarrassment of tackling the local chemist's counter. I doubt that my father ever noticed that slight dent in his stock, but if he did, he never mentioned it. How could he? How could he indeed, for unlike some boys' fathers who were, it seems, ready with the odd coarse remark in the form of encouragement for their son, a sort of thrill-by-proxy approach, my father steered clear of that entire area.

There was only ever one exception.

I was twenty-one and had been living away from home for more than three years. I went 'home' to my parents in the outer suburbs about once a month, but I never took a girlfriend and gave evasive answers when my mother asked about such matters. Then I was offered the facility of their comfortable house for my 21st birthday party and gratefully accepted the offer. Friends aplenty were invited to make the journey from London to come to the bash... and accepted. It meant a degree of preparation, so it was only fair I went home on the morning of the party – complete with girlfriend Patricia.

Just as I had feared. she was given the third degree by my mother. Third degree? It was all 360 degrees! A practised zoologist dissecting a small victim was as nothing to my mother's precision with her 'prey'. But what was surprising and impressive was the cheerful, resilient way that Patricia stood up to the assault. She even managed to convey the impression that she welcomed genuine interest well concealed in relentless interrogation.

Like a coward, I left Patricia to her fate, and went off with my father to collect supplies. As we arrived back and I was about to carry a crate of beer up to the house, my father, looking away from me so our eyes could not meet, blurted out, 'You do *know* about modern birth control, don't you?'

Looking back on it, I'm not sure what he considered 'modern' birth control to be. Was it using coral-coloured condoms rather than an old rag? Was it buying them in bulk to save money? Or was it he really wanted to know if Patricia was on the pill, the wonder of the age, and didn't know how to ask? (I expect that, by then, inside the house, Mother had extracted that answer from her good-natured prey without the use of electrodes and bright lights.)

Whatever he meant, I assured him that I did and he hurried off, clearly greatly relieved. Relieved that he'd had a positive response and that the ordeal of having to deal with 'bedroom' issues was behind him. He went into the house and I continued to unload the car and carry supplies up the steps from the drive.

As I reached the kitchen, I heard my father say to my mother in that conspiratorially lowered tone of voice, 'It's all right. I've had a word with him.' Job done.

SCHOOLDAYS

The first thing one noticed about Mr Humphreys were his eyebrows. Two dense arcs of grey-brown hair which came to a point in the middle and stuck out from his face like small horns. How this extraordinary facial feature did not earn him a nickname, like 'goatman' or even 'Satan', remains a mystery.

Unlike me, not everyone liked Mr Humphreys, but then, not everyone liked maths. For me, it was the almost perfect subject. For a start, it required less writing than almost every other classroom subject – a big plus if you were so completely untidy. Even today, left handers have a problem with handwriting, but back then in the days of inkwells and dip pens, being a lefty was a real handicap. We'd not quite passed the time when children were forced to write with their right hand, but at least in my school, that was not enforced. But even so, Mrs Sellars, my first teacher, rapped my knuckles with a ruler every time I smudged the page, which I did all the time. It didn't make my pages any neater but it gave me a resistance to writing longhand which I've never completely conquered. Keyboards have been my expressive saviour.

But back to Mr Humphreys. I doubt he would have flourished as a teacher under today's strictly-controlled school curriculum regime. We would start a lesson looking at long division and by the end of it, might have diverged into algebra or even calculus. Those of us who had the kind of mind made for the logical structure of maths could follow these journeys into the unknown with relish. Others, I understand, struggled and might have preferred the sing-song approach to times tables which one heard though the thin partition walls between the classrooms. I was in the B-stream for almost everything which required handwriting but had no trouble in making it to the top in maths. Under Mr Humphreys' unique marking system, it was a rare event when I only achieved a hundred percent in the end of term exam: a hundred and ten or fifteen was more common. Extra marks for showing the workings perhaps. Almost anything in my case (except neatness)!

If he had favourites, he certainly never showed it. His love, it was clear, was the logical perfection of his subject and demonstrating this on the blackboard to a room of thirty pupils. Some paid avid attention. Others might be lost or bored. It mattered not. The chalkface might be filled with concept of pi, the numerical relationship between the diameter and the circumference of a circle. That took one into the realms of irrational numbers, transcendental numbers and the abstract, like infinity.

When he got to the right-hand edge of the classroom-wide blackboard, he'd rub out the workings on the left and continue. That cinematic cliché of a blackboard filled with a scrawl of numbers and mathematical symbols was a reality for those of us who attended Mr Humphreys' performances.

I don't remember anyone misbehaving in his class. Not because we were all well behaved but because he never made that an issue. Not that he was oblivious to his pupils: if you put up your hand because you didn't understand, he'd go back over the point carefully. I suppose those who were totally lost didn't ask questions but merely coloured in the little squares in their exercise books. For one's maths exercise book was not on lined paper like most of the others. The pages had a faint blue grid of lines to help one lay out the mathematical symbols using both horizontal and vertical alignment.

It helped, too, when we had to draw triangles. Oh! Triangles! A source of inspiration. That led one on to Pythagoras, trigonometry and beyond.

In every lesson, we wrote in workbooks which had a cover of blue card with the name of the school and the local authority printed on them and a space for you to write your name, the subject and class. Years later, I discovered a stash of my completed books in a box in the attic. Handed over to my mother, no doubt as certain proof of her son's scholastic failings. Smudged, untidy, badly written, poorly spelled. Red crossings-out galore. Low marks and 'could do better' comments from the teacher. Where were the maths books, though? Mr Humphreys would have been witness to a different story.

RENTAL JOB

Almost the whole of one wall is filled by a beaten copper panel. It depicts a bull elephant, charging into the room in three dimensions. I have never seen anything even remotely similar and am appalled and, at the same time, transfixed.

'It's great, isn't it?' Barry says proudly, as if that alone would be a reason to rent the house.

'Great,' I say meekly, suppressing the rest of the sentence which has formed in my mind '*if you like that sort of thing*'.

I follow him through to the kitchen and he demonstrates the built-in gas hob. 'Modern cooking job,' he boasts. Now he is showing me around the rest of the house. I'm easy to please for it is not as if I am looking for a place to spend the rest of my life. I need somewhere to stay that is more than the B&B where I first went, or the room in a shared flat where I have been staying more recently. I don't really know where I will end up, but I am slowly rebuilding a different life now that my wife and I have just separated. This is convenient, affordable and available. It is not as if I've too many other options just at the moment.

I follow Barry back into the lounge-come-jungle where his assistant, Dawn, is sitting on the dark brown leather-look sofa with the tenancy forms I have to sign. 'Mind you, I wouldn't want to go to sleep looking at this,' Barry says. 'Are you working at the hospital?'

He can't quite work me out. Not in my first flush of youth. Wanting a fully furnished house. I don't look like an immigrant doctor, which is what his present tenant is. But why don't I have more possessions?

It's a short term let. I'll have to give one month's notice. It'll be ready for me from the first of the month which is a week next Thursday. 'It's the perfect rental job,' Barry says as I sign the cheque for the deposit. It doesn't take much to twig his favourite figure of speech.

I think we are done. But far from it. He is now going to go through an inventory of the contents of the house, which I also have to sign, presumably so I don't make off with the copper-elephant-wall-panel.

We're back in the kitchen and he is opening cupboards and drawers, 'cutlery-job', 'plate-job', 'pans-job', ticking them off the inventory as he goes along. I'm providing my own linen so he does not put a tick besides the sheet-and-towels-job, but there still is a double-bed-job in one room and a twin-bed-job in another to tick off.

In between this, he is busy trying find out why I'm his new tenant. I've told him I work on the local paper but he clearly wants more and for me, it has become a kind of game. I know exactly what he is after but I'm making him work hard for it, giving opaque answers.

He now knows that I have a daughter, but still no possessions to speak of. I've told him I've been living with friends but want to move into my own place. Can't he work it out for himself?

It's Dawn who asks the sensible, direct questions, and prises out of me that my marriage is over and we have separated. Suddenly, everything drops into place for Barry.

'Oh! A re-marriage job,' he beams, triumphantly.

THE PARTY'S OVER

The bathroom sink is hanging off the wall, the bottle of my father's 'Bokma' special old Dutch gin has gone missing from where he had hidden it, there's a burn mark on the table and I am eighteen years old and one day. At the moment I feel more like eighty.

Jenny is helping me clear up, but we are not really speaking. Grunts, 'yes', 'no', that sort of thing.

I can't quite remember when it all started to go wrong, so wrong.

What I can still remember clearly are the weeks of painstaking planning and preparation. Endless lists. Parents, huh!

'If you're going have a party, we need to know who is coming.'

'Why so many?'

'They're going to drink *how much?*'

I am left thinking if that is what it is like to be an adult, stop the clock right now!

Then it is the day itself and we are off to buy beer, cider and a little wine, my father letting me drive and silently regretting that he has agreed to the whole project in the first place. His son still a child in his eyes. Perhaps always will be. Then there is Mother's ambitious spread of largely unwanted delicacies, made because I cannot convince her that no one will expect more than crisps and nuts. I have negotiated her down to quiches, salads, canapés and those bread rolls you can buy in bulk. I could not talk her out of the cake in the middle with my name in different coloured icing. Eight or eighteen. Makes little difference. Just count the candles.

It gets a lot better when I pick up Jenny from the station, an overnight bag so small it doesn't need those little wheels at all. Her long hair frames her wonderfully symmetrical face, just a touch of dark eye make-up. A loose blouse I've not seen before showing off her figure to great advantage. We hug tightly and there in the station carpark, she gives me my present: a neatly wrapped slim book of love poetry. Written inside: '*À Steve, le poète de la vie*', and three kisses. In French because it is more *romantique*.

Then there is the interrogation she endures with bravery when she meets my mother for the first time. 'I like your parents,' she tells me when the grilling is over. I am surprised she has come out of it alive.

Now it is already early evening and I'm looking at my watch conspicuously, willing my parents to go. They drag things out, but eventually they are ready, sorry they agreed to stay with relatives for the night. 'I'll ring to see everything is OK,' my father says, getting into the car. His anxiety is so heavy I wonder if he'll make it down the road without crashing.

I have a feeling of gaiety which comes as soon as they have gone. Just me and Jenny. I want to 'fool around' as she calls it. She wants to put up some of her own decorations, move furniture, be the responsible adult. She wins: makes a cup of tea for us both. I'd suggested opening the bottle of sparkling stuff... 'Keep that for later,' she says, too wise for her years.

The guests start to arrive but not, of course, at 7.30. David and Jane, Doug and Sue, Pea and Brian... Fred, my best mate with his new girlfriend, Sandra. Straight upstairs to change. Up there for quite a while. They ask if they can stay over. Of course, I say, but I haven't thought this one through.

It is all flowered shirts and bell-bottoms, hot pants and minis, more bottles of wine. And prezzies, which I open and put down somewhere. I've already had two glasses of wine, but I can't see where my glass is again so I have to start yet another.

Martin is doing the music. He's gone for his own faves, as if he's forgotten it is <u>my</u> party. (Actually, it's an act of kindness because no one could dance to Bob Dylan or Bert Jansch). We and the music spill out onto the terrace, enjoying the warm evening air I'd taken for granted. Still they come, Jill and Carl, Mel and Pete. Moody Mandy. Jasper on his own because Petra is unwell, but he wouldn't miss this one for the world. Tony and Dorothea. John and his wife whose name I never remember. Me and Jenny. Actually, where is Jenny?

I'm whirling wildly, it is dancing of sorts but anything goes. Then I'm sitting at the side in the dark by the low wall feeling distinctly unwell. Another glass of wine. There's Jenny. Carries on without me... I don't remember inviting Anthony!

It is getting to the blurry bit now. I've been drinking much too much, much too soon. Bravado? No, I can because now I'm 18? Who am I trying to impress? Jenny's seen it all before. Perhaps she's been sensing it will go badly. Who invited Anthony? I don't even like him.

There's a big gap in what I can remember but it's very late and carloads of gate-crashers arrive, moving on from another party somewhere. I know one of them vaguely and they bring that sinister Jack who does drugs. We all know him, don't we! They go upstairs. I think it is Jenny who phones the police.

They have slipped away again before the police arrive. The bathroom is a mess but I don't notice the damaged sink. Maybe neighbours are complaining about the noise, car doors, loud music, that sort of thing. 'Keep it down,' we are told.

And others are drifting away, the spell broken, the gaiety gone.

She is asleep in the spare room when I find her this morning, my head throbbing like it should, after so much alcohol.

For me, it is strong black coffee, surveying the mess. The patio doors have been wide open all night, the front door never closed properly. Ugh! Cigarette butts among the leftover food, a small table on its side, thankfully not damaged. Cans, bottles, half-eaten food, paper plates, a little broken glass, the detritus of the celebration. Not too bad considering.

I have been quietly straightening the house to little effect for more than an hour when she comes downstairs. She makes herself breakfast as if she's been doing it in our house for years. Toast, tea, a little cereal. Hardly a word. No kiss.

And now the recriminations: 'You were so drunk, it was horrible. You should have seen yourself.'

'I thought you were going to come to bed with me.'

'What? In that state? No thanks.'

'Who were you dancing with?'

'What's it to you?'

Clearly no longer *le poète de la vie*...

She fills the sink with hot water and some liquid soap and starts sorting things out efficiently. Washing glasses, clearing plates, emptying food into the bin. Without needing to be told where anything goes.

'I'm going to catch the 11.32, if you can take me to the station.' It is the longest sentence she has said to me since she came downstairs. I'd been hoping she'd stay all day, even another night.

'I thought...'

'I've got to get back,' she says. I know it is hopeless.

At the station, I try to arrange something for the following Wednesday but I know a brush-off when I get one. Ouch!

By the time I am back at the house, my parents have returned and are doing the last bit of tidying up.

'I slipped getting out of the bath,' I lie when they ask about the sink. Father has already polished out a cigarette burn, relieved that there is not more damage.

'How did it all go?'

'Where is Jenny?'

Maybe grunts are better after all.

On paper, I might now be an adult but my parents know better than that, and this is slowly dawning on me, too.

WHAT DO YOU KNOW?

There is a particular burden which comes from being an undisciplined child born to brilliant parents. They may work hard at hiding their disappointment. Indeed, they may even, somehow, conceal it from themselves. But underlying everything is an expectation that their offspring is going to be an even brighter light in the firmament.

Many of us may be familiar with that self-deluding parental sentiment – 'I just want you to be happy.' But it's a downright lie. 'Happy', perhaps. But not 'just happy'. It goes far, far deeper than that! You want your child to be successful. Perhaps somewhere on the scale between 'moderately' and 'exceptionally'. And wouldn't many parents gleefully trade a few small notches down on the happiness index for a few big notches up on the success scale?

My problem was that I was as unscholarly as they come, with parents whose academic achievements were formidable. And as a second child, I trailed in the wake of an older sister who was clearly much more of a chip off the old block. Indeed, if my mother had not been present at my birth, she might well have thought I was the fabled gift of the gypsies, at least in terms of scholastic application.

Miss Sellars was the first to experience my lack of prowess in the classroom. Neat handwriting, indeed almost any writing, was not to be found in the pages of my primary school workbook. Smudges there were in abundance. I blame a combination of being left-handed and having to use a dip pen. Modern scholars who have not experimented with the contents of a desk ink-well and a scratchy pen know nothing of the challenges of shaping even one letter of the alphabet in this way. While the friars may have mastered illuminated manuscripts of awesome beauty, this five-year-old managed to get more ink on himself than on the paper (and sometimes still does!)

Her solution was the carefully aimed 12-in ruler across the knuckles... A swift blow and a critical comment: 'Not like that, Stephen.' 'Don't make such a mess, Stephen.' 'Write along the line, Stephen.' No modern educationalist would support Miss Sellar's sadistic approach and for good reason. It did nothing to improve my handwriting and instilled in me a hatred of writing by longhand which persisted throughout my schooldays and quite possibly contributed to my lack of academic prowess.

I remember nothing else from my year with Miss Sellars, but I can picture her still: younger than the other teachers at Smitham County Primary, black hair, a severe, unkind face and the always prone wooden ruler.

Mrs Oriel in my next year was a complete contrast and a big improvement. Older, gentler, kinder. But what mattered to my parents was scholastic progress and a gentler regime did not automatically equate to better results. From what I can recall now, my mother did show suitable pride when my crayoned picture of a windmill made it to the classroom wall. (I wonder if, briefly, she flirted with the notion *'if not Einstein, perhaps Chagall?'*) Mrs Oriel was followed by Mr Campbell, a former policeman, who though both tough and kind, did little to stimulate my unconventional approach or get some order into an unruly mind. And then Mr McMaster, who used the slipper – an old plimsoll actually - almost as readily as Miss Sellars had used the ruler. But by then, I was more adept at avoiding attention, except once when Pigtail Sarah sitting next to me annoyed me so much I bit her. Slipper across the bottom. Try not to cry in front of the whole class.

It is wrong to suggest that I was not interested. I was *very* interested; just not often in what the teachers were trying to get across. I doubt that any school system has been devised that could cater for a child like me: bright, quick witted, impatient, undisciplined and still with that inability to write neatly in longhand. School seemed to me to be more about neatness on the page than the quality of what was being written; not that I could make any great claims for the quality of the content either. Still to this day, my mind works faster than pen or fingers, so that quite often I (....) words out.

A quick, easy way to all the right answers: that is what I was looking for. And the opportunity to learn from my own experiments. Which is why, some years later, my room was filled with mains radios and old black and white TVs, all bought for a few pence from a church jumble sale (the forerunner of today's car boot sale). They were all in the process of being brought back from a state of uselessness to a state of semi-uselessness. The summer I was supposed to be revising for my O-levels, I was actually watching Wimbledon on a 7in black and white TV screen, the picture slowly scrolling up and up and up, frame after frame, while Margaret Court and Billy Jean King played in the final. Either that or Gary Sobers receiving the bowling from Fred Trueman...

My 'repairs' did not amount to more than taking the back off the one-shilling (5p) purchases and fiddling with a few internal components, my fingers never far away from tubes with lethal voltages. But hitherto blank screens would limp back to a half-life, old radios might briefly crackle enough for me to listen to *The Navy Lark* or *Beyond Our Ken*. They might work for a few weeks or a few months. It mattered not, there were always fresh supplies awaiting in other church halls.

Had I not come from such an academically-focused lineage, I might possibly have emerged from my school years as a technician. But no good Jewish mother talks about her son the TV repairman, now does she?

Amazingly, by a series of flukes, I managed a handful of O-levels: just enough to scrape into the local College of Further Education on an A-level course. It is a measure of the success of the accidental – or not so accidental – brainwashing that went on at home that I did not stop to think why I was enrolling? A bit of me was still hoping to emulate my father/hero, the research scientist.

A year later, the scenery was very different. As well as the maths and physics lectures, we also had to attend something called 'liberal studies'. It was there that a short, stout, disputatious, lecturer awakened in me latent feelings about reason, injustice and inequality. The stopper was out of the bottle... I skipped A-level lectures to attend a whole series of other events which fed my growing political appetite.

By the end of the first year, the college told me my attendance record had been insufficient to go on to Year Two, and I would have to repeat the year or leave. It was a guilty secret I carried throughout the long summer, taking full fraudulent advantage of the generous 'long vac.' afforded to students who need to recharge their batteries for the intellectual demands of another year of study. Finally, sometime in September, I guess, my parents asked me why I wasn't back to my studies. The nearest I got to the truth was when I told them I had left.

'Left? Left? How can you have left?' my normally mild-mannered father demanded.

'I've left. I don't want to go on at college. Life isn't all about maths and physics.' *Big mistake*. Not a good thing to say to a research physicist and university professor. And I certainly couldn't tell him I'd been kicked out!

'How can you have Left? Tell me what you know about anything?'

So here comes my new-found power of reasoning: 'That's not fair, who can say everything they know? What do you know?' Oops!

My father started listing a long series of advanced scientific theories I'd hardly heard of – and I fled to my room in tears.

About a week later, my mother sheepishly slipped me a copy of *The Pan Book of Careers for Boys*... but that's another story.

<u>ROAD RAGE</u>

Typically, the large lollipop sign on the motorway asks me to slow down to 50mph: 'Obstruction Ahead', it glows in poorly formed digital lettering.

I do slow down (but not to 50mph) so that every other road user can now rush past me, lorries included. Three lollipops later, the sign suggests that the road is now clear. Needless to say, I have not passed any type of obstruction. There was possibly one three hours ago and 'they' (whoever they are?) have forgotten to turn off the displays. Either that or some well-meaning road user reported what they thought was an obstruction, but perhaps it was a blob on their windscreen.

The truth is that no one ever pays much attention to these signs any more. I have a slightly uneasy feeling that one day, we will all be caught out because the sign will say something that is true and current. But it has never happened yet.

It is now half-an-hour later and no lollipop has warned me that all traffic is at a standstill. I see the queue, a necklace of red brake-lights well ahead and slow down, trying to discern which lane will offer the least delay.

I'm in the 'pre-queue weave zone' where most arriving motorists make snap judgements. Advanced

318

studies by a behavioural psychology researcher at the *University of Onceapoly* have shown that there are three main types of 'weavers', ILSs, FLFs and MLDs.

ILSs, the Inside Lane Stalwarts, through experience, have come to the conclusion that the nearside lane, full of lorries, will keep trundling along slightly more evenly than other queues.

FLFs, Fast Lane Fiends *always* plump for the outside lane, come what may. These, of course, include everyone in big black shiny SUVs with tinted windows. They are in the outside lane already, doing a steady ninety and never move over for anyone. Only slightly slower, white van man can be found here too.

MLDs, Middle Lane Ditherers, find that they have arrived at the back of the queue faster than they can make a choice of where else might be best. In any case, many of the members of this group regard the inside lane as the lorry lane into which they will only go to leave the motorway and the outside lane as the overtaking lane, only to be used in extremis and with great trepidation.

So here I sit, surreptitiously glancing sideway to check if the man in the red Nissan-with-a-spoiler who joined his queue at the same time as me is now ahead or behind.

For a few minutes, we all patiently wait our fate. But nothing is moving: we inch forward, not so much because the blockage is now free but more because we are all squeezing more tightly together, as if for comfort! Ha! Ha!

Now, new groups emerge, not yet identified in the study of our researcher.

The man in the Nissan is half out of his door, peering along the central Armco barrier to see if he can tell what is happening ahead. He is sharing his new knowledge with the cheerful man in the white Volvo two behind, who also cannot see anything moving, but who tells him that he was stuck on the M58 for three hours last week because of nothing more than a heavy rain shower.

The large, overweight man in the black tinted window Porsche Cayenne SUV is also busy trying to identify the cause of the blockage. He is using various electronic devices in his vehicle which came as expensive extras. His in-car system, however, is annoyingly unhelpful because, he now discovers, *someone* failed to update the chip last month. He's on the phone to his secretary trying to blame her, or the firm's transport manager or just anyone. And he is doubly irritated because his 11-year-old daughter sitting in the back, has used a cheap phone app, possibly called something like ZimZam (about which he knows nothing) which tells her that her friends, the diaeresis twins Chloë and Zoë, are in another car slightly forward in the queue and that the outside lane is closed several miles ahead. 'Is it, dear?' he says in the same patronising tone that he often uses when talking to his trophy wife.

For a while, nothing much moves at all. Only the lorries in the nearside lane inch forward, tighter and tighter. The lady of uncertain age in the blue Berlingo with a rainbow sticker across the back, who never goes over 55mph so she can save the planet, is now feeling quite rightly intimidated by the towering Scania a few centimetres from her back bumper.

And now we are in the next phase: snatch and switch.

All three lanes move forward and then stop again. Never all together. Never in any type of predictable sequence.

Red Nissan man is switching queues every time there is movement, nipping into ludicrously tight gaps in the next lane, causing jerks and jolts. The sequence is well known to him but it makes no difference. He will never learn. Stop… then go, accelerating hard: the road ahead must be clear now. Oh! No! It is not. He must stop again unless he nips into the next lane, which then immediately stops just as the one he has just left gets going again… He is angrily aware that his dangerous manoeuvres have actually disadvantaged him. The white Volvo is now well ahead of him. His girlfriend, sitting next to him, chewing something he has not been offered, has been told to shut up. (Prediction: When the journey is over and they are back in South Acton, she will elect to become his ex-girlfriend.)

Meanwhile, the man in the big-black-job is busy sending a text message to someone he knows in government who *could* find out what has happened, but actually won't reply. He is so distracted looking at his iphone that there is now a lengthening gap in front of him. Others in the lane start hooting their horns. He lowers a tinted window to make a rude sign with his fat hand, his Rolex glinting in the sun.

And now I have reached high-viz and cone-land. A small army of policemen are gesticulating wildly, indicating that many drivers must change lanes. Big-black-job needs to be in the middle lane, where he has rarely been in his whole life. He moves over without any thought to the fact that there might be other vehicles there already. He misses me by inches, only because I sensed he would come across without another thought. The outside lane is now closed and everyone is rubbernecking. Inside the coned-off area, there is a small car with foreign number plates and a caravan which seems to be embedded in the central barrier. There are multiple ambulances and police vehicles. On the hard shoulder is another small group of cars with steam coming from under bent bonnets. I know not if they were involved in the accident with the Estonian Renault or perhaps (more likely) they bumped into each other while looking at the crash and not the road... it is called rubbernecking.

Up front, another frantic policeman is waving his arms, urging me on, as if it is my reluctance to go faster which has caused a 40-minute delay for thousands. Big-black needs no urging and he is already in the outside lane again, his German engine propelling him almost silently way beyond the national speed limit.

Seven miles further on, an illuminated lollipop tells me that the A5758 is now closed at Sefton, just outside Bootle, which is only 214 miles away.

And now of course, I have reached the road works. They have been going on here for three years. A Department of Transport sign tells me they are delivering a smart motorway.

About the Author

Steve Hoselitz was born in Sheffield shortly after the end of WWII. His family relocated to the Surrey suburbs when he was five. He failed to thrive at school and crashed out of full-time education half way through his A-levels.

By a series of flukes, he managed to find a job on a technical journal while still in his teens, progressing to be deputy editor. By then, he aspired to work in more mainstream journalism and worked in Fleet Street for a while before taking what today they would call a 'career break'.

He spent a year working as a freelance editor in India in his early twenties, before returning to the UK and joining a daily newspaper in the north of England.

In the late seventies, he moved to South Wales, where he still lives, and worked as a daily newspaper editor before setting up his own media consultancy with a colleague from TV news.

He is married, with one daughter and wonderful grandchildren. He still works as a freelance journalist and is a keen craft potter.

Printed in Great Britain
by Amazon

21728495R00185